Journey to Glory

Carrie Rachelle Johnson

Psalm 37:4

Carrie Rachelle Johnson

DEDICATION

I dedicate this novel to my Beloved Cameron and Allie
who have filled my life with joy and made my journey even better.

CONTENTS

ACKNOWLEDGMENTS

First and foremost, I would like to thank God for being my Inspiration, my Guide, and the One and Only Ancient One. I thank Jesus Christ who died for my sins not because I deserve it, but because of His great love for me.

I would like to thank my mother, Donna, and Aunt Pam for being my first readers who constructively advised and encouraged me. I also thank my church family for being my test group and encouraging me to seek publication.

PROLOGUE

IN THE CENTER OF THE WORLD

Deep in a fiery chasm at the center of the world where black smoke billows and chokes, there dwelled a most cruel creature. He was a hideous, monstrous dragon with scaly, red flesh and fierce, orange eyes that held hatred and loathing. His name was Diablo though it had not always been. He had once been one of the Light Warriors who lived in the Glory of Glories under the benevolent reign of the Ancient One. The eternal Ancient One had created all in the world. The Light Warriors were human-looking servants of the Ancient One and soldiers at His command. Through Him, the Light Warriors could use mysterious powers.

Diablo had been Lucero, one of the higher-ranking Light Warriors. He was strong and handsome. He was a valiant champion and never lost a battle nor failed a mission. However, Lucero's pride grew with every victory and soon he desired even more power. His heart began to ache for dominion over all. Yet Lucero knew that he could not rule as long as the Ancient One sat on the pure white throne.

Lucero began to speak secretly among the Light Warriors seeking allies who would rise up against the Ancient One with him. Many were eager to join Lucero for they knew he was strong and had never failed. They were also under the belief that Lucero would rule better than the Ancient One due to his commanding, heroic presence as a warrior.

Lucero and his followers armed themselves and marched toward the throne room where the Ancient One was always present. With armor thick and swords drawn, the rebels approached the glistening throne.

The Ancient One, though merciful and compassionate, would not tolerate anyone trying to dethrone Him for He had always been and everyone else was His creation. Though He knew this was coming, the Ancient One first felt sorrow then anger at the approaching traitors. The Light Warriors still loyal to Him stood on both sides of the throne watching their former friends enter the throne room. Campion, one of the higher-ranking Light Warriors, stepped forward ready for a battle, but the Ancient One told him to stand down for He would handle His enemies.

Lucero stood before the throne feeling powerful and undefeatable. With a battle cry, the army rushed forward. However, the battle was short. The Ancient One using His glorious, unquenchable power flung His once Light Warrior Lucero out of the Glory of Glories into a dark hole at the center of the world known as the Chasm of Misery.

As for the followers of Lucero, they were cursed to follow him forever away from the Ancient One. Their beauty was stripped away. In its place was pale gray flesh, cold stony eyes, and pointed ears. Rags hung on their bodies and they became known as Demoni or the Cursed Ones.

As for Lucero, his cruel heart and malicious spirit transformed him into a monstrous dragon. Lucero chose Diablo as his new name and existence for it meant devil which fit him well. Diablo's new purpose became vengeance against the Ancient One. He lay fuming in the chasm, devising schemes to use against those whom the Ancient One loved. These people had been rightly named the Beloved.

The Beloved were people who had travelled to Mount Glory and pledged their allegiance to the Ancient One. Then they had returned into the world to do their Lord's bidding. Diablo hated all that the Ancient One loved and sought to hurt Him through them. The Demoni went throughout the world implementing the plans of the evil dragon. Diablo laid waiting in his Chasm of Misery with fury eating away at his heart even further. No one seemed safe from his endless rage and the misery that he plagued the world with at all times.

CHAPTER 1

LAILANI

Thousands of years after the Fall of Lucero, the world had become a dark place in need of light. The sky was always gray and no lights shone in the heavens. The people of the world were scattered. Many of them lived in Terra, a huge prosperous city where everyone looked out for themselves. The rich got richer and the poor had to struggle to survive. Crime ran rampant and the Demoni walked the streets tormenting people especially those who were known Beloveds of the Ancient One.

Living in a filthy, damp alley among splintery crates and boxes was a young woman whose name was Lailani. She was barely eighteen and far too skinny for a woman of her age. She had long fiery red hair that she kept in a single, low ponytail. Her dark green eyes sparkled like emeralds when she smiled which was not very often. Though her face was plain and held no noticeable marks of beauty, Lailani had a humble and trusting personality. People seemed to like her if they ever gave her a chance, yet many did not have the inclination to talk with her.

The young woman had lost her family in a fire when she was a small child and she had no peace from her loss. Daily she longed to have her family back safe with her. Since the fire, she had gone around begging for food and work, but no one would truly help her. Yes, sometimes there were small handouts usually from people who were Beloveds, but never anything lasting. Lailani mended clothes for some of the middle class families and was usually paid with a meal or old fabric to wear. Still she struggled daily to survive.

As Lailani sat on a stone step outside a tall white building mending a dress for one of the noblewomen in the city, she hummed to herself and thought about how she wished she could see her family again. She missed her parents so much. Her heart ached for the love and safety that they had provided for her. Tears brimmed in her eyes and she took a deep breath to regain her composure.

Suddenly, a feeling came to her that was so strong it took her breath away. Lailani had a sense that she needed to look up. She glanced into the gray sky and gasped. A light glistened brightly to the north. The woman had never seen anything so beautiful in her life. No light had ever been in the sky before and its magnificence caused her to gasp.

Jumping to her feet, Lailani pointed and exclaimed, "Look! There in the sky!"

People passing by stopped and looked up glancing in different directions as if searching for something.

Lailani kept pointing, but the others seemed confused. A wealthy man in a golden robe shook his head. He had a bald head and was overweight from never having to go hungry.

"There's nothing up there, stupid girl. You're seeing things."

Lailani frowned, "You don't see the light?"

The man guffawed loudly. He motioned to the others.

"She sees a light. Here in Terra?"

The others began to taunt and laugh as well. An old man that Lailani had known for many years came up.

"Now, ladies and gentlemen, Lailani is just playing a joke. She doesn't see anything because there's nothing to see. Isn't that right, Lailani?"

The young woman wanted to argue, but the look in her friend's eyes told her that it would only end in more trouble.

"Yes, I wasn't serious. Sorry to disturb you."

The man in gold scoffed and walked away muttering. The other people walked away as well, speaking to each other and going back to their business.

"Cornelius, why did you do that? I wasn't making it up."

The old man turned back to Lailani. He was a short man with a hunched back from years of hardship. He had short white hair and a white bushy beard. Lailani had been his friend for many years and he was the only family she knew now that her parents were gone.

"I'm sorry, Lailani, but you were attracting too much attention to yourself. The wrong kind if you get my meaning."

Cornelius looked away to a group of Demoni who were causing a ruckus nearby. The gray demon-like creatures were stealing from a vendor and daring him to do something about it. The man bowed his head and endured the abuse. Lailani was tired of seeing the Demoni oppressing and tormenting innocent people. Yet she trembled at the thought of the evil creatures coming over to her.

"You're right, Cornelius. I didn't think. The light just surprised me. I have never seen anything like it."

The old man sat down on the stone step.

He smiled, "I have seen it for many years. However, I have never met anyone else who could see it."

Lailani sat down next to him and picked up the dress she had been mending. Now she would have to wash it before returning it to the owner.

"Do you know what the light is? What does it mean?"

Cornelius shook his head.

"I have no idea."

"It is the Bright Morning Star of the Ancient One."

Lailani and Cornelius were startled at the sound of the new voice. Standing before them was a tall woman with dark skin and long black hair that was braided in multiple braids. She wore a bright yellow gown that wrapped around her and flowed at the bottom. Her face had a pleasant smile that made her look very radiant.

Lailani was enthralled by her beauty, but Cornelius peered at the woman suspiciously.

"Who might you be?"

The woman smiled more brightly.

"My name is Ziona. I am one of the Beloved who serve the Ancient One."

Lailani glanced around to see if anyone had noticed them talking to this woman. The Demoni were no longer in sight. She felt a little braver.

"What is the Bright Morning Star? Why can't everyone see it?"

Ziona smiled, "The Star is only seen by those who are called by the Ancient One. When you see the Star, you must make a choice. You can either ignore the Star or follow it to the Ancient One who dwells on Mount Glory."

Lailani had never left Terra so she didn't know anything about the landscape or places beyond the city walls.

"Where is Mount Glory?"

Cornelius leaned forward eager to hear the answer as well.

Ziona replied, "There are many paths to take once you are outside of Terra, but only one way will lead you to Mount Glory and that is by following the Bright Morning Star. I am heading to Mount

5

Glory now to bring something precious to the Ancient One. I can travel with you if you choose to go."

Lailani felt her heart swell at the idea of leaving her miserable life behind and going to a place where she might start a new life. She was still young though and unsure about what to do.

"What do you think, Cornelius?"

The old man stayed quiet for a few minutes staring up at the Star.

"I have heard stories about the Ancient One and I have always wanted to meet Him. I will go to Mount Glory if you will go with me."

Lailani felt a desire to go to the Ancient One. It was a feeling she had never felt before and its strength surprised her.

"Yes, I want to go to see the Ancient One."

Ziona motioned for them to join her on the road. Oddly, neither felt like they needed anything to take with them on their journey. They left their meager belongings behind and started down the path with the Star as their guide and the Beloved as their companion.

As the trio left Terra, a Demoni by the name of Monstre hissed and cursed. He quickly headed for the Chasm of Misery to tell his lord Diablo about the Beloved who was guiding some of his slaves to the Ancient One. He trembled at the thought of the dragon's reaction.

CHAPTER 2

VICTOR

The sound of clashing swords filled the ears of Victor. He lay on the ground struggling to regain consciousness. His eyes refused to open and he couldn't breathe.

Victor had been raised in the great city of Terra, but had gone to the Ancient One when he was a teenager in order to serve Him as a knight. The Ancient One had lovingly accepted his service and sent him back into the world as one of His Beloved. Victor had trained with others becoming a knight.

Now several years later, he had been in a battle for many days against the Demoni. Fierce, relentless attacks had slammed against the army of the Ancient One. Weary and worn, Victor had been hit in the head and his mind had reeled into darkness.

Victor tried again to open his eyes. He noticed that the sounds of battle were becoming quieter. Soon only silence was heard. Victor used his hands to push himself up. He opened his eyes which widened in shock at the sight of the battlefield. The ground was soaked in blood and littered with mangled, crumpled bodies. Heads and other body parts were missing from several of the corpses which caused the young knight to cringe.

Looking around, the young man saw that there were no survivors from his army. The Demoni had left, no doubt whooping in victory. Victor felt his stomach lurch as hot tears streamed down his face. Gagging, he fell to his knees retching and sobbing.

Unbeknownst to the shattered man, there was one warrior watching him from afar. It was Davo who was a high-ranking Demoni in the evil dragon Diablo's army. He had spent many days slaughtering the Beloved soldiers of the Ancient One taking great pleasure in their anguished screams and fearful eyes. Davo watched Victor and smiled deeply. *Such a weak creature.*

Killing him would put him out of his misery. Instead Davo wanted the young man to suffer. He put his bloodstained sword in its scabbard.

Walking over to Victor, Davo mocked the fallen hero.

"Oh, my! You didn't fight very courageously, did you?"

Victor looked up at the Demoni and fear shone in his eyes for he knew that it would be no challenge for this enemy to kill him.

Davo sneered, "Don't fear me, weakling. I won't kill anything so pathetic."

Victor hung his head in shame.

"My, how you have failed the Ancient One. He must be so disappointed in you and regret choosing you as one of His knights."

Tears rolled down Victor's cheeks. His face and neck flushed red with shame. *He's right. I'm pathetic.*

"How could you ever serve the Ancient One and make any difference in the world? You should go back to Terra and forget about your decision to be a knight."

Davo walked away laughing as Victor stayed on his knees reflecting on the Demoni's words.

After a moment, Victor struggled to his feet and picked up his sword which had been shattered in the battle. The hilt was intact, but the blade was short and ragged. The despairing man put the broken sword in its scabbard and began to search the sky. He saw the Bright Morning Star clear in the sky. It was the same star he had followed to find the Ancient One years before. Now it was shining to lead him back to his Master. His heart ached for the love of the Ancient One yet his fear of rejection took control.

"I won't go where I am not worthy."

Victor headed for the path that led toward the city of Terra and away from Mount Glory.

Davo stood at the edge of the battlefield. He felt full of pride at his deceit.

"Don't look so smug, Davo. It is not over."

Davo frowned and turned to see a strong, handsome man standing all in pure white with a radiance of light surrounding him.

"Well, well. Campion. A little late, aren't we?"

Campion who was one of the Ancient One's Light Warriors smiled, "Oh, I follow the Ancient One's plan so I am never late. It is by His timing that I do anything."

Davo scoffed, "Of course. Keep believing His lies."

Campion's hand went to the hilt of his sheathed sword.

"Careful, Davo."

Davo waved him away.

"I don't have time for your threats today, Campion. I must go to my dark lord Diablo and tell him of this massacre. It is a great victory for my people."

As Davo walked away, Campion called out to him, "Enjoy it while it lasts, Davo, for the final victory shall be ours!"

The Demoni visibly trembled and scurried away. Campion looked to the path where Victor had gone. With a sad shake of his head, the Light Warrior hurried to report back to the Ancient One.

CHAPTER 3

SIMON

The great knight sat ready on his white steed with his shield in one hand and his sword in the other. The approaching invaders rushed at him yet the knight thrust his sword into the air saying... "Simon!"

The ten year old boy blinked at the sound of his name. He looked at the stone fence he was straddling and lowered the piece of firewood he had raised in the air. He was small for his age with a mop of brown hair and pale blue eyes hidden by a dirt-smudged face. He wore a brown sack that was too big for him. His feet were covered in dirt and sores from never wearing shoes.

"Simon!"

With a groan and a sigh, the boy climbed down from the fence and headed for the house. The house was large and extravagant though Simon knew that it would never be home. He was a slave to the rich man Aurelius who was haughty and cruel. Aurelius lived in the mansion with his wife, Keikari, his heir and son, Vano, and his vain beautiful daughter, Korskea. All of them treated Simon horribly. The boy had to endure verbal taunts, cruel shrieks, and occasional beatings. He hated living in Terra with the wealthy family and dreamt of one day going on an adventure. He wished to become a true knight who helped people with no one to stand up for them. People like him.

"Simon!"

Simon reached the back of the mansion just as Keikari screamed for the third time. Keikari was a large woman with short curly brown hair and fierce brown eyes. She always wore elegant gowns and spent piles of money on all her jewelry and possessions. The woman stood at the back door with her hands on her hips. Her voice was always shrill and her words always held superiority in them.

"Where have you been? I've been calling you."

Simon lowered his eyes as was his custom to show his inferiority to his masters.

"I was out by the..."

"Oh, hush. I really don't care. Get inside and start packing."

10

Simon came inside with his eyes still on the floor.

"Packing?"

Keikari snorted, "Yes. Aurelius has this foolish idea that we should leave Terra. He thinks we need to see the world as a family before the children are grown and leave home. Fool of a man."

The woman walked off muttering. Simon thought it was odd to travel now since Vano and Korskea were already young adults who probably had no intention of leaving home where they were spoiled with anything they desired. He began to pack all of the clothes and items that Keikari had left out on the table.

"Simon!"

The boy jumped at the harsh deep voice of Aurelius. He scurried out to the foyer near the front door. Aurelius was standing just inside the doorway dressed in his favorite golden robe. He was a large man with a bald head and a sour expression. He glared at Simon.

"Start putting the bags in the wagon. Hurry up!"

The child ran out to the wagon. Gula and Avidez were standing near it with their horses. Simon had seen them visit the house several times over the last few weeks. They were hired by Aurelius as bodyguards. Both were known for their love of money, so Aurelius had probably paid them well for their services.

Avidez was a tall, lean man with straight, long, brown hair. He wore dark brown clothes with a cape and had a patch over one eye though no one seemed to know what had happened to his eye. The warrior wore his sword on his back as an archer wears a quiver.

Gula was tall and more muscular with straight, long, black hair. He wore black metal armor with a matching cape. The man had a sword hanging around his waist.

Simon nodded at the men who grunted and returned to their conversation using hushed whispers. The boy put each bag, no matter how heavy, into the large wooden wagon. He wished that he could go on an adventure. It would be so glamorous to travel the world and experience all that lay outside of Terra. If only the family would let him go too, but they never took him on trips with them. No, he would be forced to stay behind locked in the small closet they called his room and hope that they returned before he starved to death. *Dogs are treated better.*

Simon sighed at what his life had become.

11

Aurelius stepped out of the mansion with Keikari following him. Both looked red-faced and angry as if they had been fighting which was not unusual for the couple.

Vano came out yawning lazily. He was a tall, strong young man with a muscular physique and handsome facial features. His hair was blond and his eyes a bright blue. He wore a white tunic and white pants with a golden belt. Around his neck flowed a blue cape. The man looked perfect, but his attitude was one of superiority as if all should worship him. He looked down at Simon and pushed him aside before climbing onto his brown stallion.

"Daddy!"

The whiny screech of Korskea made Simon flinch. She stomped out of the mansion. The young woman now in her early twenties was tall, beautiful, and very thin. Her blond hair was long and always in perfect shape. Her eyes sparkled blue. She wore a fancy pink dress and had a silk shawl around her shoulders.

Aurelius turned and sighed, "What now, Korskea?"

The young woman scowled, "I think you should let me stay here. I have no desire to travel in that wilderness."

It was Keikari who answered.

"Young lady, if I am going, we are all going. Now get in the wagon."

Korskea stomped in a huff and climbed into the wagon.

Aurelius helped Keikari climb up into the wagon where she sat beside her daughter. He then climbed onto the driver's bench. With a jerk of his head, the large man glared at Simon.

"Simon, you will walk. Keep up with the wagon."

Simon gasped. He was going with them on their journey. He couldn't believe it.

"Yes, sir. I will."

Gula and Avidez rode their horses in the lead. Vano followed closely with his nose in the air in case anyone should see him and question his importance. As the wagon rolled away, Simon followed it filled with excitement. *I am finally going to have an adventure!*

12

CHAPTER 4

DEVIN

In the upper chambers of the Chasm of Misery, Diablo laid waiting for news from his Demoni. His minions kept him up to speed about what was happening in the world outside of the Chasm. Diablo only left his caverns when absolutely necessary. He mainly would go to the fiery depths below to torture those who had been captured or wandered into his lair. The great beast delighted in tormenting them.

Movement caught Diablo's eye and he saw Davo approaching.

"Ah, Davo. What news from the battle?"

Davo knelt on one knee and bowed his head.

"My lord, I have excellent news. His army has been destroyed. Only one survivor who feels so worthless that he has abandoned the Enemy for good."

Diablo hissed in amusement.

"Perfect…And you, Monstre. What news from Terra?"

Monstre gulped and approached the dragon warily. He had hoped to not be noticed for some time with all of the other Demoni in the room, but the dragon had sensed him and now he couldn't blend in. Monstre knelt down trembling.

"My lord, I have not so good news as Davo. It appears that Lailani and Cornelius of Terra have seen the Star."

Diablo raised his head in expectation.

"And? What did they decide?"

Monstre gulped again.

"Well, they were ignorant of the meaning of the Star and seemed to just sit and look at it."

Diablo growled happily. Monstre decided it was time to get the bad news over with.

"But Ziona approached them."

Diablo lowered his head until his face was close to Monstre's face.

"Ziona! And?"

Monstre closed his eyes ready for the deathly blow that he was sure would follow the end of his news.

"And they have left Terra with Ziona and are following the Star."

The roar of the dragon was deafening and struck fear in the hearts of all of the Demoni. Monstre held his breath waiting for his demise. When nothing happened after a few minutes, the creature slowly opened his eyes and saw that Diablo was no longer in his face. Instead the dragon had moved back inside his cave and was fuming out of sight. A harsh whisper moved Monstre into action.

"Summon Devin."

Devin had been eavesdropping on the gathering and now moved away to return to his chambers. He was a twenty year old strong-willed human. His face was handsome and his body strong. His hair was black and his eyes green. He was always keen to wearing black from head to toe. He had always been a rebel and refused to be controlled by the Ancient One even from a young age. Devin had chosen to serve Diablo who gave him more of a free reign to do as he pleased. He was an excellent swordsman and had the gift of spying to find information that he could use to manipulate others. Occasionally, the warrior had to run errands for the dragon or kill someone who defied Diablo, but he considered it a good life. It didn't matter whether or not he was happy. There was no way to leave the dragon's service now unless it was as a meal for him or worse as a new toy for the creature to torture in the fiery depths below.

Devin entered his chambers and sat on his bed waiting for Monstre to come retrieve him. He knew in his heart what the dragon would ask of him and he welcomed the chance to leave the Chasm for a time.

A knock came on the door. Devin opened the door and faced Monstre who still looked shaken by the reaction of Diablo.

"Lord Diablo summons you."

Devin nodded. He followed the Demoni smiling at the thought of Diablo's displeasure at the creature. The young man did not like the monsters that served the dragon and wished to stay away from them as much as possible. Any moment where the creatures were humiliated or frightened by Diablo brought amusement to the man.

Devin entered the gathering area near the cave where Diablo had slithered. He approached the cave and was about to announce his presence. However, it was not necessary.

"Ah, Devin. Enter…Alone."

The last word was spoken harshly to the Demoni who had followed Devin over. The creatures backed away as Devin entered the cave. It was pitch black inside, but he could hear the dragon breathing. He stopped as he saw the fiery lit-up eyes staring at him in the darkness. Devin's throat closed up slightly and he began to feel nervous. The man tried to speak, but the words wouldn't come.

"Devin, two have seen the Star and have left Terra. They are heading to the Mountain. I want you to find them and convince them to return to Terra or better yet wander here."

Devin nodded, "As you wish, my lord. And if they won't be swayed?"

The dragon growled deeply causing Devin to force himself to stand in place and not flee.

"If they will not turn from their journey, then I want you to kill them."

Devin smirked and bowed before taking his leave of the dragon.

Diablo laid his head on the cave floor still fuming. He would not allow the Ancient One to obtain any more Beloveds. If he had to destroy Ziona to reach them, then the dragon was more than willing to take her out of the picture.

CHAPTER 5

CROSSROADS

The road leaving Terra had the occasional hoof print or wagon wheel impression, but it wasn't near as busy as the roads inside the city. In fact, Lailani had been traveling for a couple of hours and had yet to see anyone other than her fellow travelers. The path so far had led them through an open field with tall yellow and brown grass with an occasional tree. Though it did not appear beautiful, Lailani was thrilled to see land so different from the gray buildings and cobblestone streets of Terra. She occasionally looked up to see if the Star was still there. Her heart swelled with joy each time the woman saw it still blinking ahead of her.

Cornelius had not spoken much as they traveled down the road. He kept looking behind them watching his home of many years grow smaller and smaller in the distance.

Ziona walked tall and practically bounced as she hummed happily. Lailani was constantly in awe of the Beloved. She was so beautiful and graceful. She seemed to be full of joy no matter how far they traveled. Ziona's energy did not seem to lessen as they went farther from the city.

The dirt road went on straight until the trio came to a fork in the path. Ziona stopped and cocked her head to one side as if listening for something.

"Why don't we rest here for a bit?"

Cornelius plopped down on a grassy bump on the side of the road and took several deep breaths.

Lailani stepped closer to the crossroads. She looked at the left road. The redheaded woman saw a smooth path with more fields and no signs of danger. Lailani looked to the right path and saw a much different sight. The right road had a rough, rocky terrain and scraggly trees bending above, creating a dark canopy. Strange growls and howls came from the shady woods.

Lailani shivered as she turned from the road to the right.

"Which way do we go, Ziona?"

The dark-skinned woman looked up into the sky. Then her eyes fell on Lailani. Before she could speak, the sound of a wagon approaching stole her attention. The road that they had just come down was now the path for three men on horseback and a wagon. The horses stopped and the men looked at the old man and the two ladies curiously.

"What's the problem, Gula? Avidez? Vano?"

A large man dressed in a golden robe walked in front of the paused steeds. Lailani groaned at the sight of him for she remembered the man who had mocked her. She glanced at Cornelius who looked equally annoyed. On the other hand, Ziona smiled and approached the men. The three men on horseback climbed down.

"Good day, gentlemen. We mean you no harm. We are simply travelers resting here at the crossroads. Where are you all going?"

The man in brown and the man in black exchanged amused glances at her declaration of meaning them no harm. The young man in blue and white snorted at her speech. However, the large man in gold spoke.

"Out of our way, Woman! We don't have time to waste talking to you."

Ziona smiled more deeply and stepped to the side motioning the men forward.

Lailani frowned at the man in gold as he stepped forward to look at the crossroads.

"Which way, Aurelius?"

The man in gold turned and was about to speak when Ziona called out to him.

"Be careful of your choice, Aurelius, for it could be your last!"

Aurelius glared at the woman as he stomped back to the horses.

"Mind your business, Beloved, for your mouth may get you into trouble."

Ziona laughed loudly and musically. Lailani was surprised by the woman again. She returned her attention to the men and was startled to see a small boy standing there wearing a brown knit sack.

Simon had been taking in all of his surroundings as he walked beside the wagon. When the wagon had stopped, the boy had waited for orders. None came for some time.

Finally, Keikari snapped, "Simon, go see what has delayed us!"

Quickly and eagerly, Simon hurried forward his mind reeling. He wondered if thugs and bandits had stopped them. Maybe he would see Gula and Avidez use their swords to protect their employers. Yet he felt disappointment and surprise when he reached Aurelius for all he saw was an old man and two women. One lady with dark skin and wearing yellow was laughing to the annoyance of Aurelius. The other woman had long red hair and wore poor, ragged clothes. Simon wondered if she was the laughing woman's slave. As he looked at her, the woman's gaze fell on him. She seemed startled to see him.

Aurelius glared at the dark-skinned woman. Gula and Avidez seemed amused, but Simon knew that his master was about to explode. The boy sidestepped trying to get away from the large man for Simon knew from experience that he would be the one Aurelius would lash out at in his fury.

"Stop your laughing, Woman! I've had enough of this nonsense!"

The woman in yellow smiled, "I am sorry to have offended you. My name is Ziona. This is Cornelius and Lailani. We are travelling to Mount Glory to see the Ancient One. You are welcome to join us."

Simon was in awe at her courage and compassion for people she didn't even know.

"We have no intention of going in the direction of the mountain."

Ziona nodded, "You may not intend to go there, yet your path may still wind in that direction."

Aurelius growled in frustration. Simon smiled at the woman's boldness. He wished that he was that confident.

Simon frowned as he saw movement on the path to the right. He squinted trying to see more clearly. His heart beat in excitement as he saw a man come to the crossroads. *It's a knight!*

Victor had been hiding behind a tree listening to the exchange between the two groups at the crossroads. At Ziona's introduction and mention of the Ancient One, the man's heart ached with longing to be in His presence. However, the Demoni's words echoed in Victor's mind. No, he couldn't return to Mount Glory. The knight continued walking toward the crossroads. He came out and instantly drew the attention of the people gathered there.

The large man Aurelius snorted, "Now what?"

The red haired woman Lailani turned with surprise. The old man Cornelius stood up.

"My goodness. A knight."

Victor did not speak a word, but Ziona was not so quiet.

"Welcome, Sir Victor. You seemed to have seen hard times."

The young man started at the use of his name, but since she was a Beloved, he assumed that she had seen or met him at Mount Glory.

"I have recently been in a battle."

The people seemed to wait for the knight to elaborate, but he said nothing else.

Ziona smiled affectionately, "Where are you heading now, Sir Victor?"

The man winced for he did not like the title she used to refer to him which he now felt unworthy to hold. Victor looked at the roads before him. The road to Terra was partially blocked by Aurelius' horses and wagon though he did not really want to go back there for it was a reminder of where he had been before finding the Ancient One. The other road seemed easy to travel and it would not lead to Terra or Mount Glory. He did not know where it would lead nor did he care. Without a word, Victor headed down the road toward the unknown destination.

Lailani watched the knight walk down the left road feeling curious about his life. She returned her gaze to Aurelius and the conversation at hand.

Ziona sighed, "Well, Sir Victor has chosen his path. Have you chosen yours, Aurelius?"

Her voice held disappointment and her face seemed sorrowful.

Aurelius turned away from her and addressed his men.

"We are going left."

The three men climbed up onto their horses and Aurelius began to walk toward the wagon.

"What about you, Simon?"

Lailani saw Ziona looking at the young boy.

Aurelius turned to see the boy standing by Vano's horse.

"He's going with us. He's our slave and we won't let you steal him."

"It is your choice, Simon."

Aurelius shook his head, marched over to the boy, and dragged him to the wagon.

Lailani walked over to Ziona.

"How did you know his name, Ziona?"

The other woman looked at her and smiled, yet she did not answer the question.

The horses galloped forward. Both women stepped out of the road and watched them head down the left path. As the wagon rolled by, Lailani heard a woman snapping at Aurelius. The man's face was scrunched up in a sour expression. Lailani couldn't help but grin at the man's discomfort. However her satisfaction vanished as the end of the wagon came by with the boy walking behind it.

The redheaded woman's eyes widened. First, she saw a rope tied from Simon's hands to the back of the wagon. Then she saw the tears streaming down his face where a bruise was forming on his right cheek. He looked at Lailani and Ziona with a look of surrender.

"Oh, Ziona, can't we do something for him?"

Ziona paused as if listening for something. When she spoke, her voice held hope and love that Lailani had never heard before.

"Do not worry about Simon for another will intervene for him and the child shall be allowed to make his own choice whether Aurelius wants him to or not. Oh yes, someone has been sent who will help Simon."

Lailani looked at the retreating back of the child and truly hoped that all Ziona said was true.

CHAPTER 6

FOREST OF MALICE

Simon wiped the tears from his face awkwardly. The path was smooth which made the boy grateful since he was barefoot. His right cheek hurt. He knew it was probably bruised.

When Aurelius had dragged him back to the wagon, the man had grumbled about what Ziona had said. Then spitefully he had yelled at Simon.

"How dare you think about going with her!"

Without waiting for an answer, the man had backhanded the child. Then Simon was tied to the wagon and had to struggle to keep up. The boy saw Lailani and Ziona watching him, but all he could do was briefly look at them.

In his heart he had wanted to go with them to this place called Mount Glory. He was curious about the Ancient One who had to be better than his current masters. Looking up into the sky, Simon saw a light shining off to the right. *It's so beautiful!*

He wished that he could follow it, but Aurelius would never allow that.

Darkness surrounded the wagon and Simon glanced around noticing for the first time that they had entered a forest. Tall, ancient trees towered over them and the eerie darkness frightened the boy. He kept walking, though he stumbled over tree roots and sharp rocks. His feet began to hurt. Simon wished that Aurelius would stop, so he could rest. But why would he?

Suddenly to Simon's surprise, the wagon indeed stopped. Walking to the right side of the wagon, the slave boy saw that there was another path. Up ahead, their road continued on. Gula shouted back to the wagon.

"Which way, Aurelius?"

The large man grumbled and climbed down again.

Simon watched as the four men gathered and began to discuss their options. Soon, their voices grew louder and angrier. Simon struggled to hear. However, in the next moment, everyone in the forest could hear their conversation.

"And I say we are going straight through the forest. This is my family and my money."

Avidez stepped forward.

"If you want to go straight on through this miserable forest, then we want more money."

Aurelius yelled, "Absolutely not!"

From the wagon, Keikari screamed, "Don't you give any more money to those weasels!"

Gula growled, "Who are you calling a weasel, you penny-pinching troll?"

Aurelius screamed over his wife's retort. "Watch how you talk now! That's my wife!"

Avidez grunted, "Well, no one else would want her."

Simon was shocked at how cruel and angry the argument was becoming. It was almost as if the forest was having an effect on them.

"More money or we'll leave you and your horrible family."

Gula's face was red and his expression frightened Simon. Avidez nodded in agreement.

"Fine. Leave! We will manage without you."

Aurelius marched back to the wagon. Gula and Avidez returned to their horses and headed back toward the crossroads muttering about other money-making schemes they could implement back in Terra.

Keikari screamed at her husband.

"You fool! What will we do if we are attacked? Tell them we will pay double."

Aurelius huffed, "Gula! Avidez! I will double your wages if you will continue on with us."

Simon watched the two men stop and turn their horses. He saw Gula wink at Avidez who mumbled, "All too easy."

As the group of men gathered to discuss their plan once more, Simon felt a craving inside so deep that he almost couldn't stand it. It was a strong desire to go on the side path. He looked at the path and didn't see anything different about it. He looked up and saw the light gleaming in the sky. It was in the direction of the side path. The feeling to go down that path was so strong that Simon was willing to do anything to go that way. The boy squeezed his hands around and wrenched them out of the rough rope. He glanced at the men talking

22

and saw Keikari leaning to hear their discussion. Slowly he tiptoed toward the path. He was getting closer and closer.

"Daddy! The slave is loose."

Simon froze. He had forgotten about Korskea. Her scream alerted the men. Aurelius stormed toward the boy. Simon lowered his eyes and fell to his knees.

"Running away, you ungrateful runt?"

Out of the corner of his eye, Simon saw Aurelius raise his hand. The boy closed his eyes waiting for the blow. It didn't come.

"Unhand me!"

Simon opened his eyes and was startled to see a hand holding Aurelius' wrist. His eyes moved to see his rescuer. Surprise covered the slave at who he saw.

Standing there before them was a knight. It was not the knight from before whom Ziona had called Sir Victor. No, this knight did not look anything like Simon would have imagined. His armor looked like it had once been iron, but it now was covered in dents and rust. His hands were covered in metal gloves. He had a sword hanging on his waist in its scabbard. His visor on the helmet was up and the face held no outward majesty.

The man had scraggly gray hair and beard. He also had a bushy, gray mustache. His face was worn with age. When he spoke, his voice held boldness and strength in it.

"Lower your hand from that boy and I shall unhand you."

Aurelius glared at the stranger and pulled his hand back. The knight let go then turned to Simon who was still kneeling on the ground with eyes wide open and his mouth ajar.

"Are you alright, boy?"

Simon was too stunned to speak so he nodded. The knight smiled warmly. For the first time in his life, Simon felt safe.

"Now see here, Knight. This is none of your business. What I do with my property is none of your concern."

The knight faced Aurelius.

"I assure you, sir, that the abuse of children is everyone's concern. I shall not stand by and allow you to hurt anyone especially a helpless child."

Simon's heart swelled with hope and gratitude.

"He is my slave and I will beat him if I see fit."

The knight touched the hilt of his sword.

"No, you will not. If the boy wishes to go down that road, then you will not stop him."

Aurelius turned pale at the reminder of the sword. He glanced over at his bodyguards, but Gula and Avidez just shrugged and watched from afar.

"Fine! Take the worthless runt! He eats too much anyway."

Aurelius stormed back to the wagon.

"Let's go!"

Simon watched the wagon roll away with the people he had always known as his masters. Disbelief filled the boy as he looked back at the knight.

"Thank you, sir."

The knight looked at Simon and said, "You are welcome, son. Now I will have you know that I do not force anyone to go with me. It is up to you, boy. Where do you want to go?"

Simon had never been given a choice before. He looked at the wagon and then at the path. The boy then looked back at the knight.

"Will you teach me about being a knight? I would love to be one."

The knight smiled warmly, "Of course I will. I will also lead you to Mount Glory where the Ancient One may accept you as a knight."

Simon felt his heart jump.

"I will follow you to the mountain. My name is Simon."

The knight smiled and helped Simon to his feet.

"I have many names, Simon, but you may call me Cristo."

Victor had traveled down the road and rested where a new path met the old path. He had thought about which way to go. On seeing the Bright Morning Star above the new path, the knight had decided to continue straight. As he stood to be on his way, however, he heard the horses and wagon coming down the path. Quickly, Victor hid behind a tree in hopes that no one would see him and try to talk to him about the battle or knighthood.

The knight listened as the men argued and shook his head as Gula and Avidez tricked the family into more money. He had watched the boy get loose from the rope and tiptoe to the path. Victor had stepped forward ready to stop the large man Aurelius from hitting the child when he saw the knight. He seemed to have come out of nowhere. The knight wore rusty armor and did not appear noble, but Victor realized that he himself couldn't talk for he was far from noble and chivalrous. Still something about the knight was familiar as if they had met before, but the younger man couldn't quite place him.

Aurelius and the knight had words. The confrontation ended with the boy being left behind by the family as they continued straight down the path they were on. Victor was ready to continue that way as well until he heard the knight promise to teach the boy about being a knight. The former knight couldn't bear the thought of the child being led down a path that he himself had gone and ended up being a failure.

Victor decided that the boy needed to know the full truth even if it meant that he himself had to follow the path guided by the Bright Morning Star for a time.

"I will follow you to the mountain. My name is Simon." *I will help you before it is too late, Simon.*

"I have many names, Simon, but you may call me Cristo."

Victor came out from behind the tree and approached the other two people. The boy looked at him excitedly and the knight turned to see who was coming toward them.

"Ah, a fellow knight. I am Cristo and you are?"

The younger knight glanced at the elder knight and replied, "I am Victor. I am going down this path and would like to join you if I am welcome?"

Cristo laughed jovially, "Of course you are welcome. The more the merrier."

The trio set off down the right path following the Bright Morning Star. Victor kept telling himself that he could turn back as soon as he convinced Simon that being a knight was not what he hoped it to be.

CHAPTER 7

SWAMP OF SORROW

The right path of the crossroads had looked so frightening to Lailani when she first saw it. Yet the darkness and rough terrain transformed into a more pleasant road after a mile or so. The path the trio walked down now was smooth with the landscape being tall brown and yellow grass with the occasional tree again.

The road was quiet except for Ziona's constant humming. She would switch songs without pausing and her musical voice cheered Lailani up so much that she believed that she could go on forever. Cornelius seemed to be almost skipping as they walked. The redheaded woman couldn't remember the old man ever looking so joyful.

Lailani's attention was captured when silence filled the air. The young woman glanced at Ziona noticing that the other woman was no longer humming. Instead she had slowed her pace and was staring straight ahead. Lailani turned to see what had drawn her attention.

A tall, handsome man stood by the side of the road leaning on a broad tree. The man had black hair and sparkling green eyes. He was dressed in all black with a sword placed in a scabbard secured to his waist. The stranger was watching the trio approach with a curious look on his face.

Ziona stopped, leaving a large gap between her companions and the man.

"Greetings. I am Ziona. This is Lailani and Cornelius. We are on our way to Mount Glory. Who are you and where are you headed?"

The man smiled warmly during this introduction. He stood up straighter and stepped towards them.

"It is nice to meet you. My name is Devin. I am also traveling to the mountain. I was hoping to find some fellow travelers, so that I wouldn't have to continue on alone. May I join you on your journey?"

The man's voice was mildly deep which gave a slight music to his words.

Lailani felt drawn to the man. She noticed that Cornelius also seemed to trust Devin. Ziona, however, frowned at the man suspiciously. She opened her mouth to respond, but stopped. She cocked her head to the side as if listening to something. The woman took a deep breath before opening her mouth again.

"Yes, Devin. We would love for you to join us on our journey to Mount Glory."

The man looked confused and doubtful as if not expecting this answer.

Devin had left the Chasm of Misery heading on the most direct path to get to the travelers from Terra. On a hill near the path, he could see people down the road heading his way. Quickly the minion of Diablo scurried down the hill and leaned against the tree looking as if he was waiting for someone. Soon he saw the lady and old man, yet he was startled to see that they were not alone. He had heard Monstre and Diablo talk about two people, but he had failed to overhear about the third. By the look of her, the man knew that she was one of the Beloved.

Stopping, the woman introduced herself and her fellow companions yet her face looked unsure about the man.

Devin tried to change her mind about him through his introduction. He wanted to sound like he truly wanted to go to the Mountain. Panic hit him as Ziona suspiciously opened her mouth to reply. Confused, he saw the woman close her mouth and cock her head to the side.

After a silent moment, Ziona spoke, "Yes, Devin. We would love for you to join us on our journey to Mount Glory."

Suspicion crept into his mind for he knew that she didn't really want him to come along. *So why did she agree?*

Devin's mind reeled as he considered what the Beloved could be up to. He forced the smile to stay on his face and clapped his hands together once.

"Wonderful. Shall we go?"

The other three stepped forward and continued down the path. Devin followed them. He thought of all of his options and schemes as he walked. He almost didn't notice the red haired woman, Lailani, moving to his side.

"Devin? When did you see the Star?"

Devin watched her look up into the sky.

The man easily lied, "Oh, it was a couple of days ago. Luckily, I had heard my parents talk about the Ancient One so I knew what to do."

Smirking, the young man looked up in the direction she was staring. He was ready to pretend that he really saw the Star too. Devin nearly choked as his eyes beheld the Bright Morning Star in all its glory. Shock filled him and he felt panic hit him like a punch in the stomach. *How can this be possible?*

The warrior had no intention of really going to Mount Glory and yet here was the Star serving as a guide to him.

His mind raced as he thought about his life now where he was safe from Diablo and his monstrous minions. What if Diablo found out that he could really see the Star? That would mean instant death or eternal torture for the young man.

"Devin? Are you alright?"

Devin brought his eyes down from the Star and looked into Lailani's green eyes.

"I'm fine. I just forgot how beautiful the Star is. It always surprises me when I look up and see it again."

Lailani smiled warmly, "I feel the same way."

The travelers continued on the road talking and admiring their surroundings except Devin who kept silent, fretting over what he was going to do now. He felt rushed and didn't have the strength to try to convince them to turn back, not that they would with Ziona advising them. *No, the best way to get rid of them would be to kill them, but how?*

A plan did not enter his mind until he saw the place that they were about to enter. Then an evil grin crossed his face for he believed that the answer had come at last. *Perfect.*

The path led into a wet, dismal swamp. Green, mossy paths led through the wetlands. Large pools of murky water clung to the sides of the paths begging someone to take a wrong step and fall into the endless depths to their doom. Unbeknownst to Lailani, the waters held a secret that could capture the hearts of any who looked into the pools.

Lailani followed Ziona unsure about the swamp. It looked so dreary and dangerous. However, the other woman walked through confidently. Cornelius was right behind Ziona and he kept glancing back at his friend to see if she was still following safely. Lailani reassured him with a smile and continued to follow her companions. She could feel Devin behind her and she felt blessed to have met him for he seemed like a nice man. The woman had been excited at his choked up reaction to the Star. She felt so overwhelmed and joyful about its appearance as well.

"Lailani, did you see that?"

Devin's voice came in a low whisper and Lailani was curious at what he had seen.

"What is it?"

She stopped walking and turned to the man.

Devin pointed at the water.

"In there. I saw something."

Lailani glanced ahead and saw Cornelius and Ziona still walking, but it was at a leisurely pace. Surely she and Devin could catch up quickly.

The young woman edged her feet to the tip of the path so that they almost touched the water. She leaned over slowly. Surprise hit her. In the water, she saw the faces of her parents who had died so long ago.

"Oh, Devin, I see my mother and father!"

Lailani couldn't bear to take her eyes off her parents to look at the man, but she heard his reply clearly.

"I know of this place. People say that if you pull a person out of the pool, then he or she will be alive again. Try to pull them out."

Lailani's heart beat loudly and she gasped for air. Could it be true that she could have her parents back? Her heart longed for them so much. Without thinking further on the matter, the desperate woman reached into the water. The reflective faces of her parents vanished. The woman felt something in the water and she instantly pulled on the object. Her hand came out of the water and to her excitement she saw that she was grasping a hand by the wrist.

"Keep pulling. You have your mother!"

Devin's excited whisper moved Lailani into action. She pulled harder and soon an arm was coming out attached to the hand. If she kept pulling, then her parents would be back with her and they could go to Mount Glory with her.

Suddenly as Lailani continued to tug on the arm, she was startled as the hand she was grasping grabbed her wrist. Fiercely it pulled back and she felt her feet sliding closer to the water. Lailani screamed in surprise.

The woman slung her head in the direction of Devin, but he was gone. She twisted her neck the other way and saw Cornelius hurrying back for her. Ziona was farther up ahead and appeared to not have heard her scream.

The hand pulled harder and Lailani fell to her knees. She felt herself growing closer to the water that now appeared to move in hungry waves as if ready to eat the foolish girl who had fallen for its mirage. Desperately, she cried as a hand grabbed her other arm. This time she was grabbed from behind and her hero was pulling her away from the water. However, the pool was not even close to surrendering its prey.

Devin couldn't believe how easy it was to convince the girl to grab her parents and pull them out of the pool of treacherous water. Of course, Lailani was now being dragged into the deep water that would be her doom. Diablo would not have to worry about her joining the Ancient One.

Cornelius scurried over to help Lailani. He hesitated when he saw what had happened. The old man seemed indecisive and turned ready to yell for Ziona. Devin couldn't allow that, so he approached the man and whispered in his ear.

"Cornelius, grab her and pull. You can save her."

The old man hurried to her side and grabbed her free arm. With all of the strength he could muster which wasn't much because of his age, Cornelius pulled on the girl.

A tug of war occurred between the elderly man and the water. For a moment Devin thought the old man might win. The younger man couldn't have that. He walked close to Cornelius and leaned toward his ear.

Devin smirked, "You can't win against the arm. It is too strong. It will take Lailani. Why don't you quit fighting it and go with her?

You don't want to lose the only person you have left in your life, do you? Go with her and you won't be lonely here."

The old man sobbed and gasped. He stopped pulling and just clung to his friend.

Devin watched as most of Lailani's body went under the water. Only her head and the arm that Cornelius clung to, was still above the pool.

"Cornelius, pull me out, please."

The old man wailed, "I can't. I am too old. I have no one, but you. I have to go with you."

Lailani's head went under the water and Cornelius sobbed more violently. His cries echoed through the swamp. The old man's feet touched the water.

Devin smiled, "Mission accomplished."

The minion of Diablo turned and began to walk out of the swamp. Now he could return to the Chasm of Misery and abandon the path that the Star was guiding him to follow.

Blurry water swished in Lailani's eyes and she struggled to hold her breath. She could barely see that her other arm was now under the water meaning Cornelius was being dragged under as well. Hopelessness filled her and she felt guilt for killing her friend by her foolishness.

Lailani closed her eyes and waited for her body to drown lost in the deep, cold waters of the swamp forever. She thought she heard music as she sank further into the pool. It surely was her imagination. *How can there be any music in the swamp water?*

As she sank, Lailani noticed a tug on her arm. *Poor Cornelius! He is still trying to help me.*

Then a light tried to pierce through her closed eyes. She squeezed her eyes tighter not wanting to see what was going to happen to her. Perhaps some monster was going to lure her to let go of her breath and then devour her under the slimy water. It was too late already though for the woman realized that she was out of air. With a gasp, expecting to taste the water, Lailani was surprised to find that her lungs took in air.

"Lailani, open your eyes!"

31

The young woman quickly opened her eyes and saw that she was no longer in the pool, but lying on the mossy path. Cornelius was huffing and puffing over her with relief on his face. Next to the old man, Ziona was leaning over her.

"Ziona, how?"

The dark-skinned woman smiled, "I had help."

Ziona glanced to the side. Lailani turned her head and saw a man standing before them dressed in pure white with a light radiating around his body. He had a sword and scabbard around his waist and was smiling affectionately at the gasping woman.

When he spoke, he had an attractive voice that made her feel safe once again.

"Hello, Lailani. My name is Campion."

Devin heard music as he left the swamp. He recognized the voice as Ziona's and he spun around in desperation. Surely she wouldn't be able to pull the two people out of the swamp pool. The woman was standing by the pool looking at Cornelius as he was being pulled into the water. Her song was too distant, but she seemed to be waiting for help.

Devin smirked, "There's no one to help you, Beloved."

As he was about to turn, the man saw another man rushing toward Ziona. *Where did he come from?*

There had not been anyone else in the swamp. Devin hurried to get closer so that he could hear and see more clearly.

The man was dressed in white and seemed to shine. He took hold of Cornelius and pulled on him. Devin was shocked to see that it didn't take much energy for the man to get Cornelius back out of the water. The old man's hand still clung to Lailani. The man took the girl's arm, but Cornelius still wouldn't let go. Ziona put an arm around the old man's shoulders and kept singing. Cornelius looked at her and let go.

Devin watched the man pull on Lailani's arm and easily bring her out of the pool as well. The girl was laid on the moss and gasped for breath. Ziona stopped singing as she and Cornelius hurried over to check on their friend.

Devin tried to suppress a growl as Lailani spoke.

"Ziona, how?"

The other woman who Devin now hated with a passion smiled, "I had help."

Lailani looked at the man who spoke jovially, "Hello, Lailani. My name is Campion." *Campion? That name sounds so familiar. Why do I know that name?*

Devin's mind reeled as he tried to think about what to do now. *How can I join the group again? What excuse can I give for my actions?*

"Devin? Are you going to join us?"

The young man started at his name. He looked and saw that Ziona had walked over to him. She was smiling warmly at him which made him suspicious again.

"Uh, sure."

Devin walked over averting his eyes from Lailani and Cornelius. He saw Campion exchange a glance with Ziona.

The woman whispered, "We will be fine."

Campion nodded, "Of course."

Devin gulped, "So will you be joining us, um, Campion?"

The other man stared at him uncertainly before replying, "No. I must be going. You are in good hands."

Campion looked at Ziona again who motioned for him to go. With a slight glare at Devin, the man left quickly through the swamp heading in the same direction that the travelers were going.

Ziona smiled motioning to the path, "Shall we?"

Devin knew that she was up to something, but what?

Ziona's Song

Oh, sorrow strikes me hard all day,
My soul aches for those I have lost
I yearn for them to return
No matter what the cost

Despair pulls me down so low
I cannot escape the sorrow
But He restores my joy today
So I can live for Him tomorrow

My Master is full of love for me
He doesn't want me to despair
For He made me to be forever His
On Mount Glory I will meet Him there.

CHAPTER 8

GARDEN OF TEMPTATION

A cool breeze blew over the travelers on the side path. Simon shivered slightly for he still wore his brown knit sack and no shoes. He walked a little behind the two knights because he still felt unimportant and lowly compared to them.

Cristo had fetched his horse shortly after meeting Victor. The horse was gray and looked as old as its rider. It tromped along at a leisurely pace and seemed almost worn out or melancholy. Cristo walked beside the horse patting it affectionately on the head.

Victor walked on the other side of the horse which made it so no one could talk to him conveniently. Simon wondered why the knight wasn't walking on their side so they could talk about knighthood and his adventures.

"Simon."

Cristo stopped walking and turned to regard the boy. Simon looked at the man expectantly.

"You must be frozen, my boy. Let me see if I have anything you can wear in this cool wind."

Simon protested, "Oh no, sir. I am fine. I don't want to be any trouble."

Cristo smiled warmly, "You could never be any trouble, child."

The knight untied a bundle that was attached to the horse's saddle. He opened it pulling out a tunic, pants, and a pair of boots all of which looked to have been made just for Simon.

"Here. Put these on. You will be much warmer."

Simon changed clothes and couldn't believe how much better he felt. The tunic was pale blue with a golden mountain in the center. The pants and boots were black. All of the clothes were warm and comfortable. Simon's feet felt so much better now that they were protected from the elements of the road.

"Thank you, sir. I am very grateful."

"My pleasure, Simon. Are you tired?"

The boy hesitated not wanting to appear weak.

"Of course you are tired. You have been walking for many hours. Here. You can ride on my horse. His name is Feliz."

Simon tried to protest, but Cristo would not let him walk anymore. He hoisted the boy up onto the saddle and showed him where to hold on to it.

Simon thanked him quietly and looked over at Victor. The younger knight was walking with his gaze straight ahead. The slave boy wished that he would talk to him, but the knight didn't seem interested in conversation. As they continued down the road, the sky grew darker and Simon's eyes began to close.

The three knights sat on their horses facing the huge army. They were vastly outnumbered. However, they drew their swords ready to fight for their ruler the Ancient One. The youngest charged forward and found himself falling and falling...

"Simon!"

Simon opened his eyes and found himself in Victor's arms. The knight looked startled. Cristo rushed around Feliz and came to their side as Victor set Simon on his feet on the ground.

"I'm sorry. I fell asleep."

The boy lowered his eyes as was his custom, but a hand raised his eyes back up. He looked into the eyes of Cristo so full of compassion and mercy.

"No apology necessary, dear boy."

Simon smiled weakly. He glanced over at Victor.

"Thank you, sir."

The young knight shrugged, "No problem, but don't call me sir. It's Victor."

Victor stood up from his kneeling position.

"Well, why don't we camp for the night? Over here is a nice little area."

On the side of the road was a grassy spot that was smooth and almost looked like a large green blanket. Victor gathered wood for the fire. Simon tried to help, but the knight told him to rest a bit. Cristo searched his bundle again and found food for the trio. He set out three metal plates and cups. Simon marveled at all that could fit in one bundle.

When Victor returned with wood and made a fire, Cristo began cooking the food. The younger knight took over quickly. The older knight leaned back on the grass smiling with gratitude. Simon thought about his dream. He so wanted to be a knight.

"Cristo? What do you need to have to be a knight?"

The older knight looked at him thoughtfully. Simon saw Victor tense at the question. He didn't understand why. *Being a knight has to be so wonderful.*

"Well, Simon, a knight has to be of noble character. Not noble blood, mind you. The poorest person in the world can be a knight. You must have honor and integrity. You must be courageous and brave. You have to be willing to work with other knights to protect the Ancient One's kingdom. You have to be compassionate and generous. You have to care about other people. Most of all you have to have heart. It is a wonderful kind of service with its own rewards."

Simon smiled as he listened. He thought that maybe he fit some of those characteristics. He told the truth and cared about others. He was willing to work with other knights and serve the Ancient One. He knew that in time he could be more courageous and be of noble character. *Perhaps I can be a knight!*

Victor cringed as Cristo told Simon about the traits of a knight. He remembered hearing the same speech when he was in training as a knight. The man watched the boy's eyes light up in excitement and he knew that he should say something. After all, he knew that it was not a wonderful service.

"Why don't you tell him the truth, Cristo?"

The older knight gently turned his gaze on Victor. The boy gaped at him, but Victor ignored him. He was doing this for the child.

"What truth do you mean, Victor?"

"You make it sound like all good times. Simon ought to know about the horrors of being a knight."

Cristo continued to look at Victor calmly. The young man wondered why he was being so kind to someone who was calling him a liar.

"Why don't you tell him, Victor?"

Victor wondered if the elder knight was setting him up. He turned to Simon ready to tell him because after all that was why he had come down this path in the first place. Once he said it, then the man could go back away from the guidance of the Star.

"Fine. Simon, what Cristo says is what a knight should be like, but the life of a knight is not glamorous. The battles you face are loud and frightening. Everything moves quickly and you don't have time to think or make decisions. You have to act and hope you don't make a mistake. The enemies are fierce and bloodthirsty. They won't hesitate to kill you and they actually enjoy it. The battle I was just in was a complete massacre. I was the only one who survived. The dead bodies were hacked and desecrated. Many of the dead knights were unrecognizable. It is not worth it!"

Victor watched the boy as tears formed in his eyes and rolled down his cheeks. He felt terrible, but he kept telling himself that it was for the boy's own good. Glancing at Cristo, Victor saw that the older man was watching him coolly. There was sadness in his eyes, but he didn't correct the younger knight. Victor turned back to cooking the food on the fire.

Simon wiped the tears from his face. He looked at Cristo.

"Is that true, Cristo, sir?"

The older man sat up and took a deep breath.

"It is true that being a knight is not always glamorous. There are battles where you can be injured or lose your life, but there are also battles where the knights are victorious over their enemies. There are times when you don't think you will make it, but then the wind changes and you come out as the champion. No matter what you do in life, though, there are troubles. There is nowhere in the world that you can hide from bad times, no matter how hard you try."

As he finished talking, Simon saw Cristo look at the younger knight as if directing the last statement to him. The boy saw Victor tense again, but remain silent cooking the food. The trio ate in silence. Simon reflected on what both knights had said. He lay down in the grass ready to sleep and looked up into the sky. The Bright Morning Star still shone brightly in the heavens. A heavy sleep fell over Simon and his dreams soon took him to happier thoughts.

As the sky lit up to a pale gray instead of pitch black, Victor quietly gathered his gear ready to sneak back down the path away from the Star. He walked gently down the path hoping that the boy would be alright.

"Leaving us, Victor?"

The man stopped and sighed. He should have known that the older knight would catch him. He should have left in the night. Victor turned and regarded Cristo who stood by his horse reattaching his bundle.

"Yes. I'm going the other way now."

Cristo nodded, "Running away from Him won't make you happy."

Victor cringed, "I'm not running away from anyone. I have places where I need to be."

The old man laughed, "Oh? Where are you going then, Victor? What places are you traveling to where you need to be?"

The young man turned back to the road and started to walk.

"Don't worry about me. You just take care of Simon. He needs you."

"Simon needs you too."

Victor turned again curious.

"Oh, how so?"

Cristo stepped away from the horse and advanced slowly on Victor.

"That child has had no friends for his entire life. He has been beaten and abused since he was small. Now he has the chance to be loved and protected. Your words last night meant something to him. I can tell that he likes you and he needs you to be there as times get tough again which will happen sooner than you think. I cannot be with him all the time for there are moments when I will need to scout out the terrain. Shall I leave him by himself in this dark world? You know what lurks in the world outside of Mount Glory."

Cristo put a hand on Victor's shoulder as the young man looked over at the sleeping child who would stir soon and be ready to continue his journey. His heart ached to help Simon for he knew that the boy would need someone. But how could he help this innocent child when he felt like such a failure? The boy stretched and opened his eyes. He sat up and looked around.

"Are you leaving?"

Cristo looked at Victor who sighed.

"Yes. We're continuing on to Mount Glory today, aren't we?"

The boy jumped up ready to travel again. Cristo smiled warmly.

Victor leaned over and whispered, "This is not permanent. I will be turning back soon."

Cristo nodded, "As always, it is your choice."

As Simon joined the others, he thought he heard horses. Surely Feliz couldn't make that much noise. He turned and saw a sight that made his heart freeze.

Gula, Avidez, and Vano were coming down the path followed by a wagon that Simon had hoped he would never see again. Victor turned to see what Simon was looking at and frowned. He positioned himself in front of the child. Simon felt safe, but it didn't calm his nerves. The boy glanced at Cristo who was still standing in the same spot looking at the group curiously.

"Father, you won't believe what we found."

Vano turned his head in the direction of the wagon.

"What? We need to keep moving."

Aurelius in his wealthy golden robe pushed past the men on horseback. He looked at the trio with disdain and disbelief.

"Well, it's the fake knight and the slave thief."

Simon saw Victor's hand stiffen on the hilt of his sword.

"Greetings, gentlemen. I see we are going in the same direction. Shall we travel together for a bit?"

Cristo smiled at the men who exchanged glances.

Aurelius huffed, "I think not."

Gula interrupted, "Come on, Aurelius. It's just for a bit. They might come in handy if trouble arises."

The bald man seemed to be debating with himself. In the end, he decided that they could combine forces for a day or so, but no more.

Simon wasn't sure this was going to work. He knew these men and their cruel ways.

"Cristo, maybe we shouldn't," he whispered.

Victor regarded him protectively and Cristo walked over laying his hand on his shoulder.

"It will be fine, Simon. Remember that a knight has to get along with others even those who are not very pleasant."

Victor snorted, "Well, these people definitely fit that category."

Cristo laughed quietly, "Definitely."

The group traveled for a couple of hours before they came to another crossroads. The Bright Morning Star hung above the path that went straight. The travelers rested at the side of the road gulping water and taking relaxing breaths. Cristo climbed onto Feliz and took the reins in hand.

"I am going ahead to scout. Stay here and I shall return as soon as I can. Remember stay together. There is strength in numbers."

Feliz galloped down the road. Simon suddenly didn't feel as safe. He must have moved slightly because Victor put an arm around his shoulders.

"Fear not, Simon. No harm will come to you while I am here."

The others sat resting and talking quietly. Occasionally, Keikari would glance over at Simon and say something to Aurelius, snapping at the man. After a couple of hours, the group grew tired of waiting for Cristo.

"Why don't we go down this path and see where it leads?"

Keikari looked around to see what the others thought. Simon felt unsure. Cristo had said to stay at the crossroads.

"I say that's a good idea, wife. Let's go."

The others climbed on their horses and into the wagon. Aurelius glared at Simon and Victor.

"Well, are you coming?"

Simon looked up at Victor who seemed uncertain as well. The boy saw him glance up at the sky.

"Yes, we are coming."

Simon was confused. Shouldn't they follow the Star? It was pointing the other way.

"Victor…"

The knight leaned down.

"We will follow them just for a bit, and then come back for Cristo. He did say to stay together. It will be fine. Trust me, Simon."

Simon nodded and walked beside the knight though he still didn't think that they should leave the crossroads against Cristo's advice.

The side path was to the left of the main road. The landscape on the path was the usual brown and yellow grass. There were more trees, but they were spread out evenly so it wasn't really a forest as before. At the end of the path, the travelers were surprised to see a giant, stone wall. An opening was in the side of the wall and anyone could easily enter for there was no gate or door. Through the opening, they could see a castle and lots of color.

Walking cautiously, Victor followed the group through the entrance and gasped. They had entered a garden which held so many flowers of a variety of colors that the knight had never seen anything like it. The sky was so sunny and bright that Victor could only remember one place that pleasant and he was avoiding it like a plague. There was a magical feel to the garden and the group was drawn in further. Victor looked down at Simon and saw that the boy was in awe just like everyone else.

Approaching a pavilion in the center of the garden, Victor saw a woman standing behind a table. She was enchanting with pale, white skin. Her long black hair flowed down her back in curly ringlets. She wore a long sparkly white gown that flowed outward at the bottom. On her head, the woman wore a silver crown. A necklace with six colorful jewels was draped around her neck. She smiled brightly with red lips and her voice had an addictive quality to it.

"Greetings, Friends. I am so glad that you have come to my humble abode. I am Queen Tatianna and you are welcome to stay here as long as you like. Perhaps you would like to join me for a banquet. I do not usually have such pleasant, worthy company."

Aurelius and his family were enthralled and eagerly joined the queen at her table. Gula and Avidez looked around as if seeking treasures to steal before taking a seat.

Victor was suspicious, but the look Tatianna gave him enticed him so much that he found himself sitting at the table as well. He didn't know that anyone else was there because his eyes were fixed on the beautiful, intoxicating queen. She laughed gently and sat across from Victor pouring her guests wine from a silver pitcher. The group began to converse with the woman who seemed to enjoy their company and attention. *Maybe we can stay here for a while.*

CHAPTER 9

HALL OF MIRRORS

Simon couldn't believe his eyes. Everyone even Victor seemed to be under a trance by Queen Tatianna. They had not questioned whether they should be here or not. Instead, they had eagerly joined a complete stranger in a dangerous world for dinner. The boy avoided the gaze of the queen and asked if he could look around the garden.

"Of course, dear. You may explore that old castle over there as well. Lots of knight armor and royal items in there. All things I am sure a sweet boy like you might find interesting."

Simon watched her turn back to her attentive guests and he was sure that she had no interest in a small boy.

The garden smelled so sweet and pleasant that Simon found himself yawning as he walked down the rows. Shaking his head, the boy decided to go inside the castle in hopes of waking up and becoming more alert. The door was wide open and the castle was very quiet. Simon walked through several rooms: a plush, extravagant throne room complete with a silver throne; a room full of armor, swords and other weapons; and another room with priceless tapestries and paintings.

Simon was awed by all of the rooms, but nothing captured his attention like the hallway that he found past the tapestry room. His mouth flew open. He stared at the hallway walls which were covered with a single mirror so that when one walked down it he or she saw their reflection on both sides as they walked. The boy smiled and walked down the hallway slowly taking in everything that he saw.

About halfway down the hall, Simon caught movement out of the corner of his eye. He stopped and turned toward the mirror. Beside his own reflection, the boy saw the reflection of a girl. Startled he turned around searching the hallway for the young lady, but no one was there.

Simon looked back at the girl in confusion. She was about ten years old with dark skin and black hair braided with purple ribbons. Her dress and shoes were also purple. She waved at him and spoke, but her words were inaudible. Simon stepped closer and tried to read her lips, but he couldn't make out what she was saying.

The girl put her hand on the mirror. By reflex, Simon placed his hand on the mirror to match hers, palm to palm. A sweet smile crossed her face and her eyes twinkled causing Simon to smile shyly. The next thing that happened shocked the boy for the girl's fingers came out of the mirror and grasped his hand.

Simon backed away gasping and the girl held tight allowing him to pull her out of the mirror. There she stood fully in the hallway for real. Simon's eyes widened in surprise and he found himself speechless.

The girl giggled, "Thank you! You rescued me! I can never repay you! My name is Harmony. I am a princess of Mount Glory."

Simon stuttered, "A princess? You...um...I mean..."

Harmony giggled at the shyness of the boy.

"Perhaps you should start with your name."

"Simon."

The girl smiled, "Hello, Simon."

Simon looked over at the mirror then back at Harmony.

"How did you get in that mirror?"

Harmony frowned, "Tatianna lured me here with her pretty flowers. When I was picking them, she came to me and took me inside her castle to show off her royal rooms. Then she cast a spell trapping me inside the mirror. My fate is better than the others."

Simon gasped, "Others?"

The boy glanced at the mirror again hoping to see other people to help.

Harmony nodded, "Other princesses. Tatianna boasted to me about how she had captured six princesses and trapped them inside the jewels on her necklace. Only the Ancient One can release them. We must get that necklace away from her."

"How? We are just kids. Wait a minute. Victor can help. He's a knight."

Harmony giggled, "A knight. Oh, good! Then we are saved. Where is he?"

Simon pointed, "Down in the pavilion with the others."

The girl replied, "Others. Oh, no. Tatianna has lured more people. They haven't drunk the wine from the silver pitcher, have they?"

Simon frowned, "Most of them have. I don't know if Victor did."

Harmony grabbed Simon's hand and pulled him down the hall the way he had come.

"Hurry, Simon! She will transform soon and then it may be too late."

"Transform into what?"

The princess did not answer, but continued running. She only stopped when they came to the weapon room.

"Oh, Simon, grab a sword. Not that one. Grab the one with the golden handle. It comes from Mount Glory. It will help your friends."

Simon clasped the hilt of the golden sword and was surprised at how light it was though it was large in size. He followed Harmony as she began to hurry once again. They exited the castle and headed through the garden to reach the pavilion. Simon halted in shock.

The openings of the pavilion were covered in thick white ropes. It took Simon a moment to realize that it was in fact webs that blocked the entrances. Inside the pavilion, Simon saw his group of people laying with their heads on the table dozing in a deep sleep. He leaned in to see Victor, but the man was not at the table. Frantically, he looked around the room and his heart skipped a beat when he saw a cocoon-like object hanging on one of the webs.

"Harmony, I think Victor is in that cocoon," he whispered sure that she could hear the fear in his voice.

The princess nodded and pointed quietly to the opposite corner where Simon saw a creature so horrible that at first he couldn't believe it was actually the beautiful queen. Huddled in the corner was Tatianna with gray flesh and stringy black hair. Her eyes were sunken and from her mouth hung two fangs. But what took Simon's breath away was the fact that the lower half of her body was now in spider form. Great fuzzy black legs crouched under her, ready to finish off her unsuspecting prey. Around her neck hung the necklace with its six jewels. Simon's stomach turned at the thought of the trapped princesses.

"Simon, use the sword to cut the web by Victor. Then free him quietly and he can help us with the others."

Simon was surprised at how calm the young girl was and instantly he felt courageous. Clutching the sword, the boy crept

45

quickly, but silently to the side of the pavilion where the cocoon hung. Taking the sword close to the web, Simon cut it carefully keeping his eyes on the spider woman. The web broke easily and without a sound. The cocoon fell gently down the web as he cut and finally it was on the ground.

Simon cut thinly so as not to cut his friend. A soft mumble came from the cocoon and the boy hoped that Victor wasn't hurt. The cocoon webbing busted making Victor visible. His eyes were alert, but his mouth was bound with silk strings similar to the web.

"Victor, I'm going to cut the string around your mouth. Then you can get us out of here."

Simon put the sword near the knight's mouth and tenderly cut the silk strings. A shriek frightened him and he looked up in fear. Tatianna was stretching and heading for the guests at the table.

Victor grabbed his hand and Simon's eyes bolted to his face.

"It's okay, Simon. I'll take care of her. You get the others out of here."

As Simon was exploring the garden and the castle, Victor had been mesmerized by the enchanting beauty and unending charm of Queen Tatianna. He sat at the table eating and listening to the chatter. However, when he was offered the wine, the knight remembered his vows he had made to the Ancient One. Though he was no longer following that Master, Victor decided to decline the wine. Tatianna did not seem pleased that her guest refused the wine, but she let it go for a bit. The others slurped down great gulps of the red wine and jovially kept up the party conversation.

Tatianna offered refills of the wine and again tried to convince Victor to drink some. When her eyes flashed in anger at his refusal, the young man started to wonder what was going on. It seemed suspicious that the woman was so determined to have him drink her wine. A third time she refilled their cups and begged him to try her fine vintage. This time Victor refused out of suspicion and the queen's cheeks flushed red with fury. She tried to pretend like it didn't matter to her and hurried around the table attending to her guests.

It was then that Victor remembered Simon. He began to search the garden with his eyes wondering where the boy had gone. The chatter at the table died down. Victor looked at the other guests. Each one had their head on the table sleeping. Before Victor could react, something hit the back of his head and he fell into unconsciousness.

When he awoke, Victor was stuck inside a silk case of some kind. He tried to call out, but his mouth was covered. He tried to move, but the case held tight. Despair filled him as he waited for the end to come.

Surprised, Victor suddenly saw a light in the case that was getting bigger. He felt hopeful again when the case opened up and he was facing dear little Simon, safe and brandishing a sword.

"Victor, I'm going to cut the string around your mouth. Then you can get us out of here."

Victor cringed as the boy put the sword near his mouth yet Simon carefully cut the silk strings.

A shriek echoed through the pavilion. Victor saw Simon glance up quickly. He gently grabbed the child's hand and Simon's eyes bolted to his face.

"It's okay, Simon. I'll take care of her. You get the others out of here."

The boy released the sword to Victor who hoped that he would be able to stop the queen. He stood quietly and turned to see the queen, but what he saw was not the beauty that had enchanted him and the others. This creature was part spider with the top half of her looking like a gray skinned hag.

Victor gulped and gently pushed the boy to the side toward the table as he stepped forward ready to defend Simon to the death.

"Tatianna!"

The creature turned and pierced Victor with her gaze. She spoke with a screech of a voice.

"How did you get out?"

Victor stepped closer.

"Your reign of terror and cruelty is over!"

Tatianna laughed a hissing laugh throwing her head back in glee.

"Oh, are you going to stop me, little man? You are not worth the time it will take me to destroy you. However, Diablo will be pleased that I killed a knight of Glory. So come and fight me. The battle shall be swift."

Victor yelled, "By the name of the Ancient One, perish!"

The man charged forward and the creature shrieked in rage.

Tatianna scurried around trying to get behind Victor, but he kept turning so that she had to face him. In fury, she crawled backwards up the webs on the openings of the pavilion as the knight swung the sword at her legs and abdomen. Horrible shrieks escaped her throat as she tried to get the upper hand, but Victor wasn't giving her a chance to hurt him or the others.

"Tatianna!"

The creature turned at the voice of a girl. Victor was curious also, but he ignored the speaker long enough to stab Tatianna in the stomach. A shrill of pain filled the air as the creature fell to the ground. She threw out a leg and knocked Victor down.

As he crawled for the sword that fell from his hand in the fall, Tatianna sprung to her feet clutching her bleeding stomach. The monster leapt toward the table. Victor tried to get to his feet, but he felt like he was in slow motion. He had to stop her before she reached Simon.

In awe, Simon watched Victor charge toward the spider woman. He shook his head in amazement before running to the table. The boy shook and pinched the people trying to get them to stir. Each began to wake up slowly and groggily.

Simon called to them, "Hurry! We have to leave. Look! Tatianna is a monster!"

The boy pointed to the opening in the cut web. Gula and Avidez staggered quickly out of the broken web on seeing the creature. Korskea screamed at the horrid appearance of the once beautiful queen before she too hurried out of the pavilion. Vano and Aurelius didn't seem to understand what was going on, but the reaction that surprised Simon the most was Keikari.

"You little insect! Can't you see that we have it good here? Her Majesty is going to let me wear some of her clothes and jewels. I will be her apprentice and one day I will be the queen of this garden. All will worship me. Leave you say! Never! I will never leave!"

Keikari advanced on Simon angrily. She put her hands on her hips and glared at him. The slave boy knew that he would not be able to change her mind, so he turned to the two men who still seemed confused and uncertain.

"Simon!"

On hearing Victor's cry, the boy turned and saw Tatianna leaping over to the table. Simon jumped back and the claw-like hands grabbed the nearest person who happened to be the delusional future queen.

Keikari screamed, "No, you said that I could train to be you someday. Please, you promised!"

Tatianna hissed, "I lied, you fool!"

Silk strings wrapped around Keikari as the creature bit deeply into her neck killing her.

"I shall eat you later, little queen. You were right. You will never leave," Tatianna cackled.

Aurelius and Vano screamed as they ran for the broken web stumbling over each other still groggy from their wine-induced slumber. Simon started to follow, but noticed the necklace glistening around Tatianna's neck. Her back was to the boy as she finished wrapping up Keikari's body. He thought maybe he could reach the necklace. With more energy than he thought he could ever muster, the boy leapt on the table and snatched the necklace.

Tatianna screeched and swung around causing the necklace to break off of her own neck. Her clawed hands grabbed the other end of the necklace.

The monster hissed, "You released Harmony, didn't you, pesky brat? You will pay for that."

Fear struck Simon. He would have let go of the necklace if he hadn't been thinking about the other princesses that this monster had trapped.

Taking a deep breath, the boy yelled, "I won't let you keep them prisoner any longer. They will be free like Harmony!"

Tatianna pulled on the necklace as she used one of her legs to come up and hit him. However, it never made it for a sword slashed through first the queen's leg, then swinging around it chopped Tatianna's hand from her arm allowing the necklace to come to Simon completely.

Tatianna shrieked in pain and rushed out of the opening in the web fleeing to her castle. Simon looked at Victor amazed. The knight stood in full majestic valor and smiled warmly at the child.

"Are you alright, Simon?"

The boy nodded and took a deep breath trembling slightly. Kneeling down, Victor held out his arms. The child gratefully hugged his hero. The older man held him tightly and took several deep breaths himself before he spoke. His voice was a whisper and his tone held relieved worry.

"Why did you stay for that necklace? You could have been killed."

"Because Simon is as much a knight as you are, Sir Victor."

Both males turned to regard little Harmony who was practically beaming.

"You have saved us all, Sir Victor. And you, Sir Simon, have rescued the trapped princesses. Now we can take the necklace to Mount Glory where the Ancient One will release them. Our eternal thanks."

Simon saw Victor look at the girl uncertainly.

"Her name is Harmony and she is a princess of Mount Glory. We have to help her get back to the mountain now."

Victor replied sarcastically, "Oh, great!"

Harmony frowned at the knight and looked him over uncertainly.

"We better catch up to the rest of the group and head back to find Cristo," mumbled Victor still out of breath from the fight.

Harmony's eyes lit up.

She exclaimed excitedly without further explanation, "Cristo! Oh, how fortunate!"

CHAPTER 10

LABYRINTH OF CONFUSION

Victor and the two children caught up to the rest of the group right outside of the garden wall. Weary with their minds racing, the travelers walked down the path heading for the crossroads where Cristo had left them.

As they came to the place where they were supposed to stay, Victor saw Cristo and his horse Feliz waiting. The elderly knight sat on a boulder on the side of the road while his horse munched some grass.

"Ah, there you are! Where have you been?"

Cristo looked at Victor curiously yet the younger knight had a feeling that the elder knew the answer.

Taking a deep breath, Victor replied, "We grew tired of waiting and went up this path. We entered a garden and dined with Queen Tatianna. We were tricked and barely got away with our lives. Keikari was killed. We should never have disobeyed your orders."

Victor hung his head in shame waiting for the older knight to answer.

"What would have been only for evil, I see the Ancient One has used for good. Greetings, Princess Harmony!"

Victor looked up and saw Cristo smiling at the little girl who ran forward excitedly.

"I have missed you, Cristo!"

Harmony hugged the man who happily returned the embrace laughing.

"I have missed you as well, sweet Harmony."

"Look, Cristo! See what Simon and Victor did!"

Harmony held up the necklace.

Cristo's face lit up even further.

"Wonderful! Wear it and keep it safe, Harmony, for the princesses will be released at their appointed time. Well done, Simon."

The boy smiled shyly as Cristo turned back to Victor.

"Well done, Sir Victor. I knew I could count on you."

Victor nodded solemnly, but inside he felt such pride and joy. Maybe he could still serve the Ancient One and live the life of a knight of Mount Glory. A feeling of refreshment filled him as Cristo announced the path was clear and they should travel immediately.

As the travelers continued down the path, Victor looked up into the sky and saw the Bright Morning Star glistening brightly. For the first time since his defeat at the battle, the knight felt happy to see it shining in the sky leading them. He finally felt within his heart that he was truly ready to go home to the Ancient One.

Already in a dark mood, Diablo watched as his Demoni gathered again to report on the going-ons of the world. He listened to several reports that interested him only slightly as he waited for Davo to arrive. The Demoni had been ordered to check up on the progress Devin was having with Ziona's group. The instant he got there, Diablo would be ready to hear his news.

"My lord?"

Diablo looked up and saw Monstre kneeling before him. The creature had not been allowed to leave the Chasm since he gave the news about Ziona and the two slaves.

Diablo glared at him, "What do you want, Monstre?"

"My lord, Tatianna is here with some news. Do you wish to see her?"

Movement caught Diablo's eye and he saw Davo entering the area.

"No. Tell her to wait. Davo, approach!"

Monstre slunk off to deliver the message to Tatianna. Davo passed him and proudly walked over to the dragon.

"My lord, I followed Devin and saw him trick the girl and the old man into one of the pools in the swamp."

Diablo hissed in laughter, "Excellent. I knew I could count on him."

Davo took a deep breath.

"My lord, there is more."

The dragon raised his head expectantly.

"They didn't drown. In fact, Ziona began to sing and then Campion pulled them out of the pool."

A ferocious growl grew in Diablo's throat.

"Also, my lord, I think that Devin has seen the Star. I saw him glancing up into the sky many times."

A sly smirk crossed the dragon's face.

"No, Davo. Devin is merely a better actor than you would think. He doesn't really see the Star. As for his mission, I have full confidence that Devin will succeed long before they reach the Mountain."

Davo bowed, "Might I go and help him succeed, my lord?"

Before the dragon could answer, a high screechy voice filled the air.

"How dare you tell me to wait!"

The crowd of Demoni shrunk back and cringed in the presence of Tatianna as she stormed into the cavern and advanced on the dragon. Diablo, however, glanced at her calmly. Davo stepped to the side waiting for further orders.

"What do you have to report, Tatianna?"

The woman was in her beautiful form yet she was missing a hand and was limping slightly.

"I was entertaining some guests at my pavilion. However, they got away."

Diablo yawned rudely for he did not care if some insignificant people escaped the woman.

"One was surely a knight of Mount Glory for he attacked me so skillfully and valiantly."

The dragon sat up higher and listened intently.

"One was a mere boy, but he had such courage and boldness. He somehow released Princess Harmony."

The mention of the princess brought Diablo's eyes to Tatianna's neck in search of the necklace that was her prized possession.

"Where is your necklace, Tatianna?"

The woman's hand flew up to her neck.

Tatianna scowled, "That boy! He grabbed my necklace and as I tried to keep it, the knight attacked me again. They have the necklace."

Diablo threw his head up and roared in rage for he had struck hard against the Ancient One by capturing His princesses. Now they would be freed and the Ancient One would be so joyful. Diablo felt like his insides were full of fire.

"Do something about this, Diablo."

The Demoni gasped and scattered deeper into the shadows for no one called their lord by his name to his face nor ordered him about.

The dragon glared at the woman and brought his face close to her furiously.

"You do not order me about, Tatianna! You are my slave! All you have is mine. I gave you your powers and your beauty. I gave you your castle and gardens! I even misled the princesses so they found you. Yet you have failed me."

"I am not a slave! I am a queen!"

Tatianna's voice transformed to a high shriek as she changed into her spider form and flung herself at the dragon. Diablo easily moved to the side. As she tried to scurry around, the great dragon turned and snapped his mighty jaws. Diablo devoured her in a single gulp.

"You are nothing!"

The creature returned to his spot and lay back down.

"Davo."

Davo returned and knelt before his master while the other Demoni tiptoed back to the area and stared in horror at their lord. Though the woman had brought it on herself, the creatures still shuddered at the power and fury of the dragon.

"Now, Davo, I want you to continue to keep an eye on Devin and his progress with Ziona's group. Let me know if anything unusual happens. However, I do not want you to assist Devin yet, for I have the utmost belief that he will not fail me."

Davo bowed and left. Diablo entered his cave feeling full and satisfied by his latest meal.

If only that Star would go away.

Devin walked behind the others. He had to come up with a way to get rid of them so he could accomplish his mission and return to report to Diablo. *But how? If only I knew where the Star was leading us, I could make a plan.*

"Don't feel bad, Devin."

The man looked and saw that Lailani was walking beside him. "What?"

The red haired girl now dry from her earlier swim smiled, "You didn't know that the hand would pull me down."

Devin smirked, "And if I did?"

Lailani seemed shocked by his answer. She looked up into the sky at the Star and then looked back at him.

"Then I still forgive you. After all, you came back."

Devin frowned at her gentle spirit. *How could she forgive me so easily? Is she really that naïve?*

The man felt in awe by her behavior as Lailani walked back toward Ziona and Cornelius. He shook his head sharply. *No. I have to get rid of them. All of them.*

The path swung around a large hillside and the group stopped when they saw what was around the bend. A huge, vine-covered stone wall towered over them. Off to the side was a broad opening without a door.

"This is a labyrinth, a great maze that has only one correct way through," Ziona explained calmly.

Devin smiled to himself because he had heard of this labyrinth and the creatures that lurked in the shadows. *Perfect.*

"Where is he?"

Devin turned his gaze on Ziona and watched her curiously.

"Who, Ziona?"

The dark-skinned woman smiled at Lailani then cocked her head as if listening.

"Oh, I see. Let's go."

Ziona walked happily and boldly to the entrance of the labyrinth. Lailani shook her head in awe and followed her. Cornelius frowned at Devin. The younger man realized that the old man probably wondered why he was watching his prized friend so closely or thinking about the earlier deceit. Devin smirked and followed the path to the entrance aware that Cornelius was trailing him.

Inside was a dark, tunnel-like maze with walls rising far above the travelers. Eerie sounds echoed through the labyrinth bringing a smile to Devin's face. All he had to do was find one and his troubles would be over. Ziona continued on and Cornelius joined her no longer paying any attention to Devin. Lailani seemed to be falling behind taking in all that she saw.

Around the corner, a large mirror with a silver frame hung on the wall. Devin watched the girl stop and look into the mirror. This was his chance! The minion of Diablo saw movement out of the corner of his eye. Moving stealthily, the man followed the movement knowing what it was that was sneaking about the labyrinth.

"Diablo has orders for you!"

Devin used a harsh whisper hoping only the creature would hear. A growl came from the shadows ahead.

"He wants you to kill the girl at the mirror."

A hissing sound echoed in the tunnel followed by quick movement. Devin knew that his mission was about to be accomplished. First, get rid of the girl and then Ziona and the old man. Diablo would be so pleased.

Lailani had expected to see her face in the mirror, but this was not an ordinary mirror. The reflection before her was one of a woman wearing a green gown and a golden crown upon her head. It took Lailani a moment to realize she was gazing at herself. A gentle giggle escaped her as she waved at her princess self. *If only it was true.*

A growl crept from the shadows behind her. Lailani spun around startled. Sensing movement in the shadows, the woman's heart pounded in fear. If only she had not tarried. Ziona and the others had to be far ahead of her by now.

A hiss followed by another growl came from the shadows. Lailani backed up a step as a brown, furry head came into the dim light. Yellow eyes glared at the girl and sharp fangs hung from its mouth dripping with drool.

A scream escaped from Lailani's mouth as she turned and ran down the tunnel. A hissing sound came before a howl. Lailani hurried forward screaming for help. Where was Ziona? Or Devin? Surely they could help her with this creature.

Quick footsteps and growls came from behind the girl causing her to panic. It was getting closer and no one seemed to be near. Lailani screamed again hoping someone would hear her. Her foot hit a rock jutting up from the ground causing her to fall to her face. Hot breath slammed against her neck.

Lailani knew that the monster had caught up to her. She rolled over without thinking and found herself face to face with the creature. Now she could see that it was some type of wolf yet it stood as if it were a man. The wolf pulled back its head with it mouth wide-opened ready to strike.

A sword flew through the air and pierced the wolf in its heart. The creature wailed and fell onto the ground. Still breathing hard, Lailani jerked her head toward the sword's origin surprised by the sight of her rescuer.

Cristo had led the group on the path which led to a tall stone wall covered with vines. An open doorway stood in front of them. Victor immediately thought of Tatianna's stone wall and wondered what they would face in this place.

A hand grabbed Victor's and he glanced down seeing Simon who looked nervous about what could be lurking behind the wall. Victor tried to smile reassuringly and squeezed the boy's hand. He was beginning to feel like a father figure for the child and hoped that he could continue to help him on this journey.

"This is one of the entrances to a labyrinth that twists for miles, but there is only one way out. Fortunately, I know the correct path to follow. Everyone, stick close to me and do not wander from the group for monstrous wolves live in the labyrinth and they are always ready to snatch stragglers."

Cristo walked through the opening. Victor followed still holding onto Simon with one hand and squeezing the hilt of the sword he had taken from the garden in his other hand. His own broken sword was still sheathed and hanging around his waist for Victor did not have the heart to leave it behind.

Harmony walked on the other side of Simon and she also held his hand with a shaky smile on her face. Aurelius, Vano, and Korskea walked wearily for they had lost the wagon and the horses when fleeing from Tatianna's garden and none had the courage to go back for them. All they had owned was gone and the trio seemed more miserable about the lost possessions than the loss of Keikari. Gula and Avidez entered the labyrinth behind the family and both grumbled about having had about as much as they could stand.

Shortly into the tunnel-like maze, a woman's screams filled the air and echoed off the walls. Cristo turned to Victor and pointed to a left tunnel.

"Victor, find her! She is that way!"

Without questioning the older knight, Victor let go of Simon, raised the sword from Tatianna's, and raced down the left tunnel. He didn't know where he was going and the woman's screams echoed too much for him to get an exact direction. He kept running hoping to find her before it was too late.

Rounding the third or fourth corner, Victor stopped and saw a young woman on the floor with a hideous, monstrous wolf in her face. The wolf stood almost like a man. It pulled back and Victor knew that it was about to attack.

Without a sound, the trained knight flung his sword as hard as he could at the wolf. It struck him right in the heart and the monster howled as it fell dead to the ground. The woman turned her head abruptly to see her rescuer and a look of recognition crossed her face.

Victor remembered the woman and struggled to think of her name.

"Sir Victor?"

The man hurried over and helped the woman to her feet.

"Lailani, isn't it?"

The red haired woman nodded and smiled in relief.

"Are you alright? It didn't bite you, did it?"

Victor tried to see if she was bleeding anywhere.

"No. I'm not bit. Thank you so much. I thought I was dead for sure."

Victor nodded and pulled his sword out of the wolf's chest wiping it clean.

"My pleasure, my lady."

Lailani smiled brightly finally catching her breath.

"Lailani!"

Victor turned as Ziona and Cornelius rounded the corner and hurried to the woman's side. Another man stood at the edge of the tunnel looking upset. Victor felt suspicious on seeing the man yet he didn't know why.

"Are you hurt, Lailani?"

The old man was wringing his hands in worry.

"I'm fine, Cornelius. I had help."

"Why, Sir Victor, what a surprise!"

Ziona smiled at the knight.

"You seem to have changed your mind about being a knight of Mount Glory."

Victor smiled not questioning how she knew he had been reluctant.

"Yes, Ziona. I am back on the right path."

"Victor!"

The young man turned again and found Simon running toward him.

"What happened?"

The boy's eyes widened at the corpse of the wolf creature.

"It was attacking Lailani."

Simon looked over at the woman.

"I know you!"

The red haired woman smiled, "Hello, Simon. Are you okay? You look well."

The boy ran over to talk to her. Victor looked back at the corner knowing Cristo and the others would be coming around soon since Simon would not have strayed far alone. As predicted, the others came around with Cristo in the lead.

"Ah, Ziona, there you are!"

The elder knight embraced the woman who seemed thrilled to see him.

"Finally, Cristo. I've been looking for you."

The man smiled warmly, "We met up at the appointed time."

Ziona nodded, "We did indeed. Harmony? Oh, Harmony!"

The woman in yellow rushed forward and hugged the little girl in purple.

The child hugged back excitedly.

"Ziona, I am so happy to see you again. You won't believe what has happened to me."

Victor turned his attention back to the others not listening to the princess' story. He noticed the man again and wondered who he was.

"His name is Devin."

Victor didn't question how Cristo knew the name of the man or the knight's thoughts about him.

"What do you know about him, Cristo?"

Silence followed. Victor turned to him.

"Everything, but all you need to know at this point is that he is traveling with Ziona and heading to Mount Glory with us. The rest shall develop as we go."

Lailani felt overjoyed on seeing the slave boy Simon. He was cleaned up and wore real clothes instead of the sack. He was smiling and seemed to feel safe. The child spoke on and on, but the woman found herself distracted by the elderly knight with the rusty armor and grizzly face. He did not seem heroic or valiant. Yet the woman felt a peace in her heart on seeing him. Ziona had called him Cristo. As he talked to Victor, Lailani watched him intently. Unlike the desperate drawing the swamp had had on her, she felt drawn to his peaceful nature as if he could provide protection in this dark place.

"Cristo is wonderful."

Lailani looked down at Simon. She kneeled down to his height and listened as he told her about the clothes and the food. Simon told her how Cristo let him ride his horse Feliz when he was tired. Then he told about Victor and how he had saved them all from the monstrous spider woman Tatianna. Lailani felt awed as the child told the story and wondered if it could all be true.

"Simon, come here, child."

The boy ran over to talk with Ziona who hugged him fiercely and thanked him for helping Princess Harmony.

Lailani stood up and her gaze traveled back to Victor though Cristo was no longer standing there.

"Greetings, Lailani. I am Cristo."

With a gasp the woman turned and saw the man standing behind her.

"Oh, Cristo, I…um…I'm sorry…I didn't mean to stare at you…but I…"

The knight smiled warmly at her and she quit talking immediately.

"Nonsense, dear lady. You are just curious about an old knight like me. I would think it odd if you didn't stare. Now, I hope you are ready to travel on through this tunnel of darkness and continue on to Mount Glory."

Lailani smiled back equally as warmly, "Yes, sir. I am more than ready."

Cristo took her arm and escorted her across the tunnel.

"Excellent. Listen please, everyone. We are ready to move on. Follow me and I will get you through the labyrinth. Stay close mind you. There are more of these wolves in the labyrinth and they will be vengeful now that their comrade has been killed."

Lailani walked beside Cristo feeling as if she would be safe even if a hundred wolves attacked her. She could hear the footsteps and mumbling of the others following close behind them.

Devin had been so confident on hearing the screams of Lailani that the wolf would easily destroy her. Yet she had been rescued by some knight traveling with another group heading to Mount Glory. Even worse, the elder knight, Cristo, seemed to know so very much about him which he did not like that one bit.

Devin stood against the tunnel wall watching all of the action and conversations of the people. As he watched Lailani speak to the boy, Simon, the man began to feel like killing her was a huge mistake. Her bright smile and kind nature tugged at his heart. Devin was unsure if he really wanted her dead.

Confused, he followed the others led by Cristo as they went further into the dark tunnels of the labyrinth. His mind reeled as he tried to keep up.

As the group headed on down the tunnel, two men decided not to go with them. Avidez and Gula made their way down a different tunnel. While everyone else had been having a reunion, Avidez had suggested that the two of them go their own way. He was tired of following these people into one dangerous place after another. No amount of money was worth facing a spider woman and monstrous wolves. Besides if they continued following that old knight, something worse was going to happen. They just knew it.

The tunnel that the two men walked down seemed less creepy and dark than the one Cristo was taking the others down. However, Avidez noticed that as they continued walking, eeriness seemed to grow in their tunnel. Darkness engulfed them and strange sounds came from the shadows. Growls and hisses alerted Avidez.

"Stand back to back with me, Gula."

Avidez faced one tunnel entrance and he noticed that Gula stood facing the other one.

"If we stick together, Gula, nothing can defeat us."

Silence followed the statement.

"Gula?"

Avidez turned and saw that he was alone in the tunnel.

"Gula!"

His friend and business partner did not answer. Fear struck Avidez for there had been no sound or movement. Gula had just disappeared.

Avidez spun quickly looking behind himself. He then turned the other way determined to not give anyone time to sneak up on him. Nothing was going to get near without him knowing it. The warrior stopped briefly on hearing heavy breathing. It sounded like it was coming from above.

Shaking in fear, Avidez looked up just in time to see a hideous, snarling wolf leap down on him. He barely had time to scream before all went dark.

Gula had been standing with his back close to Avidez's back when suddenly a hairy arm grabbed him from the shadows. He didn't have time to scream as he was yanked away from his partner. His sword had been dropped in the struggle. Gula found himself face to face with one of the wolf-man creatures. The wolf held him out at eye level while Gula swung his fists at him fiercely. The monster seemed amused before it brought its fangs close to Gula's neck. *Why didn't I stay with Cristo?*

Screams echoed through the tunnel and Simon swung around startled. Harmony grabbed his hand and smiled though she looked frightened as well. A hand squeezed the boy's shoulder and he looked up into the reassuring face of Victor. Simon tried to calm his nerves, but it wasn't easy as more screams came.

"Who's missing?"

Ziona searched the group.

Cristo frowned, "Avidez and Gula. They chose to go a different path. I imagine the wolves have found them."

Harmony gasped, "Oh, Cristo. Can we not help them?"

The old knight looked at the princess affectionately.

"They made their choice, dear one. They must live with their decision. We all can choose who we will follow, but we have to be willing to live with our decisions. Remember that for you will be faced with many options on your journey."

Ziona walked over and put an arm around the little princess who now looked so downhearted. Simon squeezed her hand comfortingly, but his heart was heavy at the loss of the men as well. Even though he meant nothing to them, the boy felt sorry about their fate. *No one should die that way.*

Growls came from the shadows. More than one creature was lurking near the group. Simon saw Victor raise his sword ready for an attack. However, the sword was not needed for a song filled the air.

Cristo was singing a song that caused the darkness to lessen and glorious light filled the tunnel forming a wall of light around the travelers. The light made the creatures shrink away and head away from the group.

Cristo kept singing and began walking again. The others followed him and the wall of light continued to encircle them as they went further down the tunnel. Simon felt his heart soar with joy and his fear disappear with the darkness.

As Cristo sang aloud, Lailani noticed that Ziona was humming the same song as she walked. The light encircling them was so bright and radiant that the redheaded woman had a feeling that they would all make it out alive except for the two straying warriors. She looked over at Simon, saw him breathing easier, and felt joy that he was doing better. The child had been through so much though Lailani wasn't sure of any details. She could tell that he was used to being scared and it made her angry at Aurelius and his family. Yet she took comfort in knowing that Simon was safer now with Cristo and Victor.

"Lailani?"

The woman smiled at Cornelius.

"He is wonderful, isn't he, Cornelius?"

The old man looked over at Cristo knowing that was who she meant.

"I don't know, Lailani. He just took over our journey and now tells us what to do. How is that different from Aurelius?"

Lailani frowned, "I feel different about Cristo than Aurelius. He guides us, but I feel like it is for our best interests. Aurelius is pompous and tends to do things for his own interests."

The old man replied, "Yeah, but at least we know where Aurelius stands. What do we know about this Cristo? How do we know that he isn't setting us up? Look at what he does with the light. That's not normal."

Lailani didn't understand how Cornelius could feel this way about Cristo.

Before she could answer, she heard Simon yell, "Cristo!"

Victor was astonished by the light though he had seen unusual things on Mount Glory. He shook his head in wonder and listened to the words of Cristo's song. A rustling sound caused the knight to turn toward a side tunnel with his sword ready.

"Victor, what is it?"

Simon's whisper caused Victor to push the child behind him by instinct.

"I don't know. Stay behind me."

Movement came from the tunnel. Victor braced himself keeping his eyes on the shadowy object as it approached. Someone crawled out of the tunnel and fell to the ground.

Victor whispered, "Stay here, Simon."

Without waiting for an answer, the man walked forward sword ready. He came to the body and kneeled down.

Slowly he rolled it over and gasped, "Avidez."

"Avidez."

Simon couldn't believe his ears.

"Whoa!"

Victor sighed, "I thought I told you to stay over there."

The boy lowered his eyes.

"Sorry. I thought you might need back-up."

Victor glanced over his shoulders.

"And exactly how were you going to help?"

Simon shrugged, "I would have thought of a way."

The knight shook his head and turned back to Avidez. Simon figured the damage was done so he knelt next to Victor and looked at the mangled, bloody body of Avidez. His clothes were ripped and bloodstained. Simon stared at the man feeling suddenly very fearful of the wolves.

A hand flew over his eyes and Victor's voice sounded exasperated.

"Simon, get Cristo!"

Simon stood up and glanced at Avidez again.

"Go on! Hurry!"

Simon ran toward the elder knight.

"Cristo!"

The group stopped and Cristo stepped forward to meet Simon.

"We found Avidez! He's with Victor over there!"

Cristo looked in the direction the child was pointing and moved closer to see the injured man.

Victor called out, "He's alive, but I'm going to need help to get him out of here."

Simon looked at Cristo expectantly. The man turned to the others.

"Victor needs help supporting Avidez. Who will help?"

Simon watched as the other men averted their eyes avoiding Cristo's gaze. *How could they be so cruel?*

The man needed help and yet no one was willing to give him a chance.

"I'll help."

Aurelius guffawed loudly at the boy.

"You? You can't help him, you little runt!"

Simon lowered his eyes feeling inferior and insignificant once again.

"Back off, Aurelius," warned Victor.

"Simon, thank you for volunteering to help with Avidez, but I have a special task for you."

The boy looked at Cristo wondering what he wanted him to do.

"Simon, I hereby appoint you as Guardian of Glory. You now have the responsibility of protecting the princesses of Mount Glory until we reach the Ancient One. As of now, you must guard

Harmony and the necklace in hopes of protecting the freed princesses at a later time. Do you accept the position?"

Simon felt so important. Of course he would protect Harmony and the trapped princesses.

Aurelius snorted, "Ridiculous. This brat couldn't keep anything safe. He's worthless!"

Simon bowed his head in shame beginning to believe what his former master said.

"That's it, Aurelius."

The slave boy glanced up and saw Victor heading for the large man.

Cristo gracefully moved in front of the younger knight.

"No, Victor. We must get out of here as soon as possible."

Victor looked over at Simon who smiled weakly, but gratefully. Then the man glared at Aurelius and returned to raise Avidez to his feet. One of the bodyguard's arms was draped around Victor's shoulder.

"Pathetic it is relying on that slave scum to protect royalty," shouted Aurelius as he walked over to his son.

Vano added, "Completely pathetic."

Simon lowered his eyes again telling himself that it was probably true.

A gentle hand cupped under his chin and raised his face until his eyes looked into the loving, kind eyes of Cristo.

"You know, Simon, there are some in this world who will always try to make you feel worthless because they think it makes them look better. Words will be said that crush you as powerfully as a boulder and make you doubt your true value. A true knight of Mount Glory dismisses these lies and holds fast to the truth. And the truth is that you are worth more than anyone can imagine. As to the position, do you accept?"

Simon was surprised by the compassion behind Cristo's words. He didn't know if he would be able to truly protect the princesses, but he was willing to do his best for Cristo.

"Yes, I accept."

Cristo smiled, "Well done, my boy."

Devin listened to the exchange between Cristo and Simon. He knew all about words crushing a person and making them doubt their value. Diablo was a master of lies and had the gift of hurting people with mere words. He could say a few well-placed insults and make Devin feel completely worthless.

"A true knight of Mount Glory dismisses these lies and holds fast to the truth. And the truth is that you are worth more than anyone can imagine."

Cristo's words touched Devin's heart for he had a sudden desire to become a knight. He didn't want to serve Diablo anymore. The confusion Devin had felt earlier melted away and he clearly saw his path. He would go to Mount Glory and beg the Ancient One to allow him to become a knight. If the Ancient One would not let him be a knight, then he would ask to be His slave instead. Surely a slave of the Ancient One was better than a warrior of Diablo.

"Well done, my boy."

Cristo turned to the others again.

"I ask again. Who shall help Victor with Avidez?"

Devin saw the other men scoff and turn away in disgust. They were not about to give the man a second chance. Devin frowned. He wanted to be given a second chance so shouldn't he give someone else a chance? He didn't know Avidez, but he seemed to have been punished hard for his betrayal.

"I'll help him."

The others swung around to the man that they probably had forgotten in his silence. Devin ignored their judgmental stares for he looked straight at Cristo who held his gaze with a twinkle in his eyes. Devin walked over and lifted Avidez's other arm placing it over his shoulder. He glanced at Victor who was giving him an uncertain look.

Devin looked back at Cristo who was still looking at him warmly. The young man began to feel embarrassed by the attention. He was so used to blending in or hiding in the shadows.

"Well, are we getting out of here or what?"

Cristo smiled, "Yes, I think we have been here long enough."

The elder knight led the group down several more tunnels. Devin felt relief as they came out of the labyrinth with the Bright Morning Star glistening brightly above the travelers.

Cristo's Song

Through the dark world I do tread.
My heart overflows with dread.
Unknown terrors lie ahead.
By my own fear I am led.

Yet in this darkness there's the Light.
He shines eternal, oh so bright.
He shines with love and never spite.
Fears and evil do take flight.

The Light He completely drives away
My dread and all the shadows that sway
The dreary dark has turned to day.
And He will still love me when all pass away

CHAPTER 11

BATTLE ON THE BEACH

"My lord, I have seen Cristo."

Davo braced himself for the fury he knew would come with the announcement.

Diablo glared at the Demoni.

"Where?"

Davo shifted his body tensely.

"He has led a group through the labyrinth."

The dragon seethed, "What group?"

"Aurelius of Terra and his two children Vano and Korskea. Two bodyguards Gula and Avidez of Terra yet only Avidez exited the labyrinth."

The dragon hissed an amused laugh.

"Simon the slave boy, Victor the knight, and Ziona's group."

Diablo felt his temper boiling.

"Where's Devin?!"

Davo smirked though not too insolent.

"Devin is with the group and I saw with my own eyes that he was helping the knight with the injured bodyguard. Also, my lord, he definitely looked up into the sky and was relieved to see the Star on exiting the labyrinth."

Diablo swung around and entered his cave roaring and fuming.

Devin couldn't have betrayed him. He wouldn't dare. Yet Cristo had stolen other slaves from the dragon before. If Devin had truly seen the Star and was still willingly following it, then he would have to be destroyed. He couldn't be allowed to reach Mount Glory. He couldn't be allowed to serve the Ancient One and become one of the Beloved.

"Davo!"

The dragon sensed him cautiously entering the cave.

"Take some Demoni and kill all who are traveling with Cristo. As for Devin, give him one chance to return to me. If he refuses, kill him as well."

Davo chose Monstre, Nefasto, Maligno, Aciagi, and Hedias to go with him. They set out and headed to catch up with Cristo's group.

Diablo hissed in amusement, "This time you will fail, Cristo, for my best Demoni will destroy your precious followers. Then all will know about the consequences of going to your Ancient One."

On exiting the labyrinth, Cristo tended to the wounds of Avidez. The bodyguard awoke groggily. He told the group what had happened in the labyrinth. As he told of the wolves, Lailani understood his fright for she had experienced the same terror whenever the creature was chasing her.

"Gula was behind me and then he was gone. I don't know what happened to him. A wolf monster jumped down on me from above and it used its claws and fangs to tear at me. I was sure I was dead, but then I heard a song and it seemed to spread light throughout the tunnel. The wolf dropped me on the ground and fled down one of the tunnels. I started crawling toward the sound of the voice singing, but I lost consciousness as I tried to stand to exit the tunnel."

Lailani was amazed by the story and wondered if Cristo had meant to help Avidez with the song. Surely it was a coincidence. Then again, amazing things seemed to happen in the knight's presence.

As if to confirm the woman's thoughts, a musical voice wafted through the air.

"Hello, Cristo."

The group was surprised to see a woman standing behind Harmony who spun around. The tall woman's long, straight black hair was adorned with a pink flower and partially fixed into a bun. She wore a light pink kimono with a hot pink sash. A pleasant smile played on her face.

"Oh, Mercy, you are free!"

Harmony embraced the beautiful princess as Cristo approached with joy crossing his face.

"Welcome, sweet Mercy."

Princess Mercy hugged Cristo with a musical laugh.

"I am so glad to be free once again."

Harmony announced, "Everyone, this is Princess Mercy of Mount Glory. She is one of the princesses trapped within the necklace. How did she get out, Cristo?"

Cristo smiled affectionately, "When Devin was merciful and willing to help Avidez, Princess Mercy was freed from her jewel prison."

Mercy giggled, "Who is Devin? I shall thank him for his merciful spirit."

Harmony pointed to Devin who seemed slightly embarrassed at the sudden attention. Lailani stifled a laugh as the precious princess hugged Devin thanking him and the man squirmed with a "sure, no problem".

Ziona stepped forward and embraced the princess. She sweetly introduced her to the others in the group. Once introductions and greetings were made, the group started traveling again with the Star shining high above them.

As they walked, Lailani marveled at how far from Terra they had traveled. Their journey had seemed so strenuous. Surely they were close to Mount Glory after traveling so far. Lailani was ready to make it to the mountain.

The road wound around and ended at the edge of a great sea. The Star shone above the sea and Devin wondered how they were going to cross it. There was no boat in sight and the sea was too large to walk around. Devin looked at Cristo who seemed at ease at their dilemma. The knight suggested that they rest for a while before continuing their journey. As everyone sat on the grass and talked, Devin had an eerie feeling that something bad was about to happen.

A grumbling sound alerted Devin. As he looked around, fear struck his heart for he saw six heavily armed Demoni coming toward them. Davo was leading them and Devin recognized Monstre, but he wasn't sure of the names of the others. He knew that they were coming to destroy the travelers. It frightened him to think that Diablo had commanded them to kill him as well.

"Look! We have trouble!"

The man did not take his eyes off of the Demoni, but heard the others moving behind him. No matter what they did, this was not going to turn out well.

"Look! We have trouble!"

Victor jumped to his feet as he saw the Demoni. The others stood quickly as well. The knight glanced over at Simon who was standing near the princesses. Victor held the sword that the boy had found in the castle and that he had used against the wolf creature. He stepped forward so that he was in front of the rest of the group with his sword ready.

"Victor, give your sword to Simon. He will need it to protect the princesses."

Cristo's words seemed odd to Victor.

Simon protested, "Oh, no. Then Victor won't have a weapon."

Cristo smiled, "He has a sword of his own."

Victor felt embarrassed, but he had no other choice than to tell the truth.

"Uh, Cristo, my sword was broken during the battle before I started this journey."

With raised eyebrows, the elder knight asked, "Oh, was it? Let me see."

Ashamed, Victor pulled the sword from the scabbard and shock filled him as he saw his sword renewed. The blade looked more majestic and stronger than ever. Simon hesitantly took the sword that he had gotten from the castle. His eyes were wide as he looked at the knight's sword.

Victor walked forward again and saw that the Demoni were almost there now. Movement caught the young man's eye and he looked to his left. Devin stood ready with his sword. Victor turned and saw Cristo still standing with the others with his sword in its scabbard.

"Aren't you going to fight, Cristo?"

The older man replied secretly, "Oh, you can handle it. My battle shall come later."

Victor looked at the other men, but none of them stepped forward. Vano yawned and sat back down. Aurelius snorted and turned to look at the sea. The women and Cornelius stood beside Feliz with the princesses.

"I would fight, but I dropped my sword in the labyrinth."

Victor looked at Avidez who was still in sore condition.

"Use my sword, Avidez."

Cristo handed his sword to the injured man who looked ready to kill something. Avidez stepped forward and stood on the other side of Devin.

The Demoni stopped and formed a line in front of the men. Davo smirked as he recognized Victor.

"Well, if it isn't the fake knight. Look, Monstre! He is the pathetic one I told you about."

The other creatures laughed mocking Victor. Shame covered the young man and he felt his face blush.

Simon shouted, "Victor's not pathetic! He beat that spider-monster Tatianna and killed a wolf creature in the labyrinth. He saved all of us!"

Victor looked at the boy and saw him standing at his right side with sword in hand. Though he was talking to the Demoni, Simon was looking at Victor encouragingly. Pride and love shone in his face. Victor felt courage and determination fill him as he raised his sword ready to defend his friends to the death.

Monstre looked at Devin who felt dread entering his body.

"Ah, Devin. Our dark lord, Diablo, is very disappointed that you didn't follow orders."

Devin suddenly felt more uncomfortable.

"Orders?"

Devin sighed at Lailani's question. He should have known that this couldn't stay secret.

"Oh, yes. Devin was supposed to convince you to come to the Chasm as slaves to Diablo or kill you if you wouldn't be persuaded."

Devin cringed.

Cornelius mumbled, "I knew it. I knew he was up to no good."

"We have been ordered to give you one chance, Devin. Return to Diablo or be destroyed like these pitiful creatures."

Devin didn't know what to do. He didn't want to die, but he didn't want to go back to Diablo and live in misery for the rest of his life. He looked around at the others and each looked either confused or angry at his betrayal. Lailani looked devastated and Devin was sure that she had figured out how he had tried to kill her twice now.

His eyes stopped on Cristo. Oddly, the elder knight was staring at him with a look of love and acceptance. Devin thought about how different he was when around Cristo. He felt more heroic around the elder knight, whereas he felt like a slave with Diablo. He even liked himself better in Cristo's presence. His desire to continue on to Mount Glory and serve the Ancient One became stronger. Devin knew what he had to do.

"I choose to follow the Star to Mount Glory and serve the Ancient One if He will have me. Even if He won't, I would rather die than go back to Diablo."

The Demoni glared at Devin.

"Then die, Fool."

Simon oddly felt very brave as he stood with the other warriors. He hated what the Demoni said to Victor. The boy remembered what Cristo had said about not believing the lies others told and focusing on a person's true value. He hoped that Victor remembered the same words.

"Monstre, you can have Devin. I want Victor. I should have killed the little worm before when he was crying like a weakling on the battlefield."

Simon glared at Davo fiercely.

"Of course he was crying. Many people were brutally killed by you monsters and he has a good heart. That's what makes him strong. Right, Victor?"

The boy looked up at the knight and found him smiling at him.

"Right, Simon."

"Nefasto, you take the injured rat. He won't be much. The rest of you, get the princesses. The slave boy won't be any trouble. He's all mouth."

Simon frowned at the Demoni and then hurried over to stand in front of Princess Harmony and Princess Mercy with his sword ready. As the Guardian of Glory, he had promised to protect the princesses no matter what. And he planned to do just that.

Monstre with crooked sword in hand rushed forward charging at Devin. The man smirked. Having been in the Chasm for so long, he had learned how to fight skillfully with a sword. He knew all of Monstre's weaknesses and he planned on using them to his advantage. Their swords slammed together in a loud clang. Devin used all of the fancy footwork that he had learned in the Chasm. He dodged Monstre's sword and jumped from side to side slashing at the Demoni who also blocked the attack easily. *He must have been practicing while trapped in the Chasm.*

The man and the Demoni slammed swords together time after time. Devin felt his arm weakening with each blow until he didn't think that he could hold on to the sword much longer. Monstre twisted around and hit the human's sword again more fiercely than before. The sword flew into the air and Devin being off-balanced fell to the ground. Monstre's hissing laughter filled the man's ears as he waited for the Demoni's sword to finish him.

Davo charged forward swinging his sword at Victor. The knight knew that the Demoni expected it to be a short battle, but Victor was willing to give everything he had to prove the creature wrong. Taking a deep breath, the man remembered his training and stepped forward to meet Davo's blade. The fight was evenly matched for Victor blocked every strike from the monster and was even able to drive him back from the others. The surprise on Davo's face was priceless.

Victor continued to move Davo back and to the side. Their swords continued to meet and clang echoing in the air. The man felt stronger than he had in days for he knew deep in his heart that he was fighting for the Ancient One again. He was doing his Master's will and it felt wonderful.

His foot slipped on the rocks causing Victor to glance downward. He realized that he was on the edge of a steep cliff with sharp rocks below and the great sea crashing against the beach. Victor looked up and barely blocked Davo's sword. In the next instant, a fist slammed into the right side of his face and the knight tumbled off the cliff.

"You can do it, Simon."

Harmony's encouragement caused the boy's fear to melt away. Even though he was facing three Demoni, Simon felt like he could truly be victorious. He swung his sword at them, but they kept their distance.

Suddenly two of the Demoni came quickly at the boy swinging their swords. Simon dodged and ducked away from their swords. He swung his sword at one of them, but the creature easily blocked with his own sword. Dodging the other Demoni's sword, the slave boy was glad that he was small and able to move quickly. He thrust his sword again and heard a curse from one of the Demoni. His sword had struck it in the stomach.

The creature backed away and the other went to his side to check for the extent of the damage. Simon couldn't believe that he had hurt one of them. Confusion hit the child as he realized that both Demoni were smirking.

"Simon! The necklace!"

The boy turned toward Harmony and saw her pointing at the third Demoni who was running away from the battle holding the necklace high in the air above his head.

The clang of swords brought Devin's eyes back to Monstre. Devin's sword had struck the creature's weapon. The man was as surprised as Monstre to see Lailani wielding the sword. Monstre quickly regained his composure.

The gray monster smirked, "Foolish woman, don't you know that I am one of the best trained warriors of the Chasm?"

Devin looked around trying to find a weapon, so he could help the young woman. However, there was nothing available. Desperation hit him for he knew that he couldn't help Lailani. More clanging captured his attention. Lailani was striking hard against Monstre. She hit his sword time after time quickly with a look of determination on her face. The creature had not expected such a strong attack. His cockiness disappeared as the woman twisted her sword causing his weapon to fly from his hand.

Devin leaped up and caught the sword. He turned back to the fight and pointed the blade at the Demoni. Monstre looked dumbfounded. His eyes darted back and forth between the two humans. Devin glanced at Lailani and her confident smile amazed him. *How could such a young skinny girl take on a fully trained Demoni?*

Devin smiled brightly, "Not too good for one of the best trained warriors of the Chasm."

Monstre glared at the man.

Lailani declared, "Your mistake was assuming that I am a weak little woman. Instead I am a strong woman who won't let anyone stop her from getting to the Ancient One and any other people that have chosen to follow the Star."

The Demoni looked at the two blades pointed deadly close to him and fled without looking back. Devin and Lailani exchanged an amused glance.

Jagged rocks below were all that motivated Victor to hang on to the bumpy side of the cliff. Above the knight, Davo was kicking off rocks with mixed results. Some of the rocks fell past the man plunging to the depths of the cliff floor, but many bounced and hit Victor's armor. He struggled to keep hold, but it was becoming more difficult as his body ached increasingly and the gravity of his armor pulled him down. With reservations, Victor used one hand to unhook his heavy armor leaving only the gray clothes that he wore underneath. The armor fell and he cringed as it crashed on the rocks below.

Without the burden of the armor, the knight felt able to hang on for a great deal longer. He began to devise a plan for getting back to safety. *If I could get closer to the top, then perhaps I could…No that would mean certain death. But what else can I do?*

Looking up, Victor saw Davo glaring at him while still kicking rocks. Yet beyond the Demoni shining like a beacon in the sky, the Bright Morning Star glistened. The knight felt hope and peace fill him as he stared at the Star.

Climbing hand over hand, Victor climbed up the rock face getting closer to the top, but also closer to Davo. The Demoni crouched down not with his sword ready, but his fist. The creature was preparing to strike the man and send him to his doom.

Taking a deep breath and mustering all of his courage, the knight pushed on the cliff face. This sent him flying high into the air flipping over the Demoni's crouching body.

As he sailed through the air, Victor saw his sword just behind Davo. He landed and rolled his body on the ground grabbing the sword with his right hand then turning ready to strike.

A sword was pointed straight at his throat.

"Not bad, worm, but you lose. Diablo will reward me greatly for killing a knight of Mount Glory."

Two swords united by Davo's throat. Victor looked in awe at Devin and Lailani who stood on opposite sides clutching swords tightly. The man smiled gratefully and felt relief course through his body.

"I wonder if the Ancient One will reward me greatly for killing a Demoni of Diablo," smirked Devin.

Davo growled and began to turn his sword for the traitor, but a third sword touched the back of his neck.

"I wouldn't do that if I were you."

Victor was amazed to see Avidez holding his sword and looking full of strength.

Davo seemed completely unconcerned as he looked beyond Victor.

"Should you be wasting your time with me? What about the boy?"

Victor scrambled around on the ground to locate Simon. Davo scurried away as the others became distracted by the sight before them. Victor thought that his heart would stop.

"Simon!"

The Demoni rushed away with the necklace and Simon felt helpless. *If I follow the Demoni, then Princess Harmony and Princess Mercy would be left with the other two Demoni. However, if I stay with the two princesses, then the other princesses would be trapped forever in the necklace and taken to Diablo the dragon. What should I do?*

"Go, Simon! I will handle these Demoni."

A man dressed in white and shining radiantly stood beside Simon. The child did not know where the man had come from or who he was. Harmony came forward.

"Campion!"

Seeing that the princess knew the man, Simon ran to Feliz and climbed on the horse.

"Come on, Feliz. You can catch that monster."

The horse neighed loudly and raised his front hooves into the air before charging after the Demoni with more strength and energy than seemed possible.

"Simon!"

Victor's voice brought hope to Simon for he knew the man was still alive. However, he did not turn to see where the knight was because he had to stay focused on the task at hand. An inner peace filled him as he held on tightly to Feliz who was advancing on the Demoni.

Without stopping to think about the future, Simon leapt off of the horse and landed on the gray monster that crashed to the ground. The necklace went flying through the air as the Demoni rolled over and punched the boy in the face. Simon covered his face with both hands not knowing where his sword was.

Suddenly, the boy heard the Demoni gasp and felt him move away. Simon opened his eyes and saw the monster running. The young man searched the ground frantically hoping that the Demoni had not found the necklace and continued running.

A quiet neigh caught the boy's attention and he was delighted to see Feliz approaching with the necklace in his mouth.

"Wonderful job, Feliz! You found it."

Gently Simon took the necklace from the horse with a smile. He patted the horse on the nose appreciatively and Feliz neighed happily.

"Simon!"

The child turned excitedly as Victor ran up to him. The knight grabbed him by the shoulders and looked him over. His hand briefly and gently touched the bruise on Simon's face.

"I'm okay, Victor."

A look of relief crossed the man's face. He embraced the boy tightly.

Concern filled his voice as he said, "Don't do that again."

Simon sighed, "I'm sorry. He had the necklace. I had to save the princesses. After all I am the Guardian of Glory."

Still hugging him, Victor breathed quickly, "I know. I know. I'm glad you got it back, but I am more relieved that you are not hurt."

Simon held on to the knight suddenly feeling very touched. He had never been cared about before. Tears filled his eyes as all of the years of abuse came to the surface. The boy tried to prevent it, but

79

tears gushed down his face and soon he was sobbing. He felt so embarrassed at what the older man would say.

Victor had never been so scared in his life. In fact his fear for Simon's life was stronger than when he hung on the cliff with his own life at risk. Relief engulfed him as he saw the child unhurt and hugged him. The boy started shaking and Victor realized that he was crying. He held the boy as sobs escaped him and rubbed his back hoping that Simon would feel encouraged and comforted. His heart ached for the pain and suffering this child was experiencing which reminded him of his own childhood.

"Simon, I don't know all that you have been through, but I know what it is like to be unloved. My mother died when I was little and my father abandoned me when I was thirteen. Only when I went to the Ancient One did I find true love and acceptance. He became like a father to me and He is nothing like my real father."

The child had stopped sobbing to listen.

"Keep heading for the mountain. The Ancient One's love is far more than any other person can give you. You deserve that kind of love, Simon. I am honored to have you as my friend."

Simon hugged him tightly. "Me too. Thanks, Victor."

Lailani sighed with relief as she saw Victor returning with Simon and Feliz. She had feared the worst when she saw the boy riding the horse after a Demoni. As she watched them approach, the young woman heard someone clear his voice behind her. She turned curiously and found Devin looking at her.

"Lailani, I want to thank you for saving my life. I could never have defeated Monstre without you."

"You would have thought of something. You always seem to have a plan."

The woman smiled warmly at the man.

"Well, maybe, but you still rescued me. Thanks."

Lailani replied, "You're welcome, Devin."

A frown crossed the face of the man.

"Why did you do it?"

Lailani mimicked his frown.

"What do you mean?"

Devin shrugged, "Why did you help me after what I did to you? I tricked you into almost drowning in the swamp. I also sent that wolf to attack you."

Lailani didn't know how to answer him, but as she looked up, her eyes noticed the Star shining more beautifully than ever. A sweet smile replaced her frown.

"I helped you, Devin, because you decided to follow the Star when faced with the consequence of death. You didn't join up with them again when they gave you one last chance. As for what you have done to me, I forgive you. None of us are perfect. I have made mistakes too. That's the great thing about this journey to Mount Glory. We all get a fresh start with the Ancient One. I am happy that you are going to Him with us."

Lailani's cheeks flushed as she said the last part. She averted her eyes to where the others were gathered.

A hand gently grasped her left hand and Lailani looked back at the man.

Devin smiled at her gratefully, "I'm happy to be going to Him with you."

Lailani smiled affectionately and squeezed his hand. Together they walked hand in hand to join the others.

"Well done, all of you! What a courageous group of knights!"

Cristo was beaming and Victor felt pride at their victory. Even though they had been outnumbered and out-skilled, their perseverance had driven back the Demoni. The man watched as Simon handed the necklace back to Harmony who squealed with delight kissing him on his cheek. Victor held back laughter as the boy's face reddened and his eyes widened. *He'll have to get used to that if he wants to be a heroic knight.*

"Oh, no! Two jewels are missing! Oh, Cristo!"

Princess Harmony began to cry. Princess Mercy and Ziona put their arms around the girl trying to comfort her.

Cristo kneeled down in front of her.

"Dry your eyes, my sweet Harmony, for no jewels are missing. I know where they are."

Victor was as curious as the others as to the secret location of the jewels.

"Where are they, Cristo?"

The knight did not answer, but smiled at the loving child.

"We are here!"

A high, beautiful voice giggled causing the travelers to turn around startled. Standing almost next to them were two ladies. Both women were tall with shoulder length black, wavy hair. One woman had a teal dress that was sleeveless and flowed at the bottom. A golden headband with a teal jewel lay across her forehead. The other woman had a lilac dress with puffy sleeves which also flowed at the bottom. A golden crown was placed neatly on her head. Their faces were radiant with joy and their laughter filled the air.

"Oh, Princess Hope and Princess Grace! You are free!"

Harmony ran to hug the two princesses. The ladies giggled happily as Mercy and Ziona joined the embrace.

Victor was amazed at their sudden appearance. He looked at Cristo.

"How did they get freed, Cristo?"

The elder knight smiled joyfully, "You had such hope on the when you remembered who you belong to, Victor. Princess Hope was cliff side freed because of you. And you, Lailani, showed grace to Devin though he tried to kill you twice and really didn't deserve your forgiveness. Princess Grace was freed because of you."

The princesses stepped forward with hugs and thanks. Victor was touched that the Ancient One had freed them based on what he and Lailani had done. His heart filled with love and gratitude for the Ancient One as he marveled at this great moment. Yet he ached to get going on the journey again as soon as possible.

CHAPTER 12

SEA OF ENTICEMENT

With the threat of the Demoni gone and the celebration of the freed princesses fading, the travelers turned to face the rolling sea that lay in their wake. High in the sky, the Bright Morning Star shone brightly in the direction of the sea. Simon watched the water slam against the beach. There was no land in sight and the water seemed to stretch endlessly.

"This is crazy! How can we sail across the sea with no boat?"

Aurelius was looking at the sea with his hands on his hips and a sour expression crossing his face. The man did not seem the least bit grateful that they had survived the attack from the Demoni. Instead, he was grouchier than ever.

With a childlike innocence, Simon's eyes lit up.

"We could make a boat."

The large man turned and scoffed at the boy.

"Silence, scum. That is the stupidest idea I have ever heard."

For the first time, Simon did not feel inferior. Instead of lowering his eyes as was his custom, the child stared up at the man.

"I don't think it is a stupid idea."

Aurelius backhanded the boy who fell to the ground. Hot tears began to cloud Simon's vision. His face flushed in embarrassment and his breathing was staggered.

"Nobody move! This is Simon's battle."

Simon felt strength at Cristo's words. All that Cristo and Victor had told Simon about his worth and real love flooded into his mind. Taking a deep breath and regaining his composure, Simon stood back up and faced Aurelius who looked stunned that the child would still confront him.

"If we must cross the sea, then a way will be found."

The large man hovered over the boy growling.

"Worthless runt! You are nothing more than a pathetic slave!"

The man's large hand hit Simon in the face again causing him to stumble, but he remained on his feet.

"I'm not a slave! I am free!"

The hand formed a fist and slammed into the boy's cheek.

Simon gasped, "And I am going to Mount Glory where the Ancient One will love me!"

Aurelius looked like he had murder in his eyes. For a second Simon almost fled from the man. The fist smashed into the child's mouth and the taste of blood trickled on his tongue as he fell to the sandy beach again.

"Do something!"

Harmony's strangled cry touched Simon's heart and he took another deep breath.

"No, not yet."

Cristo's voice was full of command yet it also held a confidence that gave Simon the courage to rise to his feet once more.

Looking Aurelius in the eye with no fear, Simon proclaimed loudly, "I am more valuable than anyone, even you, can imagine."

The large man glared at the unshakable boy and stormed away growling.

Pride filled Simon for he had stood up to the bully. He truly felt free though his lip was bleeding and his face hurt. His eyes found Cristo's face who winked at him with a warm smile.

Victor knew that it took every ounce of restraint for him to not come to Simon's aid. As he watched Aurelius backhand the small boy, the knight gripped the hilt of his sword tightly and tensely gritted his teeth. Rage filled Victor's heart as he stepped forward ready to stop the man.

"Nobody move! This is Simon's battle."

Shock hit Victor at Cristo's words and he looked at the elder knight in disbelief. Cristo was staring right into Victor's eyes as if he knew the inner turmoil that the man faced. The older man's eyes shone with such compassion and peace that Victor had a feeling that everything was going to be alright with Simon.

Still as Aurelius hit Simon repeatedly and changed from an open hand to a fist, Victor held his breath and glanced quickly between Simon and Cristo begging for permission to help.

"Do something!"

Harmony's cry wrenched through Victor's heart. He would do anything to help the boy, but he wasn't ready to give up on Cristo.

His eyes darted to the older man hoping that he would nod his approval so Victor could help the child.

"No, not yet."

Disappointment and a desire to rebel engulfed the man, but he still refused to disobey Cristo's orders.

"I am more valuable than anyone even you can imagine."

Victor sighed in relief as Aurelius marched away leaving the child bloody and bruised. The knight rushed over to Simon who stood with a smile on his face.

"Why are you smiling?"

"I did it! I finally stood up to him. Now I am really free!"

Victor frowned, "You may be free, but you sure look like a mess."

Simon nodded, "I know, but I feel great. He didn't break me."

Victor snorted sarcastically, "No, he just broke your face."

A hand held out a white handkerchief and the boy smiled shyly. Victor looked down and saw Princess Harmony.

"Oh, Simon!"

The girl had a tear-stained face and was frowning deeply.

"It's okay, Harmony. Don't cry!"

The little princess hugged him gently and Victor shook his head marveling at the crazy boy that he felt so close to now. *My, how the Ancient One has worked things out!*

Lailani watched the knight and princess comfort the smiling boy. She was furious at the way that Simon had been treated again. She was getting very tired of seeing the boy insulted and beaten.

Lailani glanced over at Aurelius who held his head high with his nose in the air in superiority. Clutching the sword that she had kept from Monstre, the woman wandered over to the man in gold who stood next to his son, Vano.

Using a hushed voice so no one else was aware of her words, Lailani said, "You're not going to hit that boy anymore."

Aurelius glared at the woman and snorted, "I will do as I please, woman."

Lailani raised the sword so that Aurelius could see it clearly.

"If you touch him again, you will regret it. I can promise you that."

Vano stepped forward.

"Are you threatening my father?"

Lailani glared at the young spoiled man, but it was not her voice that answered.

"Yeah. She is and so am I."

Devin raised his own sword and stared coldly at the man. Vano cowered under their glares and walked away leaving his father to defend himself.

Aurelius gulped, "Alright. I have no interest in that boy anyway."

Seeing that Aurelius understood, Lailani and Devin lowered their swords and walked away. An exchanged smile was their only response to what they had just done.

Leaving Simon and Harmony, Victor walked over to Cristo who had been watching everything curiously.

"Shall we continue on our journey?"

Victor looked at the man unsure of how to respond.

"Not to start the argument again, but how are we to get across the sea?"

Victor glanced over at the old man, Cornelius, who was staring out at the sea. Cornelius' question was answered by a shout.

"Look! A ship!"

Harmony's cry of excitement drew the attention of the entire group of travelers. Off on the horizon, clear white sails glistened in the sunlight. The ship was gliding through the sea pushing the water out of its way. It was heading straight for the mismatched band of travelers on the shore.

Cristo smiled, "Ah, there she is."

Victor frowned at the older knight and glanced at Simon who stood watching the ship with a bloody lip and a swollen cheek.

Disbelief and anger came upon the man as he turned back to face Cristo.

"You knew? You knew there was a ship coming for us?"

Cristo calmly turned to face the angry knight.

"Yes. It always comes here."

Victor tried not to yell and cause a scene, but his anger was growing by the second.

"Then why in the blazes did you not say something before Simon was beaten?"

Cristo stepped forward and placed his hands on Victor's shoulders. The younger knight looked into the other's face and saw such patience. Victor felt his angry fading and was replaced with sorrow at Simon's treatment.

He whispered, "Why?"

Cristo's eyes held truth as he replied.

"No one asked me."

The answer should have rekindled Victor's anger yet he knew that what the older knight said was true. No one had thought to ask their guide if he knew how to cross the sea. Cristo smiled affectionately and walked toward the sea ready to greet the ship. Victor stared after him in awe. A hand clasped Victor's and he knew it was Simon before he looked down.

"It's okay, Victor. I needed this moment so that I am no longer a slave to anyone not even my fears. Aurelius has no hold on me any longer. I am free."

Victor squeezed the child's hand lovingly.

"You are wise beyond your years, Simon. Yes, you are free."

Lailani watched in amazement as the ship advanced closer to the shore. The vessel was huge and majestic. What had looked like pure white sails turned out to be ivory with a golden mountain on each one. The deck of the ship was bright blue. A large golden wheel, the helm, stood proudly. Never a more beautiful ship had ever existed.

"Ahoy there!"

A woman came to the rail and looked down upon the travelers. She was short with brown eyes and brown hair which hung down her shoulders in two curly ponytails. She wore a white button down shirt with blue pants that matched the deck. She raised a foot up on the rail as she peered down on the group and Lailani saw a shiny black boot that went halfway up her leg. A bright smile crossed the sailor's face as she spotted the one she had been looking for.

"Ah, Cristo, a pleasure to see you again, sir."

Cristo yelled up jovially, "It is good to see you again as well, Iliana! I have some people who would like passage across the sea to Mount Glory."

Iliana nodded, "I thought as much. Welcome to my ship! I am Iliana, captain of the Blessed Hope. Come aboard and we shall be off!"

Iliana dropped a rope ladder down the side of the ship and Cristo climbed aboard first. Lailani waited her turn as the others climbed the ladder to the deck.

"After you."

Lailani smiled at Devin and nodded. Once aboard, the young woman was amazed at the beauty and size of the ship. There was plenty of room for the entire group to be comfortable. On the deck of the Blessed Hope, there were golden benches placed along the rails for passengers to sit.

Vano exclaimed, "Finally! A place worthy of us, Father."

Aurelius nodded, "Here! Here!"

As the two wealthy yet filthy men sat down on a bench with Korskea, Lailani rolled her eyes. She looked at the golden bench and then at her rags. She felt so unworthy to sit on so fine a seat.

"Lailani! Devin! Come sit by me!"

The young woman smiled at Cristo who had taken a seat in the center of a bench placed at the middle of one side of the ship. Lailani walked over and sat on the right side of Cristo. She noticed that Devin had taken a seat on the other side of Cristo.

Across from them on the other middle bench, Victor, Simon, and Princess Harmony sat taking in the beauty of the ship. On their right sat Aurelius, Vano, and Korskea holding themselves in a superior manner. However, on the left bench sat Avidez who had moved as far away from the others as possible.

Lailani turned to see who was sitting on her side of the ship. On the bench to the left of Cristo's bench sat the other three princesses giggling and talking. Mercy, Grace, and Hope seemed to be having a wonderful reunion. On the bench to the right, Ziona sat humming with Cornelius. The old man seemed worried about this new experience. Lailani herself felt excited to be trying the new experience of sailing on a ship across the sea. She looked up into the sky and saw the Bright Morning Star shining ahead of them. Joy swelled in her heart. Surely they were almost at the end of their journey.

As the ship continued to sail into the sea, Lailani noticed that the shore was no longer visible.

"Look! In the distance!"

Iliana pointed from the helm. Everyone stood and looked to where she pointed. Off in the distance they could barely see a piece of land.

"See that island? You have to go to that island before you can go to Mount Glory. It is the last stop before the great mountain. Alas! The Star isn't in that direction. We must head north instead."

Lailani felt frustration at the thought of being so close to the last part of the journey only to be taken in a different direction. She had hoped that the journey was almost over. A hand patted hers and she looked into the eyes of Cristo. He smiled as if he knew how she was feeling. Lailani felt comfort and peace. She returned the smile and sat back down on the bench. The others sat back down as well. Cristo, however, stood staring over at the one person who seemed completely miserable and alone.

Avidez sat by himself on the bench farthest from all of the others. He had his body turned toward the end of the ship. His heart felt so heavy. He felt so alone without Gula. The two friends had endured so much together.

The man noticed out of the corner of his eye that Cristo was approaching his bench. Avidez flinched and tried to ignore the knight. Cristo sat on the other end of the bench and turned his body to face the warrior.

"Why are you sitting here alone, Avidez?"

The man averted his eyes further.

"I just felt like it."

Avidez could feel the knight staring at him. He expected the older man to snap at him or become angry storming away. Yet when Cristo's words came, they held no bite.

"Loneliness affects all at different times. I know your thoughts have been on Gula today. He was your friend?"

Avidez nodded with his eyes still away from Cristo.

"Yeah. We were always with each other at least until the wolves got him."

"You both made a choice to leave our group. I wish you had stayed close to me. I would have protected you both."

Fury and rebellion filled Avidez.

He snapped, "Who asked for your protection? Gula and I have been fine all these years without you."

Avidez was ready for a retort from the scraggly knight. In fact, he almost hoped that the man would strike out at him for Avidez wanted to hurt someone so bad at this moment. Cristo had given him his sword for the battle on the beach and the warrior still had the weapon in his possession. Surely Avidez had the advantage over their guide.

"I'm sorry that you feel that way, Avidez, for I have waited so long for you to ask me for help. I just hope you don't have to suffer too much before you realize the truth. And the truth is that I am here for you, Avidez, whenever you are ready."

Avidez turned and stared into Cristo's eyes. The man saw such love and patience in the older man's eyes.

Yet before his anger fully faded, Avidez glared, "I will never ask for your help."

Cristo nodded, "As always, it is your choice, Avidez."

Cristo stood and walked back over to sit next to Lailani and Devin.

When Cristo had left their bench to talk with Avidez, Devin had taken a deep breath then moved closer to Lailani. He didn't know why, but he felt so shy when he was around her. Usually he was so suave and fearless around women. Yet this young peasant girl gave him jitters in his stomach and left him almost speechless.

"Isn't this ship lovely, Devin?"

Devin looked at Lailani and saw her staring at him with her beautiful emerald eyes. Her cheeks were slightly pink as she blushed and looked away.

"Yes. I have never seen one like it."

"Me neither. Of course I have lived in Terra my whole life and haven't seen much. Everything we have been through is so new to me."

Devin nodded, "I have been around, but this is all so new to me as well. I have never…felt like this… before."

The man averted his eyes and tried to take control of himself again. *What is wrong with me? Get it together, Devin. She's just a girl…No, she's not. She is sweet and beautiful. She is so strong and determined. And man, she can fight with a sword. She has such a trusting, forgiving nature. Who else would forgive a creep like me for trying to kill her?...Lailani's really something special.*

Something touched Devin's hand and he glanced down quickly. Lailani's hand was laying on his. Surely it was an accident. The man took a deep breath and his eyes slowly rose to the young woman's face.

Lailani was staring at him again. Her eyes twinkled and a shy smile was resting peacefully on her face. Devin's heart pounded.

"I feel the same way."

Lailani's words thrilled the man and spread from the top of his head to the tips of his toes. His heart soared and he looked up overjoyed. The Bright Morning Star shone brightly and seemed to twinkle almost as if it was winking at the couple.

Looking back down on the deck, Devin saw that the knight Cristo was approaching their bench again. Begrudgingly, he let go of Lailani's hand and began to scoot back to where he had been before.

"No, Devin. I can sit on the other end."

Devin looked at the man and saw a twinkle in his eye. The young warrior had a strong feeling that Cristo knew exactly how they both felt. He was relieved to be allowed to continue to sit next to Lailani. He could think of nothing better than to stay by her side forever.

Cristo sat and said nothing more. He just hummed jovially as the ship continued on.

Simon felt his heart pounding with excitement at this new phase of his journey. This trip was truly becoming a magnificent adventure. Though there had been many hardships and trials, the boy had never felt so alive or so free than at this very moment. His face ached as he smiled, but he ignored the pain because he knew that he had persevered and won that battle.

The warm ocean breeze caressed his face and the aroma of salt filled his nose. The gentle rocking of the ship felt almost like a mother rocking her infant. Simon leaned back on the rail and closed his eyes. He pictured what his mother must have looked like. He thought about how she probably rocked him as a baby and sang him a lullaby. The child could almost hear her voice ringing in his ears though he was too young to remember her and, of course, no one had ever told him about her. Oddly enough the singing continued and Simon began to believe that it was real. *But it couldn't be, could it?*

The child opened his eyes and saw that everyone had become silent. The warm wind seemed to have cooled quite a bit and the smell of salt had a sweeter aroma to it.

A hauntingly, enchanting voice sang and it sounded to Simon like it was coming from the sea. It was a woman's voice and she sounded almost desperate.

Simon listened to the words that the woman sang:

> Oh, to all who hear my call
> If any love in you at all
> Into the water won't you fall
> To rescue me with your all
> And I shall be yours, my all in all

The words hung in the air and the woman repeated the lyrics over and over. Simon felt an odd sensation to help the woman.

"Who is she?"

His voice came out in a hushed whisper yet Iliana heard him clearly enough from the helm.

"Her name's Aquana. She lives on those rocks that we must sail by. She serves Diablo the dragon…She is my sister."

A deep sorrow touched Iliana's words. She sighed as she peered out into the sea. Simon stood to look and he noticed that the others seemed to be doing the same.

Out in the sea sitting on a large rock was a beautiful, young lady. She wore a long, tight, green dress that looked like it was made from seaweed. Her long, blond hair flowed down her shoulders like waves crossing the sand. Her eyes were the same blue as the sea and they sparkled as she looked up at the approaching ship. A gentle smile was on her face and she seemed to be pleased with the newcomers. She continued her song as she stared up at her captive audience.

"I must caution you all."

The voice of Cristo seemed to crash through the haunting melody. Everyone turned to him sharply almost as if they had forgotten that he was there.

"Aquana may appear to be a poor damsel in distress, but she is a temptress. Her mission is to take captive any who listen to her song and try to aid her. Do not be deceived by her gentle expression or her enchanting beauty for she is very dangerous to all who seek to go to Mount Glory."

Simon watched the reaction of the others. The princesses sat back down and continued their talking as if nothing had happened. Devin listened for a minute to the song. Then looking at Lailani, he took her hand and returned to his seat. Ziona and Cornelius sat down though the old man looked very tired. Avidez had not moved from his bench during the song and his face held a darkness to it. As for Simon's former master and his children, they continued to watch the lovely lady of the sea as she sang. Simon shook his head and sat back down beside Harmony who was frowning with her eyes closed.

The song continued. Simon tried to get his mind on something else. He turned to his right.

"Victor? Victor!"

Victor listened to Aquana's song as she sang it over and over. He stood looking out to sea and was mesmerized by the beauty of the lady. He had a strong urge to help her. After all, he was a knight and it was his responsibility to help all damsels in distress. Cristo's warning made him hesitate at first, but another look at the gentle face of Aquana caused him to forget what the other knight had said.

Slowly almost as if he couldn't stop himself, Victor threw one leg over the rail and readied for the plunge into the cool sea so he could swim to the rescue of the fair lady.

"Victor? Victor!"

A hand grabbed Victor's arm and pulled. He knew that it was Simon, but he couldn't take his eyes off of Aquana. The knight balanced himself and pulled his arm away.

"Victor, don't!"

The order angered Victor for he didn't want anyone to keep him from helping the woman in the sea.

"Let go, Simon. I have work to do."

The boy responded, "No, Victor! You can't!"

Victor jerked his hand away and flung it back at the boy. The back of his hand made contact hard. Without turning, the knight returned to his plan of helping the damsel in distress. No one was going to stop him from saving her.

Simon fell to the deck hard with his cheek flaming. Tears welled up into his eyes. He couldn't believe that Victor would hit him. The older man had been a friend to him and yet in an instant he had changed. The child felt so betrayed. For a second, he felt like leaving Victor to his fate.

But then a strong urge came over him and he looked up into the sky. The Bright Morning Star shone brightly. A love for Victor rushed over Simon and he suddenly felt desperate to save his friend.

The boy watched as Victor began to fall forward raising his other leg.

Quickly, he rushed to his feet and yelled, "Help me!"

The child grabbed Victor's leg and felt himself being lifted up. Simon wondered if this would be the end for both of them.

"Help me!"

Devin jumped to his feet and hurried to the other side of the ship. Out of the corner of his eye, he saw Lailani grabbing for Simon. Devin leaned over the rail and grabbed Victor's other leg. The knight hung now with his head hovering above the wavy waters. Aquana kept singing, but now there seemed to be a greater desperation in her voice. Victor tried to kick the man and Devin struggled to keep a hold on him.

"You can't go to her, Victor! She is evil. She works for Diablo. No good can come from going to her!"

Devin desperately tried to get through to the other man, but nothing he said seemed to help. The knight was too determined to go to Aquana.

As Aquana sang her seductive song, another voice filled the air. This voice was deep and strong. Devin realized that it was Cristo for he remembered the man's voice in the maze when he had frightened the wolves away. The former minion of Diablo held on hoping that Cristo's song would help Victor change his mind before they all fell into the sea.

Victor struggled against his captors beckoning to the lady of the sea with his free hands. All he wanted was to go to her. Then a deep voice sang out from behind him and Victor felt like a fog had been blown away from his eyes. The voices of the princesses joined Cristo in his song. All of the confusion and desire to go to Aquana evaporated.

Victor stopped struggling and felt himself being lifted back up toward the rail. His mind raced as he realized what he had done. He had ignored Cristo's warning and he had hurt Simon whom he had sworn to protect. Victor's heart ached at his betrayal. How could he have hurt that poor child? Here he hated Aurelius for hurting Simon and he had done the same thing.

Victor looked around as Devin and Avidez pulled him back onto the Blessed Hope. All three fell to the wooden deck breathing hard.

Sitting up, Victor mumbled his thanks to the men who nodded in acceptance and relief. Lailani came and knelt beside Devin as Avidez stood and walked back over to his bench.

Two arms were thrown around Victor's neck so strongly that he almost fell backwards toward the deck. Simon held him tightly and Victor frowned. Why was he hugging him? Victor pushed him away so that they were eye level, but he kept his hands on his shoulders. A new bruise was on the child's cheek and for once it hadn't been caused by Aurelius. Shame filled the man as he looked at the boy's tear stained face.

"Simon, I'm so sorry. I shouldn't have hit you. Can you forgive me?"

The boy nodded with a smile growing wider by the second.

"Of course, Victor. We all mess up at times. Besides Aquana's song makes us feel like we need to get to her no matter what. You just needed help to fight it."

Victor pulled the boy back to him and embraced him gratefully. The two little arms held on tightly. Victor looked up and saw Cristo watching them nearby still singing his song. A kind, forgiving smile was on his face as he nodded at Victor. Though the younger man had not said anything to him, Cristo seemed to have heard his silent apology and accepted it.

Simon suddenly stiffened and pulled away from Victor.

"Vano, no!"

Victor turned quickly in time to see Vano jump off the rail into the sea.

Simon had been so relieved that Victor was safe. He had held his friend so tightly, but then his heart had started pounding as he saw Vano climb onto the rail and leap into the sea.

"Vano, no!"

Simon jumped to his feet and rushed to the rail of the ship. The others surrounded him at the rail looking for the young man who had jumped into the sea.

Vano resurfaced and began to swim toward Aquana's rock.

"Vano! Come back!"

The man kept swimming ignoring the pleas of the others. Simon turned to Aurelius.

"Tell him to come back, Aurelius, before it is too late."

The large man scoffed, "My son will save her and be the hero. No one else had the courage to help that poor woman."

Simon frowned at his former master and then faced the rail again watching Vano advance closer to the rock. Victor put his arm around Simon comfortingly.

Aquana stopped singing and stood up on the rock. She smiled as she dove headfirst into the sea. Her head came up and she started swimming out to meet Vano. She reached him and he stared into her beautiful face. A soft, white hand touched his face affectionately. Her smile was so radiant that Vano stopped swimming and began to tread water. Aquana brought up her other hand and placed them both on top of Vano's head. With a giggle, the lady of the sea began to push with a strength no one thought one so small could muster.

Aurelius began to yell as realization hit him. His shrieks were strangled yet he did not do anything to help his son. Vano's head lowered closer to the water, but he could not escape.

Victor's hands tightened on Simon's shoulders and he spun the boy around. Simon gasped and buried his face into Victor's shirt. The knight's arms embraced him as Aurelius continued to yell and Vano went to his watery grave.

Cristo's Song

Tempting voices to me do call.
What they say sounds so good.
They make me always want it all.
Though I know I never should.

The Satisfier of my soul calls to me.
He fulfills my every desire.
Only through Him am I set free.
And He refines me pure by fire.

CHAPTER 13

DESERT OF COMPLAINING

Victor sat on the bench with his arm around Simon's shoulders. The child had fallen asleep as the Blessed Hope continued past Aquana's rocks. He had become so exhausted in the battle with the Demoni, the conflict with Aurelius, and his attempt to keep Victor from Aquana. Victor was full of gratitude for this little boy. Simon could have given up on the knight after being backhanded, but instead he loved his friend enough to forgive him and continue to help him return to his senses. Victor was touched that Simon had risked his life to save him.

"Victor?"

The knight looked down and found Simon staring up at him.

"Rest, Simon."

The boy's eyes moved to the area to their right. Victor turned his head and saw Aurelius sitting on his bench. The man looked so miserable. His face hung low and he had a blank stare.

"I wish I could help him."

Victor returned his gaze to Simon.

"Why?"

Simon sat up with a confused look on his face.

"What do you mean?"

Victor didn't see how the question was confusing.

"Why would you want to help him after how he has treated you?"

The boy didn't answer. Instead he looked up into the sky. Victor followed his gaze and saw the Bright Morning Star blazing in the night sky.

"I just feel like it is the right thing to do."

Victor nodded as he realized that was exactly what the Ancient One would want them to do.

"Okay. We'll think of some way to help. Maybe Cristo has an idea. Go back to sleep, Simon. You're going to need it."

As the boy leaned against the man again, Victor tried to think of how to help Aurelius without Simon getting hurt. He fell asleep without any solutions.

"Land Ho!"

Lailani opened her eyes. Morning had come again and though the sky was gray, the Bright Morning Star shone brighter than ever.

"Good morning."

Smiling, the redheaded woman sat up from where she had been leaning against Devin.

"Good morning."

Her cheeks blushed at his dashing smile.

"Land Ho!"

Iliana's cry excited Lailani. She stood quickly to get a look at this land they were approaching.

Devin came to her side and pointed to the land.

"There it is!"

Lailani turned in the opposite direction.

"But Iliana said that Mount Glory is that way past the island. Why are we going farther from the island?"

The woman was so frustrated. She wanted the journey to be over.

Devin took her hand.

"I don't know. After all we have been through, I am willing to trust Cristo and follow the Star."

Lailani pushed his hand away angrily.

"All we have been through? What exactly have you been through?"

Before the man could answer, Lailani stormed away and headed for the rope ladder where Cristo was leading the travelers off the ship to disembark on the new land.

Devin stood speechless as Lailani marched away. He couldn't believe how quickly she had become angry with him and yet he was confused at what he had done.

"She is not angry at you, Devin."

The man turned and saw Ziona watching him calmly.

"Oh, yeah? Seems like she is."

Ziona smiled, "Lailani thought this would be a quick, painless journey. She is angry because she hasn't had an easy trip...Of course, she doesn't know that the best things in life are those achieved through difficulty."

The dark-skinned woman in yellow glided away.

Devin stood still, wondering if he should just give up and head off by himself in a different direction. After all, he didn't want to make Lailani's trip any more difficult.

"Are you coming, Devin?"

The voice startled the young man because he had thought Cristo had gone ashore.

"I...I don't know."

Devin's heart pounded as he waited for a scolding from the knight. After all, he was wasting time and had slowed the group down enough. Cristo did not say anything, but waited for Devin's decision.

The man thought about it and believed that it would be best if he left Lailani alone even though it broke his heart to leave her. However, he felt that he had done enough to cause her pain and make the trip more difficult for everyone.

Devin sighed, "I'm not going on."

A sad look came to Cristo's face. He nodded with acceptance.

"As you wish, Devin."

The knight turned and slowly walked toward the rope ladder.

At that moment, a dark cloud seemed to descend on Devin. A heavy burden fell on his shoulders. The weight on his heart brought the man to his knees on the deck. He lowered his head and couldn't seem to raise it up at all. Despair crashed into the man and tears sprang to his eyes. As he began to weep, a new feeling fell over him. It was a fear so strong that it took his breath away. He feared the thought of turning from his current path. He feared going out into the world alone. Most of all he feared the thought of facing Diablo and his Demoni. The fear suddenly transformed into desperation for Devin did not want to be the person he used to be or go where he used to go.

Sobbing, Devin pleaded, "No, Sir Cristo. Please don't leave me. I will go with you as long as you will have me. Please do not turn me away though I am a weak, worthless fool. Have mercy on me please."

"Devin."

Cristo's voice came so close that Devin realized that he must be standing before him. He closed his eyes with his head lowered and waited as he tried to control himself.

A hand cupped under the young man's chin and raised his face up gently. Devin's eyes burst open in surprise and he saw the old scraggly knight kneeling before him. Cristo's eyes shone with love and truth.

"Devin, I have wanted to lead you to the Ancient One for many years. I know all that you have done in your rebellion and service to Diablo. I also know your heart now and what you truly desire. I know that you think you are slowing down the group and upsetting Lailani, but they should not be the reason that you don't follow the Star. I will not send you from me. If you leave my side, it will be by your own choice. Devin, you are not weak for the Ancient One will give you His strength. You are not worthless because the Ancient One creates all and He does not make mistakes. His creations are always purposeful and full of potential. You are not a fool because you have chosen the Ancient One over the lies of Diablo and this world though it is a difficult choice...Come, son. Time to go."

Devin allowed Cristo to raise him to his feet. His heart was light and thankful. The burden that had been there moments before had faded and the fears were driven away. Cristo put his arm around the man's shoulders and led him to the rope ladder. As Devin climbed down, he felt ready to continue the journey to Mount Glory.

Simon didn't even notice that the group had been waiting for Devin and Cristo. He was watching Aurelius who was pacing anxiously. The man seemed like a caged animal ready to dart at the first chance of freedom. Simon felt such pity for the poor man. It was true that he had bullied and beaten the child, but by following Cristo, Simon had begun to have a growing love for others develop in his heart even for those who hurt him.

Taking a deep breath, Simon walked over to Aurelius who seemed oblivious to the others near him. The boy stopped near the large man and hesitated as he felt his face aching from the previous encounter. For one moment, he almost changed his mind.

"Aurelius, sir."

The man halted and swung around so violently with an icy glare that Simon almost fled for his life.

"What do you want?"

The boy visibly gulped.

"I…I'm sorry for your loss."

Aurelius harrumphed, "Why do you care? You should be happy they are gone."

The man turned away and stared ahead.

Simon replied, "I care because no one should die that way."

Aurelius grunted, "The wealthy should not be the ones dying. That's why I have lost my wife and son because I have money."

"They died because they didn't heed Cristo's warnings."

Aurelius spun around with murder in his eyes. He stormed toward Simon.

He answered, "What do you know about it?! You are nothing, but a wretched peasant!"

Simon took a step back and gulped, "I'm sorry. I just wanted to tell you that if you need anything…"

Aurelius backhanded the boy who fell to the ground.

"What? You'll do what? How could you help me?"

With each question, the large man kicked the trembling child. Simon had dropped his sword in the grass. Aurelius snatched it and swung down on the boy. The child closed his eyes tightly confused at how quickly his good intention had turned bad.

"Simon!"

"Simon!"

Victor rushed to the boy's side and pulled him back from Aurelius who was glaring daggers at Cristo. The knight had easily blocked his attack with Devin's sword.

"Mind your business, Knight!"

The scraggly face of the knight seemed slightly amused.

"The boy is my business, Aurelius, because he chose to follow me to Mount Glory."

Simon struggled to his feet holding his side and favoring his left leg. Victor put his right arm around the child, but kept a hand on the hilt of his sheathed sword.

"You have a choice to make too, Aurelius. Are you going to follow me?"

Victor noticed Simon was holding his breath. He squeezed the child closer. The boy's hand came up and held onto Victor's arm. The knight looked up as Aurelius lowered the sword and threw it on the ground.

"I will never follow you, Knight. I want nothing to do with you or these fools who trail after you. Where is that Star you say is in the sky?"

Victor glanced up and saw that the Bright Morning Star was shining over the path to the right. Cristo pointed at the road to the right without a word. Aurelius turned and headed for the left path.

"That road leads to the Chasm, Aurelius."

Victor and Simon turned and looked at Devin who had his full attention on Aurelius. The large man gave a wave of dismissal and trudged down the left road. He didn't even glance at his daughter, Korskea, who was examining her mud-splattered pink dress.

Cristo watched the man leave with his head lowered a bit.

"I'm sorry, Cristo. I only tried to help, but I made it worse. I failed you, my lord."

Victor glanced down and saw Simon lower his head in shame. The man was about to speak comfort to his little friend, but Cristo beat him to it.

"Why do you think you have failed me, Simon?"

The rusty old knight kneeled to the level of the child.

"You spoke truth to Aurelius even though he would hurt you. You felt love and concern for a man who has always considered you beneath his feet. I am so proud of you, Simon. You have a kind, caring heart and I am thrilled to be leading you to the Ancient One."

Simon raised his head and Victor smiled at the man's words. Cristo looked up at Victor. His face lit up and his eyes twinkled.

Then standing up and addressing the rest of the group, Cristo announced, "It is time to go on."

Simon limped heavily as he followed the travelers. He had slept so well on the Blessed Hope, but his exhaustion was increasing as they went down the right path. He stared ahead as he kept moving his feet forward.

The young knight stood next to his father, Victor, who stood in full armor. They drew their swords ready for the army of Demoni that was advancing on them. The older knight turned calmly and spoke to his son, "Watch out!"

Simon opened his eyes as his feet hit something and he stumbled forward. As the ground got closer, Simon threw his hands out in front of him to catch himself. Yet he never hit the ground. Strong arms caught him around his waist. The wounded boy cried out in pain at the sudden force on his bruised sides. He was set on his feet. The hands that had saved him moved to his shoulders gently spinning him around. Simon knew it would be Victor even before he saw the knight.

"I'm sorry, Simon. I didn't mean to hurt you."

The man looked stricken at causing the boy more pain.

Simon smiled reassuringly, "I'm okay, Victor. Thanks for catching me."

Relief crossed the knight's face.

"I can carry you for a while if you want," offered Victor.

Simon didn't want to appear weak, but his dream of Victor as his father was still fresh in his mind and he was just so tired of walking. The boy nodded. As Victor picked him up, Simon wrapped his arms around his neck and laid his head on his shoulder. He felt Victor's strong, loving arms holding him tightly as the knight began to walk on again. Slowly and peacefully, Simon's eyes closed again with a smile on his face.

Lailani felt her dark mood deepen as the Star led them even farther away from Mount Glory. She had purposely walked away from the area where Devin was. She felt a little guilty about snapping at the man, but she couldn't bring herself to apologize. The red haired woman decided it would be best to just avoid the man. However, she kept glancing over at Devin as they walked. Yet to her surprise the man stared straight ahead and didn't seem to be noticing her at all. Lailani felt a little annoyed as she began to dwell on his lack of attention.

The group of travelers came through the forest. Lailani groaned at the appearance of a vast desert. As she looked out across the dry, hot sand, the young woman sighed in dismay. Above the desert shone the Bright Morning Star instructing them to cross the unending sand. Frustration filled the woman and her mind filled with thoughts of going back.

"Behold the next part of our journey."

Lailani crossed her arms frowning at Cristo's words.

"Take heed, my friends, for the sand shifts suddenly if you are not alert."

The annoyed woman rolled her eyes and began to follow the others across the desert.

The heat of the burning sun beat down on the travelers as they trudged across the scratchy sand. Lailani felt the sweat drip down her face and drench her long hair. Her mouth became dry and her throat parched. Her body was not the only thing that was growing hotter. Every minute her temper was becoming fiercer than a glowing ember among flames. *Why are we going so far away from the mountain? Why do we have to endure all these problems and hardships? Why do we have to be hot, tired, and thirsty? Why...*

The sand beneath Lailani's feet shifted and a scream escaped her lips as she fell downward. She threw her hands up as she fell knowing that this would be the end. She would never make it to the Ancient One now. Hands quickly grabbed hers and Lailani looked up gratefully, but her face turned to surprise as she beheld her rescuer.

Devin's hands were slippery and sweaty as he clung to Lailani. His back ached and sweat poured down his face. The man felt so tired, but desperation filled him. He had to help Lailani.

When the young woman had screamed, Devin hadn't thought about what to do. He just did it. He ran over and grabbed Lailani's upraised hands. As an afterthought, Devin realized that the sand beside the hole would probably shift under his weight and both people would fall to their doom. Yet the sand he stood on stayed solid as Devin held on tightly to Lailani.

The young man tried to pull her up, but she seemed heavier the more he pulled. Desperation tugged on Devin's heart. He needed help. Almost instantly, the man looked up from Lailani's frightened face to find Cristo standing nearby watching as if waiting.

"Cristo, please help me!"

The rugged knight stepped closer and came to the side of the hole. Devin sighed confident that Cristo would save the day. Instead the knight looked down at Lailani and continued to wait. Devin struggled to hold the woman. Cristo held out a hand.

As he looked from Cristo to Lailani, Devin realized that the knight wanted the woman to change who she was holding onto. Devin looked down at Lailani wanting her to choose Cristo because in his heart he knew that the older man could save her and he couldn't.

Lailani hung from Devin's hands with more than half of her body in the hole. She had thought Devin could save her quickly. Yet he seemed to be struggling just to hold her. Then Cristo came over and stood above her extending his hands waiting for her to move her hands from Devin to him.

Lailani frowned. If a strong young man like Devin couldn't pull her out, then how could an old, scraggly knight like Cristo do it? The woman looked back and forth between Devin and Cristo. Her gaze fell on Devin and she saw that he couldn't hold on much longer. The love she had for the man tugged at her heart. She didn't want the man to die too.

Lailani pulled on her right hand and Devin who seemed to understand let go of her right hand. The woman moved the hand to Cristo who instantly took hold. He held out his other hand waiting again. Lailani had secretly hoped that she could have both men pull her up. Yet Cristo continued to wait without pulling.

The defeated woman took a deep breath and pulled on her left hand. She silently wished that Devin would refuse to let go and begin pulling again, but the man let go and Cristo took her other hand. Lailani waited ready for the knight to pull her up, but to her surprise again he waited. Cristo stared at her with such love and patience. The woman began to cry.

Through her sobs, Lailani wailed, "Please save me, Cristo, because I cannot save myself."

With a warm smile, the knight pulled the desperate woman with a strength that didn't fit his appearance. Lailani found herself on the solid sand feeling relieved.

Cristo knelt down and gently wiped her tears from her face.

"My child, as always it is your choice to call out to me or to try to do it yourself. The sands of life shift when you become too wrapped up in yourself. Keep your focus on me, Lailani, and trust that I will get you to Mount Glory at the appointed time."

Lailani could not speak yet she wanted Cristo to know that she was ready to trust him.

Cristo nodded, "And I will never fail you, my dear."

The knight took her hands and gently raised her to her feet.

Lailani watched him in awe as he walked away.

"Lailani?"

The young red-haired woman turned around with her heart swooning. Devin stood looking at her uncertainly. Lailani ran to the young man and encircled his neck with her arms in a loving embrace.

Devin stumbled backwards as he balanced himself. He was grateful that he and Lailani didn't fall down especially since they were still so close to the hole.

Lailani hugged him closely.

She whispered, "Thank you, Devin."

With relief, Devin put his arms around the woman he loved.

"I'm sorry I upset you earlier, Lailani. I wasn't thinking about your point of view when I spoke."

Lailani pulled back so they were face to face, but she kept her arms around his neck.

"I'm the one who should be apologizing, Dev. I wasn't mad at you. I was just annoyed that we were moving from the mountain. I'm sorry I took my frustration out on you."

Devin smiled warmly liking the nickname she had given him.

"All's forgiven."

A scream behind them caused the couple to turn abruptly.

Simon had awakened when Lailani screamed. He had watched the struggle the woman had until she surrendered to Cristo. Relieved, the boy watched as Lailani hugged Devin. He exchanged a glance with Victor who winked and set Simon down.

The happy moment was interrupted by another scream. Simon turned sharply and looked at Korskea. The tall, skinny blonde had a look of horror on her face.

"My nail! I broke a nail!"

Simon sighed and rolled his eyes. He looked up at Victor who shook his head.

"That's it! I've had it! My dress is ruined! My hair is frizzy! And look at my shoes!"

Korskea was shrieking now and glaring at Cristo. She took a hateful stomp toward the elder knight.

"I am tired of walking! I am tired of traveling with peasants! I am tired of being dirty! Most of all I am tired of YOU!"

On the last word the sand beneath Korskea crumbled and she fell with a scream of terror. Her hands touched solid sand beside the hole and she clung on for her life.

Simon rushed over to help her. He heard Victor behind him.

"Korskea! Give us your hands!"

Simon knelt by the hole. Victor joined him and both extended a hand to the young woman.

Korskea wrinkled her nose.

"Don't touch me, you filthy worm!"

Simon frowned, "I just want to help you up!"

The blond woman laughed scornfully.

"You are not good enough to help me. You are just a slave!"

Simon was speechless. Here Korskea had a chance to live and she wouldn't take it.

"Call on Cristo, Korskea."

Simon glanced at Victor who had made the suggestion. He looked back at Korskea hoping she would take the advice.

The young woman glared, "I don't need Cristo!"

The words were barely out of her mouth when the solid sand shifted and the woman fell down in the bottomless hole.

"No!"

Simon fell forward in a last hope of catching the woman's hand. His hand remained empty as the woman went out of sight. Simon's balance teetered. His eyes beheld a dark abyss as he fell.

"Simon!"

Victor barely had time to catch hold of the boy's legs. The knight pulled with his heart pounding. Oddly the child felt heavier than usual. Victor slid closer to the hole as he was being pulled in. His fingers ached and his slick grasp was weakening. Before he could call out to Cristo, Victor felt the child slip from his fingers.

"No!"

Tears sprang into the man's eyes and blurred his vision. Victor brought his hands out of the hole and sobbed as he placed his forehead on the sand. He absentmindedly dug his hands into the scalding sand and squeezed handfuls of sand so it drained through his fingers back to the ground. Anguish filled the knight and he could not speak in words, but only in groans and wails.

Eyes shut tightly, Victor felt arms embrace him. Through his sobs, he heard the calm yet strong voice of Cristo.

"Peace, my son, for all is not lost. Look into the hole."

Victor was in so much agony that he could barely crawl the few inches to the mouth of the hole. Cristo held on to him and gave him the strength to peer over the edge into the hole. Victor gasped as more tears rolled down his face.

Simon felt Victor's grip loosen and his stomach lurched as he fell. However, he didn't fall far. The sudden jolt of him hitting solid ground surprised him. Simon looked down and saw that he had landed on sand. Looking up, the child saw that he had only fallen a few feet. As he tried to comprehend what had happened, Simon heard someone crying and yelling. Then the noise decreased.

A few sprinkles of sand fell down on him as he realized that someone was moving to the hole. A smile spread on his face as Victor and Cristo's faces came to the top of the hole. Victor looked first miserable, then surprised and relieved. Cristo smiled broadly at the boy and did not look at all surprised that he was alive.

"I'm okay, but how do I get out?"

Cristo continued to smile without a word. Suddenly the sand under Simon rumbled and he was sure that it would collapse allowing him to fall to his doom. Instead of collapsing, the sand began to elevate. Simon saw that he was rising up closer to the two knights.

Cristo put his arms into the hole. When Simon was close enough, the man lifted him out easily and embraced him.

"Welcome back, my little friend."

Simon hugged him back.

"Thanks for the help, but how did the sand get there?"

Cristo pulled back and whispered, "You trusted that I would help you and I did."

The elder knight turned to regard Victor who was staring at the child in unbelief. With a smile, he set Simon down, stood up, and briefly squeezed Victor's shoulder as he walked away. Simon turned to the other knight. He saw how tear-stained and anguished the man looked. Without a word, Simon flung his arms around Victor's neck.

Victor sat speechless in shock as he watched Cristo whisper to the boy. He couldn't believe that Simon hadn't fallen to his doom. Being familiar with miracles on Mount Glory, the man didn't really question how the sand appeared or moved upward with the child, but he was still surprised.

Cristo stood and squeezed Victor's shoulder. Comfort filled the man as he stared at the little boy who he thought he had lost.

Suddenly Simon flung his arms around Victor's neck and instantly the man wrapped the boy in a tight hug. He closed his eyes tightly as tears streamed down his face.

"I'm okay, Victor. I'm okay."

Victor whispered, "Thank you, Ancient One."

"We must continue on. We are nearing the edge of the desert."

At Cristo's words, Victor released the boy. Together they followed the other travelers as they exited the desert that had taken one life and almost taken two others.

CHAPTER 14

RIVER OF FAITH

Deep in the Chasm of Misery, Diablo watched the approaching Demoni. He could tell by their faces that they had failed at least part of the mission. But what part had they been victorious?

"Approach!"

His fierce growl caused the Demoni to hesitate, but they obeyed. Davo stood the closest to the dragon with the others forming a line as they waited for the explosion.

"Report!"

Davo gulped, "We found Cristo's group by the sea. We gave Devin a chance to return to you. He refused. So we attacked them...and..."

Diablo leaned closer waiting for the results of the battle. Davo turned and pointed at Monstre.

"He failed to kill Devin!"

Monstre stepped forward outraged.

"It wasn't my fault. He had reinforcements."

Davo laughed, "Yeah, a young woman."

Monstre growled, "The same woman who scared you away."

Diablo looked from one Demoni to the other. He waited with growing fury.

"What woman? Ziona?"

Davo shook his head.

"No, my lord. Some red-headed peasant girl...And I only ran away because Devin and the girl were pointing swords at me along with the knight."

Diablo wrinkled his forehead.

"What knight? Cristo?"

Davo gulped realizing that he shouldn't have mentioned the knight.

"Victor. The knight from the massacre."

"And what happened with Victor?"

Diablo glared at Davo who suddenly had taken a step backwards.

Monstre sneered, "Davo knocked him off a cliff, but the knight made it back to the top and then Davo ran away like a human!"

Davo stepped toward Monstre glowering. Diablo reached a clawed hand out and grabbed Davo. The Demoni cowered and awaited his fate. He looked around for some way of escape. With a trembling finger, he pointed at Maligno.

"He lost the necklace of princesses!"

Diablo turned his glare to the nearby Demoni. Maligno screamed in terror.

"My lord, I was attacked and I…"

Davo scoffed, "By a boy!"

The dragon dropped his current prey and took a menacing step toward Maligno.

"What boy?"

Maligno gasped, "Just a little boy who had a sword and chased me on horseback. I would have killed him and brought the necklace back, but Victor came at me and I fled…They were supposed to get the other princesses. The ones who have been set free."

Maligno pointed at the remaining Demoni who had gone on the mission. The creatures trembled searching for the words to say to defend themselves.

Diablo growled, "More are free besides Harmony?"

"Only Princess Mercy. Well, when we left, we saw that Hope and Grace had also been released, but at the time it was only the two…well, and Ziona was there."

Diablo leaned his head back and roared so loudly that all of the Demoni even those who were not in trouble shook with fear.

"Did you succeed at anything?"

All of the Demoni exchanged a glance.

"Well?!"

No one wanted to answer the question which told Diablo exactly what he wanted to know. With another roar, he advanced on the scattering Demoni ready to destroy them with one enormous flame.

"My lord, we have guests."

Diablo froze in fury and turned his head at the Demoni who had spoken. He narrowed his eyes at the creature.

"Who?"

The Demoni answered quickly, "Aquana has come with a report and…a stranger has wandered into our territory."

A cruel smile crossed the dragon's lips.

"Detain the stranger. I will deal with him soon. Send Aquana in first."

The Demoni bowed and hurried through the tunnel exit.

Aquana entered with her head high in the air and a cool smile on her face. Diablo could tell that she had some good news to report.

"Ah...Aquana, what news from the sea?"

The blonde woman answered in her musical voice.

"The Blessed Hope lost one of their passengers to me."

Diablo chuckled, "Excellent."

Aquana's smile weakened slightly.

"It would have been a knight from the mountain, but Cristo sang his cursed song. However, I still got a vain, little creature. He jumped overboard to save me and I showed him how unforgiving the sea really is."

"Fine work, Aquana. You will be rewarded for your loyalty."

Aquana bowed and practically glided across the floor toward the exit. A man entered the Chasm area at that moment. He was a large man in a filthy gold robe. He stopped in shock as he saw Aquana then glared at her.

"You?!"

Aquana smiled innocently with a little wave before she left the Chasm. The dragon watched the haughty manner of the man. He smiled at the thought of a new prisoner. In his wisest and kindest voice, Diablo addressed the man.

"Is there a problem, sir? You seem upset."

The man turned with his nose in the air, but gaped when he saw the dragon.

"I...I..."

Diablo tried to smile warmly.

"Dear Sir, there is no need for you to be afraid of me. I am just a humble dragon who waits in his lair for rich people to help."

The man approached eagerly with such a trusting look on his face. *Fool.*

"My name is Aurelius of Terra. I was traveling with my family and we got mixed up with this knight fellow and I have lost my family. My wife, Keikari, was killed by a spider queen. My son, Vano, jumped into the sea and was drowned by that horrible woman. And my daughter, Korskea...well, I don't know what will happen to her, but I am sure it is awful."

Diablo nodded his head in sympathetic understanding.

"I see. Well, I am afraid that nothing good ever comes from following that knight. He is always on the lookout for unsuspecting wealthy people to deceive. If you are willing, you may rest here and I will restore all that you have lost. Your wife...your children...your riches."

Aurelius' eyes lit up at the thought of his wealth being returned to him.

"Yes, my lord. Please return me as I was."

The dragon extended a hand toward a tunnel to the left.

"Go into that tunnel, Aurelius, and you will not only find your possessions restored, but you will also live forever enjoying them."

Aurelius hurried into the tunnel without second guessing the words of the dragon. Diablo motioned to a Demoni to follow him and place him in a cell until the dragon could torture him later. Feeling satisfied with his new capture, Diablo imagined how the Ancient One would react to this loss.

The rolling sand dunes of the desert turned into lush green hills. The travelers were thrilled to be in a cooler climate, but a dark mood had fallen on the people. The loss of another member of the group weighed heavily on them and the thought that no one would make it to Mount Glory crossed all of their minds.

As they traveled over the green hills, Simon walked close to Victor. He was aware of the man glancing down at him periodically as if the child was merely a mirage and would disappear any minute. Simon looked up every once in a while to reassure the man with a small smile. Soon a roar could be heard in the quiet countryside.

"What's that?" Simon looked up at Victor.

"Sounds like a river."

The boy nodded and continued following the group. Sure enough, the group came to a wide rushing river. After using the water to cool their skin and quench their thirst, the travelers sat in the cool grass resting.

As he sat taking in the beauty of the river, Simon began to think about everything that had happened to him so far. He shook his head in shock as he realized that just a few weeks earlier, he had been a slave working in a mansion with that miserable family. Then he had met Cristo and Victor in the forest and everything had changed. Yes, he had been frightened at Tatianna's garden and in the labyrinth of wolves. Yes, he had worried that they would be killed by the Demoni on the beach. But then he had won his freedom from Aurelius on the beach and sailed on the most beautiful ship in the world. He had helped Victor as Aquana sang and witnessed a miracle while in a hole in the desert. Simon had wanted an adventure and now he was in the middle of one.

Suddenly, Simon started laughing. It started as a smile, then a giggle, and finally full laughter. He couldn't stop. He had never felt so happy in his entire life.

The solemn mood of the group was beginning to wear on Victor as they had continued to walk through the hills toward the river. Even after they had found the river and cooled down, the people seemed to be brooding more than resting. Victor leaned back on the grass and closed his eyes actually feeling content that he had not lost Simon. Nothing in the world seemed more depressing than losing his friend. No, by now Simon seemed more like his child than just a friend.

Suddenly Simon started laughing next to the man. Victor opened his eyes and turned his head to regard the child. Simon's body was shaking more by the second with laughter and for the life of him, Victor couldn't figure out why the boy was laughing.

"What's so funny, Simon?"

The boy was laughing too hard to answer. He tried to take a breath so he could explain, but he only giggled harder. Victor noticed that others in the group were watching Simon with a curious expression. Only Avidez seemed annoyed at the amused boy.

Cristo sat up from where he had been laying and smiled at the child.

"Simon, why are you laughing?"

Victor looked back at Simon who was taking a deep breath and stopping his laughter. A smile was still on the boy's face. Victor couldn't help but smile as he watched the child.

"I'm just happy."

Avidez grumbled, "How can you be happy after all we have been through?"

Victor admitted that it was a good question.

Simon shrugged, "That's just it. Think about it. We have traveled so far. We have faced a spider monster, wolves, Demoni, and a water witch. We have crossed a huge desert...True some of us were lost, but the rest of us are still here. We are closer to the Ancient One than ever before. I just feel happy to be here."

Victor thought about his own journey. He had felt as good as dead as he left the massacred battlefield and yet now he felt more alive than he had in his whole life. He had Simon still with him. Plus he was returning to Mount Glory to see his Master and Lord. The smile on his face grew with each of these thoughts. Soon he felt like laughing too.

Cristo chuckled happily and Victor couldn't hold it in anymore. He joined in laughing. Soon everyone was laughing except for Avidez. He smiled slightly, but then looked away. Victor put his arm around Simon who was giggling again. The group's dark mood had lifted and even as the laughter died down, smiles were beaming on most of the faces of the travelers.

A musical laugh continued when all of the others had stopped. Victor turned his gaze toward the river in surprise. Standing on the shore by the rushing water was a beautiful, young woman with tan skin. She was short with shiny, black hair wrapped into two buns on the sides of her head. Her red and white dress looked amazing with the white veil affixed to her regal head.

"Princess Joy!"

Harmony ran forward into the open arms of the giggling princess. The other princesses and Ziona rushed forward as well exclaiming their greetings. Cristo walked over with an enormous smile on his face. The princesses parted and Joy stepped into the knight's open-armed embrace still giggling.

"Welcome back to us, sweet Joy. You were released from Tatianna's necklace because our friend Simon found joy even in the most depressing circumstances."

Princess Joy curtsied to the boy.

Victor turned and took a long look at the river. The rolling, bubbly water rushed by in murky, brown waves. The water's speed was astonishing. The river was as wide as the cobblestone roads of

Terra. Victor saw that the river went many miles in both directions. He also noticed that there was neither a bridge nor a calm place to cross.

Glancing up into the sky, Victor saw that of course the Bright Morning Star was leading them across the river. The knight shook his head not knowing how in the world they were going to get across. However, he suddenly remembered his conversation with Cristo on the beach when the elder knight had pointed out that no one had asked him what to do.

Victor saw Cristo standing by the rushing water upstream a little way from him. The young man walked up the grassy shore and stood next to their guide.

"Cristo, how do we get across this river?"

The elder knight regarded Victor with a warm smile.

"Fear not for I know the only way across."

Then turning to the other travelers, Cristo announced, "We shall cross the river now. If you trust me and keep your eyes fixed on me, then you will make it across safely. Follow me."

Without another word, Victor watched in amazement as Cristo took a step onto the water and began to slowly walk on the river.

Avidez gaped at Cristo as the knight started to walk across the rolling, brown waters of the river. The man shook his head in wonder as Cristo turned and beckoned the others to follow him on the river. Instantly, the princesses along with Ziona pulled their dresses up above their ankles to keep them dry and stepped onto the river. The women stared ahead at Cristo and none of them sank nor were swept away by the furious waves. Avidez watched as Simon grabbed Victor's hand and the duo headed across the river as well. Lailani and Devin stepped out onto the bubbling water holding hands and watching Cristo. Even the old man, Cornelius, followed the knight never taking his eyes off of him.

Avidez didn't want to be seen as a coward. The downcast warrior took a deep breath, looked at Cristo, and held his foot over the water. He stepped down and was surprised to find something solid underneath his foot. He brought his other foot down and it also hit a solid mass. Avidez kept walking with his eyes on Cristo.

As he made it to the middle of the river, Avidez began to believe that the water was solid for any who crossed it, not just those watching Cristo. Still determined not to fully rely on the knight, the man decided to watch his footing and look toward the rushing water certain that he would make his way on his own.

Suddenly the river seemed fiercer and hungrier. A fear gripped the fallen warrior's heart as his feet began to sink into the water. The solid mass was gone. Avidez went deeper into the cold, furious waters. Panic seized him. No matter how hard he tried to swim and keep his head above water, the river struggled against him even harder. His head went under briefly and Avidez brought it up spluttering and choking on the murky liquid.

As he felt the river pulling him back down, Avidez shrieked, "Cristo, help me!"

His head went under deeper and his mouth filled with foul, choking water. Avidez closed his eyes waiting for the end.

A hand gripped his right wrist. Another hand tightly grasped his left wrist. A strength that put the river to shame jerked him upward. Fresh air slammed into Avidez's face causing him to spit out the filthy water and suck in the air. He coughed and opened his eyes as his feet hit solidity again. He looked into the face of his rescuer.

Cristo released his wrists and placed his hands on the man's shoulders. His eyes seemed relieved and a comforting smile was present under his bushy moustache.

"Keep your eyes on me, Avidez, and I will not let you fall."

Avidez nodded and stared at the knight as he turned and walked back toward the grassy shore where all of the others were watching in curiosity. The man followed Cristo to the shore still shaken from his near death experience. He remembered how he had hatefully told Cristo that he would never call on him for help.

"Never say never," muttered the soggy warrior as he was reunited with the group.

Simon watched Cristo as he pulled a brown, thick blanket from his bundle on Feliz and placed it around the wet shoulders of Avidez.

"I'm glad he is okay."

Simon turned to Princess Harmony and nodded, "Me too."

His eyes fell on the necklace that hung around the little girl's neck. He frowned as he saw that there was only one jewel on it. Simon remembered that there had been six jewels originally. His mind went through all of the princesses who had been released during the journey so far.

Princess Mercy had been released outside the labyrinth when Devin was merciful and helped Avidez. Princess Hope and Princess Grace had been released after the battle on the beach with the Demoni. Hope had been freed because Victor had had hope in a hopeless situation. Grace was freed when Lailani forgave Devin with grace. Finally, Princess Joy had been released because Simon had been joyful in the midst of danger and troubles. There should be two more jewels left on the necklace.

"Harmony, a jewel is missing!"

Both children glanced around the clearing not looking for the missing jewel, but hopefully searching for a newly freed princess. Their eyes fell on a tall, slim woman in a plum and gold full-length dress. Her blond hair was mostly hidden under a linen turret hat with a flat top and a bright pink scarf hanging from the back.

Simon shouted, "Look!"

The others turned sharply and looked where the boy was pointing excitedly. Harmony ran forward squealing with delight.

"Oh, Faith, welcome!"

The tall princess stooped gracefully and scooped the child up into her arms. Cristo and the other princesses hurried forward and embraced Princess Faith who was radiant with joy.

Simon smiled at the beautiful reunion. He wondered how Princess Faith had been freed.

Cristo announced, "Princess Faith was released because Avidez called on me in faith when he was sinking. He trusted that I could save him."

As Faith thanked the still damp man who sheepishly nodded, Simon turned to see where the Bright Morning Star was shining. He was ready to continue on his journey to Mount Glory. The Star shone straight ahead. The boy looked from the Star to the ground right below it. It looked like a normal forest with a green grassy field beyond it. A smile came to the child's face. Maybe the next part of the journey would be peaceful and uneventful.

CHAPTER 15

VALLEY OF STORMS

Rain poured heavily drenching the travelers. Simon sighed as raindrops flowed down his face. *So much for peaceful and uneventful.*

The group had walked happily through the end of the forest and across the soft, lazy field. The field began a slight downward slope, but not enough to slow down the group. As the people descended down the hill, small droplets of water sprinkled gently on them. Simon had not minded the sprinkles for his skin was still warm from the desert and the way the raindrops fell seemed almost peaceful. However, as the crowd reached a flat area of land at the bottom of the slope, the raindrops fell faster and harder.

Now the group was getting drenched as they crossed the soggy field with streams of rain pouring down on them. Simon had looked around him noticing that they were surrounded by upward sloping land. The boy realized that they were in a deep valley. The sky was a light gray with wispy gray clouds. The ground was mushy with chocolate-colored mud puddles and shaggy emerald grass. Simon's feet sank a little in the mud and he heard a squishy sound as he walked.

Suddenly a streak of lightning shot across the sky followed by a loud boom unlike any Simon had ever heard. The child jumped startled. His heart pounded so hard that he was sure that everyone else could hear it.

A gentle hand touched his wet shoulder and Simon looked up. Victor smiled reassuringly down at him. The knight's hair hung in dripping strands and his clothes were soaked yet his face seemed full of hope. Simon returned the smile then turned to Cristo as the elder knight spoke addressing the entire group of pilgrims.

"Listen, my friends, and heed my words. We are about to cross this valley and make our way up the steepest side. We cannot stop no matter what. This storm will get much worse before it gets better. Persevere! Do not give up or you will be stuck in this valley forever. Follow me! Stay near the group and do not lag behind."

Cristo turned and walked through the pouring rain which had become even harsher as the knight had spoken. Flashes of lightning had given emphasis to Cristo's promise that the storm would get worse.

Simon felt fearful of being left behind to stay in the valley forever. A shiver ran up his spine at the thought. His trembling hand grasped Victor's gray shirt sleeve and tugged desperately. His cheeks blushed hot and red as he suddenly felt embarrassed at his weakness. However, the loving look that Victor gave the child disintegrated any feelings of inferiority or weakness. The man knelt down to Simon's eye level placing a knee indifferently in the mud. He gently grasped the boy's shoulders.

"What's wrong, Simon?"

Simon stuttered, "I'm scared, Victor. What if I fall and can't get back up the hill? What if it is too slippery? I don't want to be stuck here forever!"

Tears sprang to the boy's eyes. He found it hard to catch his breath. He felt heavy and exhausted. Simon thought his heart would explode as it pounded so frantically.

The knight pulled him into a hug and Simon clung to him ready for some words that would make him feel better.

Silence. No words of encouragement or comfort came and Simon was devastated.

Victor held the trembling child closely trying to think of something to say that would comfort him. However, the thoughts of losing Simon plagued his heart and mind as well. Since almost losing him in the desert, Victor had not been able to get the image of Simon falling out of his head.

At Simon's words, Victor had begun to wonder through his own fears. As he held the boy, the man's mind raced. *What if Simon does fall? What if I can't catch him in time? Or hold on to him on the slick slope? What if he dies? What if…*

Victor shook his head sharply and jerked back leaving Simon with a surprised look on his face.

"No, Simon. We cannot dwell on all of the what-ifs that come to mind. If we do, we will be consumed with fear and forget all that we have learned so far on our journey. Instead, we must believe that we can do it with the strength of the Ancient One. We can make it out of this valley, Simon. Stand firm!"

The boy nodded with what seemed like a relieved smile as drops of rain streamed down his face.

"Maybe this will help in your climb."

Both turned their gaze sharply and saw Cristo standing before them grasping a white braided rope.

"Tie this around your waists and you will be less likely to fall far without the aid of the other."

Victor looked around the others and was surprised to see that they were working at tying their own ropes to their partners. Lailani was paired with Devin. Avidez was partnered up with Cornelius. Ziona was tying her rope around Harmony's waist. The other princesses were joined together: Mercy and Joy, Hope and Grace, and Faith handed her rope's end to Cristo as he rejoined the group. Oddly, Feliz, Cristo's horse, was nowhere in sight.

Victor looked at the rope in his hands. It seemed very strong as he pulled on it to test its sturdiness. He looked at Simon who had a more peaceful look on his face now. Victor smiled and began to secure the rope around his little friend. After tying the other end of the pale white rope around his own waist, the group slowly began their upward trek.

Devin stepped carefully up the sloppy, mushy ground of the sloping side of the valley. His boots slid slightly with each step and it took intense concentration not to fall. To his left, the man could see Lailani, soaked to the bone, struggling in the same way as him. The idea of slipping and causing her to fall sent shivers up his spine. Or maybe it was the cool wind slamming against the man's wet clothes. As his focus shifted to his surroundings and the storm swirling around him, Devin took another step on the slippery mud. His foot slipped and the man fell to his face. Before he could get a grip to hoist himself back up, a gushing waterfall furiously pounded in his face.

"Devin!"

With desperation, the man raised his head out of the water gasping and saw Lailani holding the rope firmly in her hands. Her feet were sliding at the man's weight. Fear struck the man for he knew that he was pulling the woman he loved down with him.

"Cut the rope, Lailani!"

"Cut the rope, Lailani!"

Lailani's eyes widened at the man's words. She frowned knowing that she couldn't cause the man to fall. Tears sprang to her eyes as her feet slid further down the hill. The soaked woman clung to the rope with both hands determined not to give up. She stomped a foot down trying to get a firm standing.

"Cut it!"

Lailani screamed back, "No! We can make it!"

Her feet still slid no matter how hard she tried to stop it. Her fingers ached and felt raw as the rope ripped into them.

Lailani looked down at Devin and gasped for the man had unsheathed his sword and was going to cut the rope himself.

"Devin, don't!"

Panic filled the woman for she did not want to lose the man she loved. She knew that if he fell then he would not make it back up. He would be stuck in the valley, forever in a raging storm. Lailani knew that Devin would need support to get out of the valley. She instantly stopped struggling against the gravity and even dropped her body in the watery mud, so that the couple slid together down the muddy valley slope. Darkness engulfed the woman as she and Devin splashed into a deep water hole that had gathered at the bottom of the valley.

Avidez fell onto his knees in the sloppy mud again. He growled as he struggled back to his feet for what seemed like the hundredth time. The man's temper was becoming fiercer by the minute. He had been paired up with Cornelius. The old man was very unstable on his feet when they were not on a muddy slope, so he was barely able to move up the valley side without falling. Annoyance filled Avidez at being partnered up with someone who was not cut out for high climbs. *I'm one of the best warriors. Why should I be burdened with the weakest*

member of the group? I would rather be stuck with one of the women or even that bratty kid than this old skeleton.

Avidez suddenly felt a strong jerk of the rope around his waist. He grabbed a clump of grass to steady himself before glaring down at Cornelius who was lying on the ground again clutching the rope tightly. Avidez's feet slid a bit and the grass blades began to tear. Surely the clump would be uprooted and the duo would fall down the valley wall. The thought of having to start the climb over or being hurt in the fall frustrated the warrior so much that he began to wish he was alone climbing the slick slope.

"Avidez, please help me!"

Avidez's eyes moved from the struggling man to his sheathed sword. Using his free hand, the fed-up warrior grasped the hilt of the sword and pulled it free.

"What are you doing? Please pull me up!"

The old man's pleas struck ineffectively on a hardened heart. Looking briefly into Cornelius' desperate, frightened eyes, Avidez swung his sword sharply and struck the soggy, off-white rope that connected the two men. The strands cut quickly and peeled away from each other leaving uneven, splintered ends.

Cornelius' cry of betrayal and horror filled the air and faded all too quickly. Avidez suddenly felt light and carefree. He began to climb the valley wall again not regretting his treatment of the old man, but justifying to himself that he would have fallen, too, if he hadn't cut the other man loose.

The climb was so much easier as the wet warrior moved closer and closer to the top. Looking up, Avidez saw that Cristo and the women were nowhere in sight. Had they fallen too? Or had they made it to the top safely? With several more minutes of crawling up the slimy slope, the top grew closer still, but now instead of mud and grass the terrain became sharp rocks.

Avidez held tightly to each jagged piece of the cliff pulling himself up. It was so difficult yet the man kept going. What he had done to Cornelius came to his mind continuously, but the man pushed the thoughts away telling himself that since he could barely make it alone, the added weight of the old man would have made this part of the climb impossible.

His hand finally touched the edge at the top of the valley wall. A metallic gloved hand stretched out to the man. Avidez took it gratefully. Cristo pulled the drenched man up until his feet struck flat land. The first thing Avidez saw was that there was no rain at the top area. Instead it was bright and sunny with green grass and birds singing. The princesses were untethered, sitting on the grass giggling and squeezing the rainwater from their hair and gowns.

"Avidez?"

The man turned with a relieved grin that changed into a sour frown. Cristo stood staring questioningly at him with the empty end of the rope in his hands.

"Where is Cornelius?"

The girlish giggles ceased and Avidez glanced over to find the princesses staring at him waiting. His eyes slid back to the scraggly, old knight.

"The rope broke and he fell."

Sadness came to Cristo's eyes as he continued to stare at Avidez.

"But Cristo's ropes never break."

Avidez returned his gaze to the princesses and noticed that Princess Harmony was now standing. Her face held accusation. Avidez's temper flared.

"Are you calling me a liar?"

The little girl did not back down from his angry glare. Instead, Harmony stuck her chin out stubbornly and placed her hands on her hips.

"If you say that the rope broke, then yes."

Avidez's hand touched the hilt of Cristo's sword which lay waiting in the furious man's sheath.

"What are you going to do? Hurt me too? Only a coward hurts an old man or a child."

With an animal-like snarl, Avidez stepped back while unsheathing his borrowed sword. A scream came from behind him, but his fury was fixated on the girl who had called him a liar and a coward. Nothing else mattered. No one else mattered.

Raising the sword, Avidez saw red as he advanced on the little princess clad in purple. Harmony stared boldly at the angry man as he came closer. Oddly, none of the other women or even Cristo came to the child's aid.

Avidez brought the sword down swiftly and shock filled him at what happened. The sword did not strike the child, but instead exploded into dozens of multi-colored butterflies that fluttered all around the little girl. Princess Harmony giggled as the butterflies encircled her.

Horror struck Avidez as the warrior realized what he had almost done to an innocent child whose only crime had been to call the man out about his lies. Shame filled the man as he stared at his empty hands and fell to his knees stunned. *I am a liar and a coward!*

Working together and taking their time, Victor and Simon made a steady climb against the pouring rain and hateful wind. Victor had touched the first rock and exclaimed in pain as the jaggedness of it pierced his hand.

"Simon, these rocks are sharp. Be careful!"

The boy nodded weakly. Victor looked at the exhausted child and knew that it was taking a lot of strength and determination for Simon to keep climbing the slick valley wall in the unrelenting storm. The child's eyes were dark and his body drenched by the ever-falling rain. He jumped at every flash of lightning and crash of thunder.

Victor wanted to help the child feel better and to lift his spirits. A tune came to his mind and though it took a minute for Victor to recognize it, he instantly knew he had heard it in the throne room of Mount Glory. The man smiled as he remembered the words clearly and thanked the Ancient One for the perfect song to bring comfort and peace to Simon. Not caring what his voice sounded like in the raging storm and strenuous climb, the knight sang loudly and joyfully. He glanced at Simon who continued to climb with a peaceful smile on his dripping face.

As Victor finished the song, his hand touched the top edge of the slope. A hand reached toward him at the same time another hand stretched toward Simon. Victor smiled at Simon who was beaming. Yes, they both recognized those familiar, strong hands. Together the knight and the boy grabbed the hands extended toward them and allowed Cristo to pull them to safety.

The calm, peacefulness of the grassy knoll at the top of the valley made Simon smile wider, but another sight froze the boy's heart. He was only slightly aware of Victor untying the rope from his own waist and then putting his hands on the knot fastened tightly around Simon.

"Only a coward hurts an old man or a child."

Harmony's voice brought both climbers' attention to the situation before them. Avidez stood facing the little purple princess with his hand on his sword. Harmony was facing the warrior with a firm stare.

Suddenly Avidez drew his sword and by instinct Simon, guardian and protector of the princesses, stepped forward. The swordsman stepped back sharply bumping into the boy who stumbled back. His feet hit nothingness. A startled scream escaped his lips as he fell backwards into the vengeful storm with the empty end of the rope swinging in front of him.

At Simon's scream, Victor dove frantically for the loose end of the rope. His fingers missed by only a couple of centimeters. The man fell to his stomach on the grass. He crawled forward hoping for one last chance to save the child. His eyes stared at the falling boy as he slid down the muddy slope becoming a blur amidst the growing darkness and pouring rain.

The knight was filled with panic, but it was different from what he had experienced in the desert. He knew that Simon was alive though he was no doubt making his way back down to the bottom of the valley once more. Taking a deep breath, Victor started to devise a plan to get his young friend back.

Lailani gasped for air as her head bobbed out of the cold murky water. She looked around her surroundings and realized that she had fallen back to the base of the valley. However, the rainwater had gathered causing a flood at the bottom of the slope. She now was floating in a large pool of water.

Lailani felt a tug around her waist and realized that it was the rope. Her glance moved in the direction of the tugging and her eyes lit up at the sight of Devin pulling the rope toward what could now be considered the shore. Lailani swam in the same direction, so they could both get out of the piercing cold water. Devin climbed onto the grassy slope and helped pull Lailani out so she was beside him. The man averted his eyes in anger.

"Devin? What's wrong?"

The man in black turned to face her with fury in his voice.

"What do you mean what's wrong? You didn't have to start over. You should have let me fall alone so you could make it to the top."

Lailani felt her temper rise at his tone, but then it faded as she replied.

"I wanted to help you get to the top."

"Why? I'm not worth your trouble. I don't want you to miss out on Mount Glory because of me!"

The harsh shout and the furious look in the man's eyes caused tears to join the raindrops on her moist cheeks.

"I'm not going to miss out on Mount Glory, Devin, because I am not going to give up. I just want you to come with me…These storms are coming on us without ceasing and it is wearing on you. But you must remember all Cristo has done for us. If he gave us this rope and told us to climb this slope, then I know we can persevere through this storm and make it to the top where I know he is waiting. Please do not give up, Dev, for we can do all things through the Ancient One."

Devin's hard, stone-like glare softened as he listened to Lailani's encouraging words. Here he had promised to follow Cristo and when it got too hard, he had just given up.

"You're right, Lailani. We can make it to the top if we work together and put our trust in the Ancient One…Ready?"

The woman smiled and the man's heart melted. He extended a hand which Lailani took eagerly. Devin pulled her to her feet. The couple stared into each other's eyes still holding hands with the rain pouring down in sheets upon them.

A scream echoed from above their heads and both travelers looked up the slope startled. Through the rainy darkness, Devin saw someone sliding down the hill. The person slid past them and fell into the watery hole that the duo had just climbed out of moments ago.

"Cornelius!"

At Lailani's cry, Devin realized that it was in fact the old man who had fallen from higher ground. Cornelius' head came to the surface of the water and he slapped his arms out trying to stay afloat.

"Hold on, Cornelius. We'll get you!"

Devin grabbed Lailani by the shoulders as she started to step forward.

"Wait! I'll get him. There's no need for both of us to get in that cold pool again."

His love nodded as he untied the rope knot around his waist and dove back into the cold water. Devin swam to the struggling old man and pulled him up so he was in a more stable position. Together they waded to the shore where Lailani was waiting, ready to pull the men out.

Once all three were safely on the muddy shore, Devin was amused at how quickly Lailani tied the rope back around his waist. The couple exchanged a smile before the woman turned to the old man who had sunk to sit on the shore exhausted.

"Cornelius, what happened? Weren't you tethered to Avidez?"

The old man burst into tears and Lailani hugged her friend gently.

Devin frowned as he noticed the rope around Cornelius' waist. Curiously, he picked up the end and examined it. The rope threads were splintered as if broken quickly and harshly.

"This rope's been cut."

The look of horror on Lailani's face matched what Devin was feeling.

"Yes, Avidez cut it with his sword."

Cornelius' anguished voice struck Devin's heart fiercely and the man felt angry. How could Avidez cut the rope and just let the old man fall? Oddly, a thought crossed Devin's mind. *You wanted Lailani to do the same thing to you.*

Devin tried to argue and justify that it was different than what happened to Cornelius, but in truth it was very similar. Devin was the one who gave up while Avidez had given up too. They just dealt with it in a different way.

"We're going to try the climb again. Come with us, Cornelius."

Devin frowned at Lailani's words not because he didn't want the old man to come, but because he wasn't sure how to get him up the slope. Two people connected would be difficult enough. With three people, it would be even worse. *How can we do it?*

As if in answer to his question, something slid past the group and landed in the deep watery pool.

Simon swallowed some of the bitter, murky water as he struggled to get his head back to the surface of the pool he had fell into at the end of his descent down the slope. His feet touched the bottom and he pushed as hard as he could. His body quickly shot up and soon his soaked head broke through the surface. Gasping for air while gagging on the sour tasting water, Simon blinked trying to clear his vision.

"Simon!"

The boy's eyes darted in the direction of the voice. On the slope he had just slid down, Simon saw three people turned in his direction. A smile of relief crossed his small, wet face as he recognized the people as Lailani, Devin, and Cornelius. The boy swam toward the shore excited that he wasn't stuck down here alone.

As he approached the shore, Simon saw Devin kneel down and extend his arm as far as he could to reach the child. The hand was almost in reach when Simon felt a tug from around his waist. He remembered the rope and shock filled his face as no matter how hard he struggled, he could not move any further.

"Keep coming, Simon. You're almost here."

Simon nodded at Devin as he grasped the rope and pulled. The rope would not budge. In fact, Simon almost thought he felt the rope tug him in the opposite direction.

"I'm stuck!"

The rope tugged again harder and Simon realized that it wasn't his imagination. He really was being tugged back. And not just back, but under.

"Please help! It's pulling…"

Simon's shout was silenced as the next pull yanked him completely under the water. He turned to see what could possibly be holding the rope. Terror filled his heart at the creature smiling at him.

"I'm stuck!"

Devin instantly began to untie the rope that connected him to Lailani. His frantic fingers stumbled around on the wet knot.

"Please help! It's pulling…"

The abrupt end of the scream caused Devin's eyes to dart back to the pool of water. Simon was nowhere in sight.

"Something pulled him under!"

The woman's scream pierced Devin's heart. Panic filled the man as he still couldn't get the knot to release him.

"He's going to drown, Dev!"

Desperate to help the child, the man unsheathed his sword and brought it down sharply on the rope that connected him to Lailani. The threads of the rope split easily.

Devin dove into the water hoping to get to Simon in time. The water, though murky, was not as dark as it should be. It had an iridescent glow that gave a haunting appearance.

Glancing up, Devin saw a bright light shining through the surface of the water. He smiled as he realized that it was the Bright Morning Star glowing and leading him from above.

The man looked back down at the watery bottom. His eyes widened in surprise. Simon was pulling away with his hands grasping the rope around his waist. On the other end of the rope was Aquana, the sea witch who had lured Vano to his watery death. She was clinging to the rope playfully.

Devin swam forward pointing the sword at Aquana who instantly let go and swam away into the shadows. Quickly the man hurried to Simon's side knowing that neither he nor the boy had much air left. He put his arms around Simon's waist nodding reassuringly at the child's startled glance.

Pushing off the bottom of the pool as hard as he could, Devin held onto the child and kicked his legs with an urgency he had never felt before. The surface was coming closer as the duo continued to kick their legs and swim upwards. Both heads broke through the surface of the water. The fresh air was so welcoming and refreshing.

Devin took a deep breath and looked at Simon who was gasping still in the man's arms.

"Are you okay?"

The boy nodded and Devin let go of him so they were both treading water.

"Let's get out of this waterhole."

As they began to swim toward the shore, Devin glanced from Simon to Lailani who was leaning forward ready to pull them out. The man smiled at her which she instantly returned. However, the woman's smile changed quickly to a frown. Devin spun around. The water between Simon and Devin was swirling and bubbling.

Aquana popped out of the water in front of the child and pushed Simon's head back under the murky liquid. Her attention was fully on the boy and her mission of drowning him. Devin didn't hesitate this time nor did he plan to give the sea witch another chance to hurt someone.

Pulling the sword out of the water, Devin swung swiftly and removed Aquana's head from her shoulders. The creature died clueless to the method of her death. Her body sank at the same time as Simon came back up out of the water again.

The child choked and coughed as he tried to fill his lungs with air again. His eyes were filled with pure terror as he looked around frantically for Aquana as if waiting for another attack. Devin sheathed his sword and waded over to Simon.

"She's dead, Simon. Hold on to my neck and I will carry you across."

Turning his back to the boy and then feeling the small, tired arms wrap around his neck, Devin swam once more to the shore. This time they reached it without any trouble. Lailani made a desperate grab to get him out.

Lailani threw her arms around Devin's neck. He embraced her around the waist. It took the man a moment to realize that she was sobbing. An amused smile played at the corners of his mouth.

"You weren't worried about us, were you?"

A slight, shaky laugh escaped through the sobs. Then as Devin had hoped, the sobs slowed before ceasing. Lailani pulled back from the man.

"Of course not. Why would I worry about you?"

A sweet, playful smile crossed her face and Devin felt his heart melt.

"Uh, Devin, sir?"

The man turned and regarded Simon who was kneeling on the shore, wet and disheveled, exhaustion all over his face.

"Thank you for saving me from her. I thought I was..."

The child lowered his head crying. Devin sighed amazed at how people outside of the Chasm of Misery were so free and open with their emotions. The only emotion shared in the Chasm was fury. His heart softened at the sight of the weeping boy.

Without thinking or giving Lailani a chance to respond, the man scooped Simon into his arms and hugged him. Simon's arms clung to his neck. Devin looked into Lailani's eyes which were twinkling at him in amusement. *Yes, I have definitely changed!*

Simon tried to calm down. When his head was under the water, he had been terrified. He had tried to struggle and escape the sea witch's grip, but Aquana was so strong. Relief and joy had filled him when he was released and fresh air could fill his deprived lungs again. Once on the shore, all of his fears flooded him and he found himself crying. He felt embarrassed to be sobbing like a baby in front of such a tough warrior as Devin.

Surprise filled him when Devin pulled him into an embrace. Comfort replaced the fear allowing Simon to control his emotions and stop crying. Looking down, the boy saw the rope tied around Devin's waist. The free end was splintered as if broken in haste. Simon pulled away frowning with guilt.

"You cut the rope?"

Devin nodded confusingly as if he wasn't sure why the boy was upset.

"How will you and Lailani get up the hill?"

Simon watched Devin pick up the end of the rope.

"Maybe we can tie the ends together."

The child wasn't sure if that would work. Oddly, an idea hit the boy that he didn't know where it had come from.

"Maybe the rope will connect if you put the ends together."

A skeptical look passed between Lailani and Devin, but they put the ends together to humor the imaginative boy. The ends fit perfectly and Simon's eyes widened as the two adults tried to pull their piece of rope away, but the rope wouldn't break. Simon touched the rope and examined it. He couldn't even tell where the threads had been cut.

"How...Never mind. Let's see if it works for your rope and Cornelius' rope."

Simon nodded at Devin's suggestion and he looked at the old man. Cornelius appeared to be completely miserable. He shook his head briskly.

"No. I won't be going."

"What?!"

Simon turned to Lailani who had approached Cornelius.

"I can't make it up the slope. I won't keep the boy from making it to the top."

The child didn't want to leave the old man behind, but he also wasn't sure that he could make it without someone to help him.

Before Lailani could speak, Simon blurted out, "I can't make it alone, Cornelius sir. I need your help."

The old man studied the child as if searching to see if he really meant what he was saying. Simon just looked back at him intently waiting for him to make a decision. Cornelius shook his head.

"No, I'm not going."

Lailani stared at Cornelius in disbelief.

"What will you do? You can't stay here. You will drown!"

The old man crossed his arms stubbornly.

"The storms will stop and the water will dry up like before. Then I will head home to Terra."

Tears sprang to Lailani's green eyes as she searched for a reply.

"What if the storms don't stop?"

Cornelius shook his head and did not answer. Lailani knelt down in front of the old man and gently cupped her hand under his bearded chin.

"Cornelius, you told me in Terra that you have wanted to go to the Ancient One for many years. Are you really going to give up when we have come so far? Each day we are closer to Mount Glory. To go back means you have to travel all that way again. Do you really want to go back to Terra?"

Cornelius listened to Lailani's words. His mind played through in reverse all that he had experienced. He thought about the slippery, wet valley and the river that he walked on by keeping his eyes on

Cristo. Cornelius remembered the hot, endless desert with unpredictable holes. He smiled at the memory of the beautiful ship called the Blessed Hope. Yet a frown returned as he remembered the battle on the beach with those monstrous Demoni. The thought of that dark, ferocious labyrinth sent a shudder up his spine. Cornelius remembered the swamp with the hands that drag people to a watery grave. He didn't want to go there again. In fact, the more he thought about it, the more certain he was that he did not want to go back the way they came. Maybe there was another path.

Cornelius thought about his life in Terra. The Demoni went around doing as they pleased terrorizing everyone. He had been starving in Terra. He had also been alone except for Lailani. If he went back to Terra and Lailani continued on to Mount Glory, then the old man would truly be alone.

Cornelius looked into Lailani's emerald eyes. He could see such pleading in them. With a smile, he answered her question.

"No, I don't want to go back to Terra. I will go where you go."

Lailani's face softened and she smiled pleasantly.

"Then let's go."

"Here, Cornelius, sir."

The old man turned his attention to Simon who was holding the end of his rope up in the air. Cornelius reached down and grabbed the splintered end of his rope.

"Here goes nothing."

The old man and the young boy touched their ropes. Pulling back to the surprise of Cornelius and the delight of Simon, the two ropes were now one.

Lailani's heart swelled with joy as the rope connected between Cornelius and Simon. Such a feeling of hope filled her even though the rain was beginning to increase again.

"Remember: No matter what happens, don't give up! Keep persevering! Even if you fall again, get up and try again."

The woman spoke with such strength though inside she was scared that they would never make it up the slimy slope. The others nodded. The four travelers, going two by two, began their ascent again.

The first few minutes of waiting were no big deal to Victor because he knew that Simon was okay and it would take time for him to get back up. The other comfort was that some of the other travelers hadn't made it up yet. Surely they would help him.

However, by the end of the first hour, the knight began to feel restless. Why was it taking so long? As the second hour began to pass, Victor couldn't stand sitting in the sunshine knowing that Simon was in the gloomy, pouring rain. He started to pace along the edge of the slope glancing down more and more frequently into the rainy valley. At the beginning of the third hour, the man couldn't take it any longer. He approached the edge ready to slide down and find the boy.

"Where are you going, Victor?"

A groan escaped his lips as the knight turned to face Cristo. The elder knight stood waiting for an answer.

"I'm going back down to find my son...I mean my child...I mean my...uh Simon."

Victor hadn't meant to say his son or his child, but as he stumbled to correct himself, the man realized that it was his heart's desire to be that boy's father and to never be separated from him again. He averted his eyes from Cristo embarrassed. Victor turned toward the edge again, but stopped as a hand grasped his arm.

"Delight yourself in the Ancient One and He will give you the desires of your heart."

Victor turned again to look at Cristo. The elder knight smiled warmly and his eyes were glowing with compassion. Victor felt that the other man knew how he was feeling and understood.

"I need to find him, my lord. I can't bear the thought of him struggling up that slope without me."

Cristo placed his hands on the younger knight's shoulders.

"Have faith, Victor, and though it is difficult, wait." *I don't want to wait. I want to help Simon.*

Yet the look that sparkled in Cristo's eyes reminded the man of all that he had done on this journey and how he was always right. The elder knight had been faithful and true to his word and honor.

"I will wait, my lord."

The smile of Cristo grew broader.

"Well done, Sir Victor."

The elder knight walked away humming a song that seemed very familiar to Victor. With a sigh, the man realized that it was the song he had sung to Simon while climbing the rainy, slippery slope together. *How did he know?*

Victor shook his head. *How does Cristo ever know anything?*

The man sat down in the grass humming the song trying hard to wait. He thought about the words of the song and felt peace fill his heart.

"My heart is heavy, full of sorrow."

Victor started at the new voice glancing around.

"I don't know if there will be a tomorrow."

The man's heart pounded as he realized the voice was not from the group who had made it to the top, but from the slope.

"Yet I can see His loving care."

The voice was getting louder or perhaps closer.

"Though I am weary, I won't despair."

A smile engulfed Victor's face as he recognized the voice.

The young man walked to the edge of the slope excitedly wanting to see the face of the singer, almost afraid that it was just wishful thinking.

"For He will fill me with His love."

Looking over the edge, Victor saw a small, wet face not more than two feet below.

"And raise me up to heights above."

A wide smile crossed Simon's face as he noticed the man peering down at him. Victor returned the smile feeling relief.

Victor's Song

My heart is heavy, full of sorrow.
I don't know if there will be a tomorrow.
Yet I can see His loving care.
Though I am weary, I won't despair.
For He will fill me with His love,
And raise me up to heights above.

137

CHAPTER 16

DANGER IN THE DARK

The first thing that Victor noticed about Simon was that he was connected to the old man Cornelius by the rope. Both looked exhausted and ready to get out of the rain. Though both appeared to be tired, Cornelius seemed to be close to letting go.

Victor extended his hand to the man who took it gratefully. From the corner of his vision, another hand extended to the old man. Cornelius took Cristo's hand as well. Both knights pulled the elderly man to the green grassy clearing.

When Cornelius was standing stable on the top, Victor let go and reached with both hands for Simon. The boy practically jumped into his arms. Victor hugged him tightly as little arms clung around his neck. *Thank you, Ancient One.*

"Good thing you waited or you would have gotten wet again for no reason."

Victor glanced up at Cristo who looked amused.

As he pulled away, Victor was surprised when Simon refused to let go and actually tightened his grip around his neck. Frowning in confusion and concern, the knight returned his arms to embrace the boy and held him closely. His eyes met Cristo's who was regarding them with sadness in his eyes.

"You two should talk for much has happened. I will help the others."

The "others" appeared at the edge of the cliff moments later. Cristo went to help Lailani and Devin to the top. Victor stood up and carried the trembling child to an area away from the others. He sat down against a large boulder with the boy on his lap still clinging to his neck.

"Simon, tell me what happened."

Silence fell on them and time seemed to drag as Victor waited for an answer.

After what seemed like hours, a shaky whisper near his ear said, "I almost died."

Shock slammed into the man as he jerked the boy back to examine him for injuries.

"How? Are you hurt?"

Simon shook his head.

"I fell into a pool of water. I tried to swim to shore, but Aquana pulled me under by the rope. Devin came and scared her away. We went to the surface and swam for shore. Then Aquana pushed me under and I couldn't breathe or get away...Devin killed her."

The fear in Simon's eyes pierced Victor's heart. He pulled the child to himself and held him comfortingly.

"You're safe now, son. I'll take care of you."

Yes, he realized that he had said son and he meant it with his whole heart. His only hope was that Simon felt the same way.

Son?

Simon frowned at the word. Surely Victor hadn't meant the word. He probably meant it as a man speaks to a boy, not as a father speaks to a son. Deep in his heart, the child truly wished that Victor could be his father and they could serve the Ancient One together.

Of course that would never happen so Simon decided to enjoy the short time that he and the knight would have together until they reached Mount Glory.

Devin took Cristo's hand gratefully and stood beside Lailani whose face was lit up with joy. The knight faced the man and woman.

"I am glad that you both persevered. Come and rest, ye who are weary."

The couple walked toward the tree where all of the others were sitting. The princesses and Ziona were huddled together talking and giggling. Cornelius was hobbling to the area and allowed Cristo to help him sit down on a nearby stump.

Away from the others, Avidez sat slumped over with a sour expression on his face. His eyes had a fierce, indignant coldness in them that caused Devin to wonder what had happened on the top area while he and the others were struggling below.

A movement out of the corner of Devin's eye startled the man from his thoughts. Simon ran by and rushed over to the women who exclaimed their welcome to their guardian. Princess Harmony patted the grass beside her and the boy blushed as he sat down.

Devin shook his head in amusement and couldn't help but smile at the shy boy. His smile widened at the thought that he acted the same way when he was around Lailani.

"Devin."

Again startled, Devin escaped from his thoughts and turned to the voice. The knight Victor was approaching him from behind.

"Uh yeah?"

Devin felt confused as the man stopped and extended his right hand.

"Thank you for taking care of Simon. He told me what happened with Aquana. You saved his life. Thank you."

The relief in the knight's voice was apparent and it made Devin feel relief as well.

Devin reached his right hand out and shook Victor's hand. "Uh...no problem."

The knight smiled, then released his hand, and headed for where Simon was speaking with the princesses. Devin watched amazed to have made another friend. *Maybe this new life will work out after all.*

Deep in the fiery Chasm of Misery, the Demoni huddled in the shadows waiting for the fury of Diablo to subside. The dragon had been told that his most useful servant Aquana had been beheaded by none other than the traitor, Devin. The roars and gnashing of teeth had filled the Demoni with terror as they fled from the creature's presence.

Diablo paced in his cave seething with rage as he repeatedly thought about what Devin had done. First he had traveled to stop Cristo and his followers. Then the man had started to follow Cristo and even survived a battle against some of the dragon's best Demoni. Now that pathetic human had dared to kill Aquana. This insolence had pushed Diablo too far because it was a stab at the very power of the dragon. Devin would have to be destroyed.

But how? Should the Demoni be unleashed on the man? No, the Demoni had failed him already. The only way to make sure that

Devin paid was for Diablo to leave the Chasm and take care of it himself.

Avidez was in a dark mood. He had quickly recovered from his regret of trying to kill the little princess and a darkness engulfed him as he sat away from the rest of the group. His mood darkened further when he saw Cristo helping Cornelius over to the stump. The old man was the reason everyone hated him now. He wouldn't have had to cut the rope if Cornelius had been able to climb the wet hill. A hatred for the old man filled the warrior's heart and he glared at Cornelius as he rested on the stump.

His fury deepened at the sight of the others who had helped the old man get up the slope especially Simon who had been hooked to him. That brat should have stayed down in the valley with Cornelius. Instead, he was smiling and everyone was welcoming him with open arms. No one welcomed Avidez or congratulated him for making it to the top. *Oh, Cornelius and Simon will pay for making me look bad.*

Cristo instructed the group to rest for the night as they would continue their journey early in the morning. As the sun sank into the horizon, the noise of the people quieted as each began to fall asleep weary from the struggles of the journey.

Lailani could not sleep though she had no idea why. She was completely exhausted physically, mentally, and emotionally. Yet as she lay on the ground, sleep did not come to her. The woman stared up into the sky at the Bright Morning Star and wondered what they would face on the next step of the journey. Would they face more struggles or more danger? Would they lose anyone else in the group? Or would they all make it to Mount Glory?

"Do not worry about tomorrow, Lailani, for there are enough troubles for today."

The woman sat up and saw that Cristo was sitting against the tree nearby watching her intently.

"Surely we have faced all of the troubles for today."

The scraggly knight motioned for Lailani to come sit beside him. The woman moved to him eagerly. As she sat down, Cristo put an arm around her shoulders.

"Life is full of troubles. It seems like one day flows into another. However, we must not worry about what is to come. We must focus on the present and rely on the Ancient One to get us through daily struggles. Do you understand?"

Lailani nodded in understanding.

"But your future is really not what tugs at your heart, Lailani. It is your past that plagues you. Tell me how you feel."

The request surprised Lailani for she never talked about her childhood nor did she think that she could do so without crying. She hoped that Cristo would see how hard this was for her and would tell her to forget telling him about it. However, the knight just sat quietly waiting for her to answer. Finally, Lailani couldn't stand the silence any longer.

"My parents died in a fire when I was little. I think about them often and I wish all the time that they were here."

The confession actually lightened a burden that had been wearing on Lailani for a long time. She took a deep breath that didn't seem so heavy and waited for what Cristo would say.

"I knew your parents, Lailani. They were wonderful servants of the Ancient One. They served him faithfully for most of their lives. When they died, both were carried by Light Warriors to the Glory of Glories. The Glory of Glories is the eternal home of those who belong to the Ancient One when they die. It is a paradise with no sorrow or pain. Your parents are there now dwelling in peace...I know you wish they were here, my dear. It is good that you miss them, but you must not dwell on your loss for it will bring you to ruin. Instead, focus on getting to Mount Glory and accepting the Ancient One as your Master, so that you may join them in the Glory of Glories when your time comes."

Tears flowed down Lailani's cheeks as she listened to Cristo's words. Her mind understood what he was saying, but her heart didn't want to agree. How could she not dwell on the people who had loved her and cared for her? Yet the woman knew that Cristo's counsel was always sound and right. If dwelling on her parents would lead to her ruin, then she was going to have to change her focus to the journey at hand.

"Trust in the Ancient One and He will not let you fall."

The whispered words of Cristo rested gently on the woman's heart and mind causing her to feel a peace that she had not felt for many years. Closing her eyes, Lailani leaned her head on Cristo's shoulder and fell peacefully asleep.

Devin listened to the exchange between Lailani and Cristo trying to stay absolutely still. His heart ached for the young woman at the mention of her dead parents.

"Trust in the Ancient One and He will not let you fall."

The words filled the man with hope and promise. A desire to make it to Mount Glory took the place of all of the desires and wants he had wished for before. Money, power, and prestige didn't mean anything to him anymore. All he wanted was to make it to the mountain with Lailani and begin his life in the service of the Ancient One.

A quiet hiss brought Devin from his thoughts. His eyes snapped open and searched the darkness straight ahead of him. Nothing was in sight yet Devin was sure that he had heard the sound. Continuing to stare, the man's heart pounded and a sickly feeling struck his stomach as he saw two orange lights flash in the darkness. He recognized where he had heard that sound and seen those lights before.

Panicked, Devin exclaimed, "Cristo!"

The man hurried to his feet and pulled his sword out of his scabbard. The knight came to his side as the others awoke and scrambled to their feet.

A growl escaped the shadows and the orange lights came closer. *No, not now. We are so close.*

The man ignored the anxious words of the other travelers as he focused on the danger ahead. Out of the shadows came the face that Devin had hoped that he would never have to see again.

"Cristo!"

Victor sat up quickly at the alarmed scream of Devin. He looked around frantically hoping to see the cause of the panic, but he didn't see anything. Simon stirred beside him and sat up rubbing his eyes.

"What's wrong?"

Victor shook his head unsure of what really was the problem.

"Uh, do you see lights?"

The man turned to the boy and saw him pointing at the darkness that was behind them. Victor stared at the two orange lights that seemed to be moving toward the camp. He had no idea what the lights were, but he had a bad feeling in the pit of his stomach.

Standing up quickly and putting his hand on the hilt of his sword, Victor faced the approaching lights. The knight felt Simon join him and he protectively pushed the child a little behind him in case something dangerous sprang from the shadows. However, Victor could never have anticipated what came out of the darkness.

His eyes widened in horror as a humongous, red dragon crawled into view and glared at the group. Though he had never seen this creature before, Victor knew from his training at Mount Glory that this was the evil Diablo, lord of the Chasm of Misery.

"Cristo!"

Lailani sat up straight at the yell as Cristo sprang to his feet and rushed to Devin's side. The woman stood up and stared into the area of darkness that the two men were facing. At first she didn't see anything. Then she saw two orange lights advancing toward the camp. Fear struck her because of the unknown source of the lights.

A hand touched Lailani's shoulder and she turned startled to see Cornelius looking at her uncertainly. She tried to smile reassuringly at the old man, but she felt as if something horrible was about to happen.

Lailani gasped as a menacing, crimson beast came out where she could see it. The woman stared in horror as she realized that the creature was in fact a dragon. The only dragon she had ever heard of was the one that Devin called Diablo which struck even more fear into her heart.

Simon's heart pounded at the sight of the dragon. The hideous monster crouched low to the ground breathing heavily. Its eyes moved throughout the camp glaring at each member of the group. Simon scooted closer and behind Victor at the sight of the creature. The knight's hand reached back briefly to pat his arm before returning to cling to his sword.

Simon glanced over at Cristo who was standing fearlessly beside Lailani and Devin. The dragon fixed his gaze on the elder knight. He spoke with a low, gravelly voice that struck even more fear into the boy. The monster's gaze was on Cristo, but his words were for the travelers.

"I am Diablo, lord of all. I am sure that you have heard of me."

His eyes flicked to Devin then returned to Cristo.

"I have heard of your struggles and how you have lost much on this journey. I thought it was my duty to warn you that you are experiencing all of this for nothing. The service of the Ancient One is full of endless heartaches and battles. Why do that if there is a better way to make a difference in the world? You may not know this, but there is an easier form of service. If you join me, then I will give you all of your heart's desires."

Diablo's eyes fixed on Victor and Simon for a moment before returning again to Cristo in an almost challenging manner.

"Everyone is accepted in my service even if you betrayed me or abandoned me."

Another glance at Devin came from the creature before he stared at Cristo again.

"There will be no pain or sorrow. There will be no lost loved ones."

Simon wasn't sure, but it looked like the dragon peered at Lailani for a moment before again focusing on the elder knight.

"You can do whatever you want and live a very prosperous life. Won't any of you choose a happier life?"

Silence followed until a gruff voice shouted out, "I'll join you!"

Shock filled Simon as he watched the speaker approach the dragon.

Avidez listened to the dragon intently. He was sick of following Cristo and his noble ways. He was tired of being treated like a criminal for wanting to make it to the top of the slope. Diablo's words sounded so good. He wanted to be prosperous and do whatever he wanted. He wanted to be free from pain and sorrow. Most of all he didn't want to lose any more friends and Cristo had never promised that in all of this time.

"I'll join you!"

Avidez approached the creature that had turned his head sharply to take in his new servant. A sly smile spread across Diablo's face as he spoke.

"Welcome to my service, Avidez! You won't be sorry for your decision. I'm sure I won't be sorry either for I know that you are a great warrior with many well-trained skills...Anyone else?"

No one else approached or spoke up, but Avidez didn't care. He knew that his new master would be far better than any other one could ever be. Life was going to get better for the warrior.

Devin couldn't believe how easily Avidez had been manipulated by Diablo's lies. The man wanted to shout out the truth about service in the Chasm of Misery, but fear filled him for the dragon was so close and held such a piercing glare. Fortunately no one else believed the lies or they were too scared to go near the dragon. Diablo glowered at the group before addressing Cristo personally.

"I cannot believe that you are still guiding these pathetic wretches. Why, Cristo, do you have any idea what your travelers have done?"

The knight's face held a look of amusement.

"Oh, what is it you accuse them of doing, Diablo?"

The dragon turned his scowl on the young knight Victor.

The dragon fixed his glare on Victor who visibly gulped.

Pointing a claw at the young knight, Diablo sneered, "He is a coward who abandoned the Ancient One after a battle where many others gladly sacrificed their lives."

Victor's heart began to pound for it was true that he had left the service of the Ancient One. The word "coward" struck him hard and he lowered his head in shame. *It's true; I am a coward.*

A hand touched his arm.

"He's a liar, Victor. Don't listen to him. Only someone brave could have faced Tatianna and the Demoni."

Confidence filled Victor at Simon's reminder. The dragon's eyes narrowed at Simon's words. Cristo spoke before the beast could say anything else.

"Even the bravest man cowers at the brutal death of others and the possibility of his own mortality...As to the abandonment charge, did you not notice that Victor is on his way back to the Ancient One?"

The dragon's eyes darted to Cristo before returning to Victor.

"But will the Ancient One accept him if he returns?"

Victor sucked in a deep breath at the question. The thought had crossed the man's mind many times along the journey and it plagued him again now. What if the Ancient One refused to take him back? What if he was banished from Mount Glory? What if...

Victor pushed the thoughts away and shook his head. He didn't care. No matter what happened once he got to the mountain, the knight was determined to keep on his current path.

"It is up to the Ancient One whether He accepts me or not, but even if He rejects me, I will consider it an honor just to stand in His presence once more."

Diablo snuffed at the man shooting smoke out of his nostrils. The dragon narrowed his eyes at Victor before turning his attention to another traveler. Victor breathed deeply in relief and glanced at Cristo who was regarding him with pride.

Lailani smiled at Victor's response to the dragon, but her smile changed to a frown as the creature turned his enormous head and fixed his accusing gaze on her.

"Well, she has hatred in her heart against Aurelius. She also would rather have her parents back than join the Ancient One."

The woman took a deep breath and thought about the dragon's words. Did she hate Aurelius? Did she wish harm on the man? No, she may have felt that way each time Aurelius had hurt little Simon, but she didn't want the man to die. In fact, she hoped that he would make it home safely and someday find happiness.

As she opened her mouth to say those very words, Lailani saw Diablo peering at her with his dangerous, powerful eyes. The woman found herself speechless. Here she felt innocent of the charge of hatred and yet the woman couldn't even defend herself.

A gentle hand touched her shoulder and Lailani instantly looked at Cristo with pleading eyes. The knight nodded with a compassionate smile. He then confidently and fearlessly focused his attention on the dragon that had begun to fidget impatiently.

"Lailani hates how Aurelius treated others, but she does not truly hate the man himself."

Diablo growled in frustration, "Well, she still wants her parents more than the Ancient One."

Lailani's eyes widened and her heart fluttered as a sudden realization struck her hard yet for once it struck in a pleasant way.

"I want the Ancient One," the red-headed woman whispered.

Diablo's glare darkened and Cristo turned to her.

"What was that, my lady?"

The knight's voice was light and pleasant. Clearing her throat, the woman found the courage to step forward and meet the monster's gaze.

"I said that I want the Ancient One in my life more than anything or anyone else in the world. I seek Him alone with my whole heart."

Diablo growled deeply with menace and murder in his eyes. Lailani held her breath waiting. A confident smile crossed her face as the dragon moved his attention back toward Victor.

Simon gulped as Diablo sneered at him for he knew it was his turn.

"He is a thief! He stole a valuable necklace."

Simon smiled at the accusation for he already knew Cristo's feelings about the necklace.

"Is that all you have on me?"

The glare that Diablo gave the boy would have melted steel. He crept forward toward the child in a hateful crawl. Victor raised his sword in front of the dragon in a warning. A deep growl escaped the monster's lips.

"Simon did not steal the necklace. He rescued these sweet princesses from Tatianna who I believe was under your command."

At Cristo's words, Simon glanced at the princesses who were frowning at the dragon.

"Rescued? Why, they were never in any danger. Were you, my dears?"

Oddly the dragon's attempt at a smile only made him scarier. Simon frowned as the creature leaned forward, his great head advancing too close to the ladies. Without hesitation the boy pulled his sword from its sheath and rushed to stand between Diablo and the princesses. A surprised and curious look crossed the dragon's face as he raised his eyebrows at the child.

"What's this?"

Diablo's eyes darted over to Cristo who was smiling. The knight did not answer, but gestured back to the boy. Simon realized that Cristo wanted him to explain his actions to the dragon.

"I have been appointed Guardian of Glory. It is my duty and privilege to protect the princesses of the Ancient One from creatures like you."

A hissing sound escaped the throat of the dragon and increased in volume as Diablo laughed mockingly.

"You?! You can't protect them, runt."

"I protected them from your Demoni on the beach."

The dragon bristled at the statement. His fiery glare returned as billowy smoke puffed out of his nostrils again.

"Demoni are nothing compared to me, fool."

Simon held the sword higher though his heart was pounding rapidly.

"Then I will die trying to protect them from you."

As if to prove that the child could not defend the princesses, Diablo suddenly snapped his fierce, powerful jaws at the boy. Simon instantly jumped to the side and brought the sword down on the beast's snout as the ladies scurried back to the tree. The dragon jerked his head back reflexively though foolishly for Simon's sword cut deeper into the flesh due to the movement.

A ferocious, anguished roar filled the air as the creature moved back from the camp slightly, snout bleeding. His piercing eyes returned to the boy whose eyes were widened in surprise. Bracing himself for another attack from the dragon, Simon clutched his sword tightly and tried to breathe. Diablo drew his neck up ready to strike at the child again.

"I wouldn't do that again, Diablo. Not unless you want me to join the skirmish. I won't have any of my followers bullied."

The dragon stared at Cristo as if trying to decide whether it would be worth it or not. Then he turned away from the Guardian and his well-protected princesses. Simon only relaxed slightly.

Devin grimaced as the dragon's steely gaze rested on him at last. Each time Diablo had turned to accuse someone, the man had held his breath and then felt relieved when the accused was someone else other than him. Yet a dark foreboding weighed on the former slave of Diablo for he knew that the beast would address him eventually if not more ferociously.

Now it was indeed his turn. Devin fully hoped that he would be able to endure the harsh words from the creature. Diablo stared at the man. Surprisingly, the dragon did not speak, but instead started to turn away. Devin couldn't believe it. He was not going to be chastised and rebuked in front of the others.

"And what is your accusation against Devin, Diablo?"

Devin turned in disbelief and gaped at Cristo. How could he purposely focus the conversation on Devin's faults?

"He is your worst sinner, Cristo. He has willingly served me for many years. He has killed many people who would have followed you. He has murdered many of the Beloved who belong to the Ancient One. He has led some people astray so that they ended up in the Chasm. The wretch has cursed the name of the Ancient One numerous times. He also has told too many lies to count..."

Diablo's eyes shifted to Lailani who frowned uncertainly at the returned attention.

"Have you all forgotten how he tried to kill Lailani in the swamp? He told her to reach into the water and pull out her parents. He knew that she would be pulled to her death. He didn't care that she would drown or that Cornelius would die trying to help her. When Lailani survived, he came up with another way to kill her. He told the wolf creature to attack her in the labyrinth. He told it that Lailani was at the mirror. Will you all really forgive him for such evil deeds?"

Devin felt a heavy burden pushing him to the ground as the dragon announced each sin. By the end of the list, the man was on his hands and knees in the grass struggling to breathe. Tears stung his eyes and trailed down his face in a stream. He knew in his heart that he had changed and he had no desire to kill or hurt anyone anymore.

Devin didn't know what to say which was good since he didn't think he could physically speak anyway. The silence that filled the air was so thick that if it were fog, one would not see anything. Devin knew that Diablo had won.

Lailani stared at the fallen, crushed man and thought that her heart would shatter. She knew that Devin had done many horrible things, though she knew that his crimes against her were weighing on him the most. The woman wanted to tell Devin that she loved him and forgave him for all he had tried to do to her, but she was unsure what Cristo wanted her to do.

"Lailani, do you have anything to say about these events that Diablo has mentioned?"

The woman smiled thankfully at Cristo's question knowing that as always the knight knew her inner struggles and desires.

"Yes, but not to him."

Lailani added extra emphasis to the last word as she glared at Diablo. The dragon narrowed his eyes at the red-headed woman as she walked over to Devin who was still crumpled on the ground with his head down. Kneeling down beside the man, Lailani spoke in a gentle, heart-felt voice.

"Devin, I know you are sorry for trying to kill me. I said I forgave you before, but I didn't truly mean it…"

Lailani caressed Devin's cheek with the back of her hand wiping some tears away as she did.

"Dev, I forgive you with all of my heart."

"Dev, I forgive you with all of my heart."

Devin still couldn't breathe, but now it wasn't because of despair but of love. Lailani truly forgave him, but how could she? He was a despicable creature who deserved to be taken back to the Chasm for all eternity.

A hand squeezed his shoulder and the man knew without looking that it was Cristo. Though no words came, Devin could feel the love and support from the knight. Instantly, the man on the ground was able to breathe. He took deep, soothing breaths. A growl came from above.

"She may forgive him, but his crimes involve more than just her. He is not fit to go to the mountain. He only fits the climate of the Chasm."

Devin sighed because he knew it was the truth.

"No one is fit for Mount Glory. We all have done bad things."

Devin's eyes widened in surprise at Simon's words. He glanced over at the boy who nodded to the man encouragingly. A weak smile crossed Devin's face.

"Besides it is not your decision who enters the service of the Ancient One, Diablo. Only He has the power and authority to control who comes into His presence."

Devin's smile grew at Victor's words who stepped forward with his sword raised. Diablo hissed menacingly.

"Simon and Victor are right, Devin. The Ancient One is supreme."

Devin's eyes shifted to Ziona whose eyes twinkled at the fallen man. Her musical voice encouraged him.

To the surprise and awe of Devin, the other princesses stepped forward one by one sharing their encouragement as well.

"The Ancient One has mercy for those who are sorry and want to be renewed," exclaimed Princess Mercy in a pleasant voice.

"His grace is sufficient to forgive all your sins," proclaimed Princess Grace.

"He bestows hope on the hopeless," sang out Princess Hope.

"And joy to the broken," Princess Joy added.

"Have faith in the Ancient One," called Princess Faith.

"And He will show you how to be in perfect harmony with His plan and purpose for you," giggled Princess Harmony excitedly.

Diablo roared horrendously and advanced on the women who wisely moved back from the monster with a high squeal.

By instinct, Simon backed up as the dragon moved closer. He clutched the sword tightly as fear struck his heart. Trying to swallow the fright he felt, the boy stood his ground and refused to give the dragon a clear path to the princesses.

"Move!"

The hateful growl slammed into the boy's ears.

Staring hard, Simon replied, "Make me!"

The dragon fumed then leapt forward mouth ready to devour the bold child.

"Diablo!"

Devin felt comfort and strength flood his heart at the princesses' words about the Ancient One. He lifted his head strongly and found Cristo's gaze readily waiting for him to look. The power in the knight's eyes gave Devin the courage to believe that Mount Glory was exactly where he needed to be. Cristo held his hands out and with no hesitation the younger man took the hands allowing the knight to pull him to his feet.

To the side, Diablo was springing toward Simon with his great, hungry mouth wide open ready to crush the boy.

"Diablo!"

The dragon's vast head swung on his lengthy neck at the familiar voice. His eyes widened slightly on seeing the man standing tall facing him, but then narrowed in hatred.

"You're not finished with me, are you?"

The creature slithered back to face the man who gulped at the massiveness of him.

"You are right, Diablo. I did all those things under your command. You promised me freedom, wealth, and power. Instead, there was enslavement, burdens, and fear. Since I have seen the Star and decided to go to Mount Glory, I have felt freer and less burdened than I ever did in your service...I would rather be a slave eating crumbs under the table of the Ancient One than the guest of honor eating the richest foods at your table."

Diablo roared fiercely and turned away stomping into the forest. Avidez looked at Devin then at the retreating back of the dragon.

"Don't go, Avidez. You will only find more misery with him. There is no happiness in the Chasm."

The warrior scowled, "Maybe misery befell you because you know nothing of loyalty and obedience."

Before Devin could answer, swift movement from the shadows came upon him. A flash of claws came into view and plunged deep into his stomach.

As Diablo stormed off into the forest, Lailani listened to Devin as he tried to persuade Avidez to change his mind. Cristo walked over to the princesses reassuring them and patting Simon on the shoulder proudly.

Lailani focused her attention on Avidez hoping the man would change his mind and return to their group. Movement from the forest caused the woman to miss the warrior's response.

Quick as lightning, Diablo sprang from the shadows landing in front of Devin. Before the woman could comprehend what was happening, the dragon stabbed his claws into Devin's stomach.

Lailani screamed, "Cristo!"

The woman didn't recognize her own voice as she moved toward the man she loved. Her feet were like heavy boulders and everything she saw seemed to be in slow motion. As the woman ran toward Devin, she pulled her sword from the sheath that Cristo had given her. It was the Demoni's sword that she had kept from the battle on the beach.

A flash of metal sped past Lailani and she halted in surprise as Cristo with sword raised above his head charged the dragon. The knight with the dented, rusty armor slammed the sword down on Diablo's clawed fingers. The creature yowled and moved back examining the shortened stubs on his paws. Smoke and flames erupted from his nostrils as he braced himself to retaliate against the knight who faced Diablo with a stern stare and sword clutched readily.

Lailani watched as Devin fell to his knees with both mouth and eyes wide in shock. As the man began to lean backwards, the woman knelt on her knees behind him and gently led his head to find rest on her lap.

Tears in her eyes, Lailani looked up ready for Cristo to destroy the monster that had ambushed her unsuspecting love. Yet the knight did not advance nor attack the dragon again.

Diablo huffed painfully and hatefully.

"You are willing to die for this wretch?"

Cristo stepped forward and replied though he spoke so quiet that Lailani couldn't hear him. The young redhead didn't care. She looked down at Devin and the tears finally fell.

Avidez stared in horror as Diablo leapt out of the engulfing darkness and attacked Devin. His shock increased at how fast Cristo made it to the dragon and cut the claws off of the creature freeing Devin.

"You are willing to die for this wretch?"

Avidez shook his head as Cristo stepped forward sure that the knight would say no. The rusty knight appeared to be so small in comparison to the great dragon.

In a quiet voice that Avidez could barely hear, the knight answered, "I already did."

Avidez frowned in confusion at the knight's answer. His confusion increased as the dragon seemed somewhat disturbed by the statement.

Diablo glared, "This is not over!"

"No, but it is closer than ever before."

Diablo paled at Cristo's words and stepped back in what appeared to be fear. Snuffing, Diablo turned to Avidez who gulped as the dragon used his uninjured clawed paw to pick him up. As the creature pushed off the ground and soared through the dark sky, Avidez wondered if he had made the right decision.

Lailani cried as she stared helplessly into Devin's upward gaze. The pain was evident on his face and it broke her heart to see the man suffer.

"Cristo, please!"

The knight came to kneel beside the injured man at the pleading tone of the woman. He examined the wounds tenderly though Devin still gasped in pain. Lailani couldn't watch the knight because she knew he would have to take the sharp claws out of the man.

Looking back into Devin's open, despairing eyes, Lailani began to hum in hopes of helping the man relax.

"What song is that, Lailani?"

Without looking at Cristo, the young woman answered, "I don't know what it is called. My parents used to sing it to me when I was little."

"Do you know the words?"

Lailani shook her head slightly annoyed. *Who cares about the stupid song? Devin is dying.*

As she continued to hum, Lailani gently caressed Devin's head by running her hand through his hair. Devin's eyes closed and Lailani's heart started to pound in fear as the man became so motionless. She was only slightly aware of Cristo humming along with her.

"Pain and regret fill my heart."

Lailani couldn't believe that she did know the words of the song, but her shaky voice began to sing along with Cristo.

"All I desire is a fresh start."

She caressed Devin's cheek tenderly wishing he would open his eyes and smile at her.

"It seems so hopeless it can't be true."

No response from the man in her arms caused the tears to flow more freely.

"I feel so lost, what do I do?"

Closing her eyes, Lailani continued to sing hearing the princesses humming along.

"But there is One who cares for me."

The young woman couldn't feel any movement from the man in her arms and it broke her heart.

"Through His love, He sets me free."

The cool breeze of the night felt good on her hot, tear-stained face.

"In Him I will forever trust."

Lailani's voice grew stronger as she continued to sing.

"Because He is always fair and just."

Lailani stopped singing, but kept her eyes closed afraid because she was sure that Devin was dead for he lay so still. *How could he have made it so far to be killed when we are so close?*

Sorrow filled the woman at the thought of losing Devin. However, the words of the song resounded in her mind and heart.

O Ancient One, I am so frightened, but I want to trust You in this. If this is the end of Devin, then let Your will be done. Please give me the strength to let go.

A hand squeezed the woman's shoulder. She smiled briefly without opening her eyes recognizing Cristo's strong, comforting grip. The hand left her shoulder, but still Lailani did not open her eyes. *Yes, I can make it without him for I said moments ago to that monster how I don't want anyone as much as You, my Ancient One. You are in control. I accept Your decision.*

Lailani felt a peace fall upon her in her sorrow.

Something brushed gently against Lailani's cheek and her eyes snapped open in surprise. The back of a finger caressed her face and Lailani's eyes trailed from the finger to the hand to the arm all the way down to the face. Joy filled her heart as her eyes beheld Devin staring up at her with bright eyes and a warm smile.

Lailani quickly glanced at the man's stomach and found that the claws were no longer there nor did she see any sign that there had been a wound to begin with. With a radiant smile, the woman returned her gaze to the man lying on her lap.

Devin's smile grew as Lailani leaned down and embraced him in a hug. As his arm went around her shoulders to return the embrace, Lailani thanked the Ancient One for His healing power and mercy on Devin.

Lailani's Song

Pain and regret fill my heart.
All I desire is a fresh start.
It seems so hopeless it can't be true.
I feel so lost, what do I do?

But there is One who cares for me.
Through His love, He sets me free.
In Him I will forever trust
Because He is always fair and just.

CHAPTER 17

OFF TRACK MISSION

As the camp grew quiet again except for common night sounds, Cristo instructed everyone to get some sleep for they would continue their journey shortly after dawn.

At first excited whispers scattered throughout the campsite as each traveler shared their reaction of the visit from Diablo. However, as before, the chatter died down and soon silence filled the area.

Simon lay quietly unable to sleep and replaying the night's events in his mind. *Did I do the right thing?*

Doubt crept into his mind. It grew fiercer the longer he dwelled on his actions.

As quietly as possible, Simon sat up hoping that he wouldn't disturb Victor who was sound asleep. Glancing around, the boy located Cristo who was leaning against a tree with his eyes closed. Simon sighed and began to lie back down.

"Come, child. Sit by me."

Simon's eyes darted back to the elder knight who was looking straight at him with an arm extended. The boy quietly yet eagerly stood and crept over to the tree. He sat down next to Cristo who placed the extended arm around the child's shoulders.

"I'm sorry, Cristo. I didn't mean to disturb you."

A quiet chuckle escaped from the knight.

"Dear boy, you could never disturb me. It is you who are disturbed this night. You must tell me your worries so that you may sleep well."

Simon nodded because this was exactly what he wanted to do.

"Cristo sir, I think I did something wrong."

Cristo's eyes seemed to twinkle as he regarded the boy.

"Oh, and what do you think you did that was wrong?"

Simon took a deep breath.

"I provoked Diablo when he wanted me to move away. I shouldn't have said anything."

"Ah, I see. You are right about watching our words. A harsh word does stir up anger. However, you did an excellent job of protecting the princesses. I am proud of you. Do not fret over what is past for I know you are sorry and you are forgiven."

A huge sigh of relief escaped the boy and caused another chuckle to leave the knight.

"Now sleep, my boy. For our journey continues soon."

Simon leaned against Cristo not wanting to return to his spot on the ground. The knight gently patted the boy's shoulder giving his permission and approval. The man hummed a soft lullaby as sleep overtook Simon.

As the sun rose and slammed into Victor's eyes, the man stretched and glanced over at the area where Simon had been the night before. His eyes widened and his heart thumped. Simon was not in that spot.

Victor swung around searching for the child as his mind reeled at the thought of the possibility of Diablo sneaking back into the camp and snatching the boy.

"He is safe."

Victor turned to face Cristo who was adjusting his armor and watching the man with a frown.

"Where?"

The elder knight pointed to the right which was where Victor's eyes moved instantly to confirm the man's statement. Relief filled the young man at the sight of Simon standing next to Feliz, Cristo's horse. *Where did the horse come from?*

Victor shook his head trying to return to the fact that Simon was indeed safe.

"What would happen to you if you couldn't stay with Simon?"

The cruelty of the question smacked Victor hard knocking the breath out of him as he turned back to Cristo.

"What?"

"If you get to the Ancient One and He decides to send Simon far from you, what will happen to you?"

The thought had not crossed the young knight's mind for he had been too worried that the Ancient One wouldn't accept his return to service. Victor gaped at the elder knight speechless as to how to answer the question.

Cristo merely raised his eyebrows before walking away leaving the man devastated at the notion that he could lose Simon even in the throne room of the Ancient One. The idea felt so unjust and cruel. Victor fought back tears as his eyes fell on Simon again.

The group of travelers now refreshed from their previous night's sleep followed Cristo through the forest that had been a hiding place for Diablo the night before. Oddly, the trees did not seem quite as ominous as they did in the deep darkness of night. Instead, the branches seemed to almost wave in welcome at the people who had come into their midst.

The path through the forest seemed to twist and turn so that one couldn't tell which way they were going. The leaves' emerald canopy overhead blocked the sun from their view. It was difficult to determine their direction without the sun.

Cornelius did not focus on where the path was taking the group. He followed after the others out of habit, but his mind and heart were not on the journey. Instead the old man kept thinking about Diablo's visit. The dragon had offered so many things and those promises had sounded so good to Cornelius. Only Lailani kept Cornelius from going with the dragon. The old man did not want to leave his friend. Though now as he dwelled on how Lailani acted with Devin, Cornelius began to wonder if he had been hurt too, which man Lailani would have comforted. Would she have left Devin bleeding at the side of the camp to help the old man? Or would she have cried for Devin and let the old man die?

Glancing up from the dirt path, Cornelius watched Lailani walk with Devin whispering and laughing. The woman looked so happy. Anger filled the old man's heart. He narrowed his eyes at the couple. He wasn't just angry about their love for each other. No, he hated Lailani for exchanging his friendship for this treacherous swordsman. How could she abandon him after all these years?

Sunshine burst into the man's eyes causing him to wince and squint. The group had exited the forest and was standing on a sandy shore with a foamy sea rolling in waves upon the sand.

Cornelius frowned as he recognized the area. The travelers had returned to the same shore that they had stepped on when they descended from the Blessed Hope's ladder days ago. In fact, the ship was still anchored in the exact spot where they had left her.

Cornelius' temper rose and he knew that his patience had faded away. With a growl, the old man threw his hands into the air in exasperation.

"That's it!"

The other travelers turned to face the old man startled by his unaccustomed outburst.

"Is something wrong, Cornelius?"

Cristo regarded the elderly man who glowered at him.

Cornelius huffed, "Yeah, there's something. Why did we have to go in a circle? Why couldn't we just stay on the ship and finish the journey?"

The warm smile that Cristo shone on the man only infuriated him more.

"Is that really why you are angry?"

The elder knight's gentle tone irritated Cornelius so much that he exploded.

"No, that's not what's bothering me. What's bothering me is you! You are just like Diablo says. You are just leading us in all different directions waiting for us to fall in deep holes or drown in stormy valleys. You have brought me far from home and lost me my only friend."

At the last word, Cornelius glared at Lailani before returning his attention to Cristo. Sadness had replaced the twinkle that was usually sparkling in the knight's eyes. Deep inside, Cornelius felt satisfaction at causing the knight pain.

To say that Lailani was shocked by Cornelius' outburst would be an understatement. She was completely flabbergasted as the old man ranted and said such horrible things about Cristo. Then her heart broke when her friend glared at her and said that he had lost his friend. Choking back tears and swallowing the lump in her throat, Lailani stepped forward.

"Cornelius, I am still your friend. How can you say that you lost me?"

The woman's eyes widened as the old man turned toward her with a cold, hateful stare. She had never seen the man like this before. There was no sign of love or friendship on the man's face.

"You're not my friend. You have chosen him over me. You spend all your time and energy with that monster."

Lailani followed Cornelius' hand which was pointing at Devin. The young man seemed uneasy at being accused again.

"Who was willing to give his life for yours in the swamp? He tried to kill you, but I tried to save you."

"Who did I try to persuade to climb the slope and not go back to Terra when we were in the valley?"

Her friend lowered his arm and turned back still glaring.

"Who did you connect your rope with in the valley?"

Cornelius spat these words at the red-haired woman with such ferocity that she backed up a couple of steps.

"Cristo paired us up. We only reconnected our ropes. I was willing to tie you to our rope before Simon came down the slope."

Lailani tried to plead with the man who had been with her for many years, but she could see the hardened look on his face and knew that he was only getting angrier. Then his expression softened.

"I practically raised you when your parents died. I have looked out for you...I love you, Lailani."

The tears could not be held back any longer. They flowed down her cheeks freely.

"I love you too, Cornelius."

The old man smiled and extended a hand toward his friend.

"Then come home with me."

Lailani tensed at the suggestion. How could he ask her to go back to oppressive Terra when she was so close to being in the presence of the Ancient One? The woman glanced at Cristo who was casually watching the exchange.

"As always, it is your choice."

The knight's simple, non-judgmental response was all Lailani needed to make her decision.

"I do love you, Cornelius my friend. I'm sorry, but I can't go back to Terra. I am bound on this journey to the Ancient One not by chains, but by love. I want you to come with me, but it has to be because you want to be with the Ancient One and serve Him with your whole heart. Either way, it is, as Cristo says, your choice."

Hope had filled Cornelius as he waited for Lailani's response. Yet it was instantly replaced by disappointment then loathing as he listened to her words. No, she would not go back with him. She had chosen the Ancient One over him.

With a scowl, Cornelius dropped his extended hand.

"I will not go to the mountain and be a slave to Him."

The old man marched away heading down the path that Aurelius had taken days before. *Let them go on following Cristo. The fools will see the truth in the end. Probably when it is too late.*

Victor watched the old man head toward the path that the abusive Aurelius had stormed down when they were on the shore days ago. He glanced at Simon who seemed sad as he watched Cornelius leave. An idea crept into Victor's mind. In desperation to keep Simon with him always, he decided to try the plan.

With a glance at Cristo who was returning his attention to Lailani, Victor knelt down beside Simon and spoke quietly.

"I wish we could do something for Cornelius."

The boy's eyes lit up.

"Maybe we can talk to him and convince him to come back."

Victor felt guilty at the innocence and hope on Simon's face, but he justified quickly in his mind that he was tricking the child so they could be together.

"Yes, let's catch up to him and talk to him."

Victor stood to his feet satisfied.

He winced as Simon shouted, "Cristo, we are going to follow Cornelius and talk to him."

The younger knight sighed and hesitantly moved his eyes to Cristo who was meeting his gaze with an eyebrow raised.

"Oh? I think that Cornelius has made his choice."

Victor could feel the man's gentle yet firm eyes burn through him. He was sure that Cristo knew exactly what Victor was trying to do.

The man cleared his throat nervously, "Well, we should at least try."

Cristo narrowed his eyes at the man who was certain that the elder knight knew the motive behind his words.

"Go ahead."

Victor smiled and suddenly felt cocky that he would get his way. He turned toward the path.

"But," Cristo continued.

Victor froze with his heart pounding.

"I shall go with you both."

Victor's heart sank even as Simon whooped excitedly.

Simon practically hopped as he waited for Cristo to start them on their little side-journey. The knight was instructing the rest of the travelers to climb aboard the Blessed Hope and await their return. Iliana, the lady captain, welcomed her guests as they approached the rope ladder that hung from the deck of the ship. The short woman scanned the group and frowned at the decreased number. However, she shook off the frown with a sorrowful shrug and replaced it with a smile.

Simon turned to speak to Victor, but forgot what he was going to say for the man stood to the side in a way that confused the boy. Pacing, Victor had his arms crossed across his chest and kept glancing at Cristo and then the path. His eyes were wide and his face looked agitated. *Perhaps he is eager to go so we don't lose Cornelius?*

"Shall we go?"

Simon started and peered up at Cristo who looked down at him affectionately. The boy returned the smile and nodded. Cristo knelt down so that he was at eye level with Simon.

"No matter what happens, my dear Simon, do not forget or doubt the truths that you have learned on this journey. Stand firm for the Ancient One for He will not let you fall."

Simon was perplexed by the knight's words.

"You'll be with me, won't you, Cristo sir?"

Sadness crept around the man's eyes and he sighed.

"That depends on some decisions that will be made soon. Do not fret, dear one, for worrying about what is yet to come will only make you weary in the now."

Simon nodded silently.

"Good. Then let's go."

The elder knight stood and turned toward the path leading his horse Feliz off of the shore. Simon hurried after him eager to find Cornelius. Out of the corner of his eye, the boy was confused again as Victor slunk beside him in a distracted manner. The trio looked like they did when they had first begun their journey together. Simon couldn't help smiling at how far they had come since then.

Victor's mind raced with thoughts of what to do now. He didn't know how he was going to get Simon away with Cristo present, but he was determined to do so. An assortment of plans swept through his mind, but none of them were fool-proof. There was a downside to each scheme. Frustration filled the man yet he was too desperate to get what he wanted to give up.

After a couple of miles walking under the forest canopy of the path, there was still no sign of Cornelius. Not that Victor cared. He wasn't out here for the old man. In fact...

"Whom do you seek, my lord?"

The shout startled Victor who stopped abruptly and grasped the hilt of his sword. His eyes glanced up to an area above them where he was surprised to see a man dressed in pure white. A radiant glow encircled the man. He was kneeling on one knee atop of a boulder and his full attention was on Cristo.

"Greetings, Campion. We seek Cornelius of Terra."

Campion frowned and stood abruptly. The man glanced at Victor then Simon. He opened his mouth then closed it uncertainly.

"Speak, Campion, for they should know the truth."

Victor narrowed his eyes suspiciously at Cristo. What did they need to know? Why was Campion unsure about telling them?

"As you wish, my lord. Cornelius of Terra has taken the road to the Chasm. He is going to Diablo."

Victor's mind raced again because now he was running out of time. Cristo would want them to head back to the ship now.

"Has he made it to the Chasm yet, sir?"

Victor's eyes darted over to Simon who had stepped forward with his eyes on Campion.

"No. He is on the road to the Chasm, but he has not reached it yet."

Victor smiled for he saw the opening he had been waiting for.

"Then we can still reach him and convince him to come back."

Cristo turned his gaze on Victor and for once it held a hard edge to it.

"As always, it is your choice. I shall go back to the Blessed Hope and await your return."

Victor noted that the elder knight's voice held no anger or persuasion. Somehow this didn't make the decision any easier, but the young man was determined to keep Simon whether the Ancient One wanted him to or not.

"I am going after Cornelius. What about you, Simon?"

It was hard to ignore the trace of disappointment that crossed Cristo's face as he gave Victor one last look before turning to regard Simon.

"I am going after Cornelius. What about you, Simon?"

Simon frowned at the question because he was confused by the sadness in Cristo's face as he looked at Victor. Was it wrong for them to go after Cornelius? But it felt so right. How could they not help their friend? Isn't that what the Ancient One would want them to do?

"It is your choice, Simon. What have you decided?"

The boy saw Cristo facing him with a neutral expression. Simon did not want the man to be angry or disappointed in him, but the desire to help Cornelius would not go away.

Taking a deep breath, Simon replied, "I am going to find Cornelius."

The child was ready to flinch at Cristo's reaction, but it was not necessary for the elder knight's face held a gentle smile and his eyes shone with approval. Confusion filled the boy again. Why was Cristo angry at Victor for going, but glad that Simon was going? How could he react so differently to the same decision?

"I shall see you soon then, my lad."

Cristo regarded both Victor and Simon.

"Remember to follow the Bright Morning Star when you are ready to return to the Blessed Hope."

Devin stood on the deck of the Blessed Hope gazing into the distance hoping to catch a glimpse of Cristo returning with the other travelers. There was still no sign of them though it had been nearly a day.

"He won't come back."

Devin frowned at Lailani thinking that she meant Cristo, but he quickly realized that the young woman was talking about Cornelius. The old man had spoken such harsh things to her. Devin knew that it was hard for her to not go with Cornelius. He had been like a father to her.

"Have hope, Lailani. Cristo seems to have a way of reaching people when others cannot."

Lailani looked up from the bench she was sitting on and Devin could see her unshed tears glistening in her emerald eyes. The man's heart ached for her to feel less anguished. He sat down next to her and took the woman's hands into his own. He didn't speak partially because he didn't know what to say, but also because he was not certain that it would help. The young woman seemed so distraught and the man felt awkward. If only he could make her feel better.

Lailani took a deep breath and tried to hold back her tears. Devin sat down and gently took her hands into his. Lailani waited for the man to speak, but no words came. He just sat silently comforting her. The woman tried to smile, but suddenly without warning the tears escaped followed by sobs. She lowered her head anguished as more tears and sobs came from her body. Her streaming eyes closed tightly. Devin's hands released hers and for a second she was afraid that he would leave her there to allow her a chance to compose herself. She didn't want to be left alone even if she was a sobbing mess. Yet Devin did not leave her. The young woman felt his loving arms encircle her in an embrace and she instantly leaned against him relieved for his understanding.

"Look!"

The scream caused the couple to separate and search for the source of the shout. Princess Harmony stood further down the deck pointing at the shore. The couple stood also and looked in the direction the little girl was pointing.

Lailani's eyes widened in shock at the sight before her.

Simon walked beside Victor trying to think what he would say to Cornelius when they caught up to him. Several ideas popped into his head and urgency filled him.

The path that Cornelius went down turned into a divided path with three routes. The Bright Morning Star shone above the path to the right. The center path was muddy and a set of footprints formed a trail to Cornelius. The left path had no distinguishing marks in appearance.

Simon stepped forward toward the muddy path in the center. A hand grabbed his arm and the boy halted confused. He turned his head so he could see Victor.

"Wrong way."

Simon frowned, "But those are Cornelius' footprints."

The hand grasping his arm pulled slightly to the left.

"We can't go that way, Simon. We must go left."

"But what about Cornelius?"

Simon wrinkled his forehead unsure of what Victor was doing.

"Forget about him. He won't change his mind anyway."

The hand pulled more strongly and Simon was dragged closer to the man.

"If we can't help him, then we need to head back to the Blessed Hope."

Simon pulled his arm toward the right path stepping closer to it. He didn't get far before he found himself anchored to the spot.

"We can't go to the mountain, Simon."

The child gasped feeling as if someone had punched him in the stomach and knocked the breath out of him. Not go to Mount Glory? How could Victor suggest such a thing? Simon spun to face the knight.

"What do you mean?"

Victor knelt down before the boy and took his other arm. Simon saw that the man's eyes were pleading.

"Simon, if we go to the mountain, then we may be separated. I want us to stay together. We have to go the other way. That way we know that we will be together. I can take care of you. We will be a family. Don't you want to stay with me?"

Simon listened to the knight's pleas remembering his dream and all that he and Victor had been through together. Tears stung his eyes at the idea of losing his friend yet he also was saddened at losing the Ancient One. However, the desperate look in Victor's eyes shattered Simon's resolve.

"Yes, Victor. I will go where you go."

The relief in the older man's eyes eased Simon's mind, but as the man and boy embraced, he couldn't help noticing an emptiness in his heart.

Victor led Simon down the left road farther away from the path that led to the Blessed Hope where Cristo had probably already returned and informed the others of the most recent events. None of this mattered to the knight. His plan was to find a quiet, safe place for him and Simon to live normal lives hidden away from adventures or duty. Surely he would never lose the child that way.

As the duo walked down the path, Victor was aware of Simon's frequent glances behind them. The man knew that the boy was looking at the Star that was beckoning them almost urgently in the opposite direction. The knight expected Simon to suddenly change his mind and try to go back the other way. However, the child kept following him and eventually he quit looking behind them.

Victor would have been happy except now the child looked so miserable and downcast that the man didn't like what he saw. Simon hung his head sorrowfully and occasionally sighed in melancholy.

Victor couldn't stand to see Simon looking so upset and his heart was moved by the child's sadness. The man shook his head. It was not worth this pain to have his own way. He wanted Simon happy. If going to Mount Glory was the only way, then so be it.

"Simon, stop."

The boy stopped and looked up at the tall man.

"I have made a huge mistake. I want you with me always, but it is more important to me that you are happy. Moving from the mountain is making you miserable and I can't stand it. We are going back to the Blessed Hope and continuing on to Mount Glory. Our future shall be in the hands of the Ancient One. Please forgive me for leading you astray."

Simon smiled, "I forgive you, Victor."

The man hugged the boy in relief. He decided to accept the fact that Simon may be sent far from him in the future, but he would enjoy his company until then. The boy tensed in his arms.

"Victor."

The frightened whisper caused Victor to push the child gently away as the man stood and spun around with his hand on his sword hilt.

The path had opened into a large meadow though Victor had not seen it before since his attention had been on Simon. The man felt like all the air had been sucked out of him for the field before him was very familiar. He was standing at the edge of the same battlefield in which he had been the sole survivor many weeks ago. The ground was splattered with dried blood and an occasional piece of armor or weapon littered the field. No bodies were still on the battlefield which was good since Victor did not want Simon to see them. The sight of blood and battle armor was not what frightened the boy though. Standing only a few feet away was a Demoni with sword in hand. *Davo*.

CHAPTER 18

INTO THE CHASM

"Run, Simon! Don't look back!"

Simon instantly turned and ran as he saw Victor pull his sword from its sheath. He hurried down the path with his eyes staring at the Bright Morning Star heart pounding. He was only slightly aware of the passing landscape and the sound of clanging swords growing faint behind him.

At the fork in the road, Simon went down the path that would lead back to the beach. He was determined to get to the ship and bring help back to Victor. He could feel that he was getting close to the end of the path. The sound of waves could barely be heard above the thumping of Simon's feet. Sunlight shone at the end of the canopied road. The child felt great hope that he was going to make it.

Suddenly, hands grasped the boy by the arms. Simon frantically glanced at both sides of him and found that he had been captured by two gray-skinned Demoni. The duo dragged him, kicking and screaming, back down the path toward where he had left Victor. Simon's attention was not on where they were taking him, but on the beach at the edge of the forest where he could clearly see the Blessed Hope anchored, shining in the sunlight so close yet now growing farther away.

"Run, Simon! Don't look back!"

Victor heard movement behind him and knew the boy had obeyed. Relief filled the man as he stared hard at the Demoni standing before him. Davo grinned at the human with a long crooked sword in his hand.

In a hoarse, superior command, the creature called out, "Catch the little one! I'll take care of this cur!"

Victor unsheathed his sword feeling helpless to aid Simon, yet hopeful that the child would make it to Cristo in time. Yes, Cristo would take care of Simon.

"We meet again, Fool. And the battle shall be short for you are truly alone this time. How foolish to stray so far from your people."

Davo charged forward and Victor advanced to meet him head on. Their swords met with a loud, metallic clang. The force of the blow caused both Davo and Victor to stumble backwards. The man struggled to stay balanced. Surprise was evident on Davo's face as he recovered and moved forward again. Victor matched him swing for swing desperate to survive so he could continue on to Mount Glory and throw himself on the mercy of the Ancient One.

The sound of struggling behind him caused Victor to lose his concentration for just a second, but it was all Davo needed. Victor felt the sword slam into the side of his head. He fell to the ground hard. His sword lay near him just within reach.

As he struggled to remain conscious, Victor slowly advanced his hand toward the hilt of the sword. A gray foot kicked it out of reach and the knight knew that he was truly defeated.

Glancing up, the man's heart broke for Simon stood before him held by two Demoni who were watching in triumph. The boy's eyes were wide with fear and Victor wanted him to look away, but no words would come.

"Take the slave boy to Lord Diablo. He will be pleased by your quarry. I will stay and finish off this pathetic creature."

Victor wanted to call out in protest, but silence ruled him since just staying awake was a struggle. Only the sound of Simon yelling truths kept him awake as the Demoni dragged the child away.

"Don't give up, Victor! You are important and loved by the Ancient One. Call on Him and He will not let you fall. He can save you! Trust Him!"

The boy's voice faded away to nothing as tears streamed down the injured man's face. He lowered his head unable to watch his own fate. His heart wrenched in fear not for himself, but for his child. A shadow fell across the knight and he closed his eyes knowing that he would be dead soon.

Silently, Victor poured out his heart to the Ancient One. *I have truly failed You, my Lord. I not only left You, but I took Your servant, Simon, with me by using deception. I know that I deserve to die for leading Simon astray and I accept that. I do not ask for You to save me, but please rescue Simon from the clutches of Diablo Your enemy. Please help him so he can return on his quest to You. He wants to be Yours with his whole heart. And so do I.*

At the last words, Victor felt his heart swell with desire to truly be in the presence of his Lord. In fact, he realized that he wanted the Ancient One to love him, forgive him, and take him back fully. Nothing else mattered. This truth filled the knight so much that he wanted to stand and face his foe even unarmed.

Victor tried to stand to his feet to face Davo, but a firm kick to his side caused the man to fall back to the ground in pain. Grunting, the knight struggled again to his knees determined to rise to his feet.

Another kick harshly slammed into his side again. Victor screamed in agony as he plopped back onto the ground. But he would not give up for he did trust the Ancient One as Simon reminded him. He pushed off his stomach with his hands and made it to his knees for the third time.

"Still trying to get up, Fool? Go ahead for my vengeance from our previous battle will be appeased by your torment."

Victor replied in a weak, yet bold, voice, "Vengeance belongs to the Ancient One."

The crooked sword came into view and Victor tried to sway away, but the blade sliced his left cheek with a force that flipped the man over onto his back hitting the grassy floor hard once more. Blood streamed from the gash and spilled down his face.

"It's over, cur. Just think of everything Diablo will do to that poor little slave boy. Torture, abuse, death. Yes, Diablo will enjoy his new toy."

Victor took a deep breath before rolling over on his stomach. He placed his hands firmly on the ground in front of him ready to push up onto his knees again.

"Diablo may be cruel and vicious. He may be very powerful, but the Ancient One has far more power and He can save Simon from that overgrown lizard-king. And He can save me from you too."

A menacing growl echoed from Davo as Victor stood to his feet and faced him unarmed. It took every ounce of strength to stay standing and his head pounded from the earlier wound to it. But Victor was determined to not cower no matter what. No, he would stand firm.

Davo raised his crooked sword ready to deliver the death blow. Victor tried to strategize what he could do, but nothing seemed possible. The sword swished through the air at an unbelievable speed. Victor closed his eyes ready to face the will of the Ancient One.

A clang of metal rang through Victor's ears, but before he could open his eyes, darkness took him and he crumpled to the ground.

In the dark Chasm of Misery, Diablo fumed at his own failure at Cristo's camp. Though he had picked up a slave to take Devin's place, the dragon was furious at the pain that he had endured from wounds inflicted by Cristo and that little slave brat. He knew that rumors had spread among the Demoni of how the great Diablo had also failed to stop the company journeying to the mountain. Humiliated and scorned, Diablo vowed that he would crush the Ancient One's followers with much pain and anguish.

A voice cleared itself behind the dragon who glared as he turned his enormous body in the cave to face the intruder. Smoke burst from the beast's nostrils as he regarded the Demoni who stood before him disturbing his Master. With a gulp, the creature spoke in a hurried squeak as if wanting to speak quickly and then scurry away to safety.

"My lord, what shall we do with Avidez?"

Diablo moved his great, frightful head closer and glowered even more fiercely. The Demoni leaned back squeezing his eyes shut in dread.

"My lord, my lord! News from Davo!"

The new voice rang out in the cave drawing the attention of the dragon much to the relief of the first Demoni.

"What news?"

"Davo and his Demoni found Victor the knight and Simon the slave in the battlefield. Davo stayed to kill the man, but he sent the others back with the boy."

The news delighted Diablo. He moved from the cave to see where the child was who had cut his snout and made him appear a fool. However, before he had moved too far, an idea hit the monster. *What if the slave boy tries to persuade Avidez to leave the Chasm and return to Him?*

Diablo turned back to the first Demoni who stiffened at being noticed again.

"Take Avidez to Devin's chamber. Tell him that all that belonged to the traitor is now his. Feed him the richest foods and keep him there until I summon him."

The Demoni nodded and scurried away as the dragon continued on his journey to the human spawn who would soon know the wrath and power of Diablo, Lord of Misery.

The sky grew darker the closer Simon was taken toward the Chasm of Misery. Suddenly a huge, jagged, black rock came into view and the boy knew that they must have reached the lair of Diablo. He was pushed through an opening guarded by two Demoni who leered at the child pleased at his capture.

Simon's captors dragged him through a long dark tunnel that seemed to slope downward no doubt taking them deep into the ground. Light suddenly appeared at the end of the tunnel blinding Simon and causing him to blink rapidly so his eyes could adjust.

Opening his eyes, Simon saw that he was in an enormous room lit by fiery torches scattered around. Hundreds of Demoni were lined up in a circle around the walls screeching and pointing at him. Fear filled the boy as he was dragged to the center of the room and thrown to the ground. Simon noticed that the rock was very warm and sharp.

A hush fell on the horde of Demoni. Simon looked up and saw Diablo had exited a cave at the far end of the gathering area. The dragon smirked triumphantly as he lumbered over toward the boy. He stopped a few feet away and towered over him. He spoke with a smooth, deep voice that was filled with mocking.

"Well, what have we here? Why it is the Guardian of Glory. My, my. I wonder who is keeping the princesses safe while you are here."

The Demoni laughed loudly at their master's jest.

Simon frowned at the creature who was encouraged by his minions' reaction.

"Oh, yes. Cristo chose this pathetic slave to protect such valuables of the Ancient One. How could he ever do harm to any real enemies?"

Diablo gurgled in merriment as the Demoni screeched and whooped in victory. Simon hung his head ready to believe what the dragon said, but then a thought entered his mind. His eyes rose to find the gash that was on Diablo's snout.

Suddenly, Cristo's words sounded in the boy's mind as if the knight was actually speaking. *No matter what happens, my dear Simon, do not doubt the truths that you have learned on this journey. Stand firm for the Ancient One for He will not let you fall.*

A smile crossed Simon's lips as he replied to the lies of the enemy.

"Then you are not a real enemy?"

The dragon's attention returned to the boy with a fiery glare.

"What?!"

A silence filled the cavern for even the Demoni could not believe what the human child had said.

Simon shrugged, "You said that I couldn't do harm to any real enemy. Since I gave you that cut, I guess that means you aren't a real enemy."

A snicker came from a Demoni, but faded quickly as the dragon's head whipped around searching for the fool who would dare laugh at him. Not one Demoni moved and several of them held their breaths.

Diablo placed his great red head so close to Simon that the boy was almost sure that the monster was going to swallow him to be rid of him for good. Yet the beast didn't. Instead he growled with little flicks of flames bursting from his huge mouth.

"We shall see who can do the most harm."

The tiny rock cell was hot and miserable yet Cornelius didn't care. The old man knew it was too late for him because he had been captured by the Demoni and put in this hole until Diablo had time to decide what to do with him.

A deep void was in Cornelius' heart that was darker than the hole he was stuck in. He felt so alone. All he had said to Cristo and Lailani replayed in his mind causing him great pain. The old man regretted how he had treated his friend, but he couldn't see any way to make amends. How could he if he was stuck in this black hole far from the rest of the travelers?

The iron door at the entrance of the hole slid back and Cornelius cringed for he knew that the great monster had decided what to do with his prey. However, above him no one tried to pull him out. Instead, someone else was dropped into the cramped pit.

A scream escaped the lips of the falling prisoner for it was such a surprisingly deep drop. Cornelius watched as the person struggled to his feet. He was astonished as he recognized the boy Simon. *How did he end up here?*

Simon brushed his clothes off, glanced up as the gate slid across the opening, and then took in his new surroundings. His eyes stopped on Cornelius who dreaded the child's reaction. He winced awaiting hateful words or the silent treatment. Instead, a smile crept up the boy's face. His eyes twinkled as he ran forward.

"Cornelius!"

Simon hugged the old man who returned the embrace in surprise.

Something soft and moist patted Victor's forehead. The knight struggled to open his eyes unsure of what could have happened. The last thing that he remembered was that he was hurt and Davo was coming in for the kill. His eyes opened. The first sight he saw was the Bright Morning Star glistening down on him. He blinked a couple of times to see if he was really seeing the Star. It did not disappear nor fade away. It shone even more brightly.

Victor tried to sit up seeking an explanation for why he was still alive. Pain slammed into his sides. He cried out in agony. A firm hand pushed him back down.

"Rest, Victor. There is no need to rise."

Tears came to the man's eyes as he recognized the voice who spoke such kindness to him. Victor turned his head to see the scraggly knight. Cristo knelt beside the man with a cloth in his hand.

"Cristo, I thought you left us."

"Ah, I never truly left you."

Victor pushed the elder knight's hand away from his forehead where he was tending to a bloody wound.

"You should have."

Victor frowned as Cristo returned the cloth without hesitation.

"Why?"

"Because I abandoned the Ancient One again and stole Simon from Him. I manipulated and lied to get the kid to stay with me. Because it is my fault that Diablo has Simon and who knows what torment he will suffer. You shouldn't be here helping me when Simon needs your help."

These words made Victor so tired that he closed his eyes. The cloth continued to pat Victor's head again. Though the man was annoyed at the wasted attention, he admitted that the cloth did feel cool and pleasant on his bruised head. He only wished there was some way to soothe his heart as well.

"Why did you lead Simon astray?"

The question frustrated Victor because he knew that Cristo knew why. He knew everything.

"Tell me anyway, Victor."

The man sighed, "Because I was afraid that I would lose him. I feared that the Ancient One would separate us. But through my own actions I have separated us. I have lost him."

Tears streamed from the man's closed eyes. His heart ached so much at the loss that he himself had caused. The regret developed into sobs as Victor dwelled on what he had done that had hurt the person that he loved as a son. Rolling to his side facing away from Cristo, the broken man covered his face with his hands and sobbed. *What have I done?*

Strong, loving arms pulled the man close.

"Peace, son, for you have been forgiven already. Forgive yourself so that you can become who you are meant to be."

Victor wiped his eyes and lay silently in Cristo's understanding embrace. The elder knight hummed quietly as the young man composed himself. Finally strength returned and Victor felt able to sit up. Cristo helped him so he wouldn't hurt his side worse.

"What happened to Davo, my lord?"

Victor looked into Cristo's eyes curious, but almost dreading the answer.

"He has fled back to the Chasm. Campion was sent here to help you and he fought Davo fiercely. The Demoni was wounded badly, but I told Campion to let him go."

Victor was unsure why Cristo would allow the creature to live, but he nodded knowing that it was not his place to question the elder knight.

Cristo smiled, "You are learning, Victor."

"What about Simon? Will we leave him in the Chasm?"

Cristo's face turned rigid and his eyes stern.

"Oh, no. I have no intention of leaving Simon to Diablo. I shall go to the Chasm and retrieve our friend. You must return to the Blessed Hope with the aid of Campion."

Victor started to protest, but stopped before he verbalized anything.

"As you command, my lord."

"Yes indeed, Victor. You are learning."

Cristo extended his hands to the younger man who eagerly took them and allowed the elder knight to lift him to his feet. Campion came to the injured man's side though Victor didn't know where the radiant man in white had come from.

As Cristo turned and climbed on Feliz, Victor was almost tempted to try to go too. The elder knight turned his gaze on him as if awaiting his protest.

Victor raised a hand in farewell before turning with Campion and heading into the forest. He didn't see Cristo raise his hand in return with a loving, proud countenance.

Simon beamed at Cornelius feeling so happy that he had found the old man even in this dark, miserable dungeon. There was relief in Cornelius' eyes, but also sadness. When he spoke, the man's voice was hoarse and dry.

"How did you get here, Simon? Where are the others?"

The boy explained, "The others are on the ship. Victor and I left the others to find you, but we ran into some Demoni and they brought me here."

"Where is Victor?"

Simon frowned as tears welled up in his eyes.

"I don't know. He was hurt when they took me away. Davo was there and he had kicked Victor's sword away. I kept waiting for Cristo to come help us, but he didn't."

Tears streamed down the child's face though he tried to wipe them away quickly with his sleeve.

"Well, maybe Victor is lucky. Least he isn't here. Cristo couldn't save us from this Chasm."

Simon looked at the man with lowered eyebrows.

"Don't say that, Cornelius. Cristo could destroy Diablo and all of the Demoni with no effort at all."

The old man gruffed, "How do you know?"

Simon smiled, "I can feel it here."

The boy pointed to his heart.

Cornelius wanted to change the subject so badly. He didn't want to talk about Cristo anymore.

"Why did you want to find me? Thought you could get me to come back?"

The boy sat down in front of Cornelius who was unsure about how he would answer.

"I wanted to find you because I was worried about you."

"Why?"

Cornelius shook his head in confusion.

"Because I am your friend and I love you."

Shock filled the old man at the strength and power of that statement. Could it be true? They hadn't known each other long and had only briefly interacted during that time.

"Yes, I am your friend and I don't want you to be alone and living miserably. I want you to be happy and safe. I believe that the Ancient One can give us peace and happiness if we will go to Him. I have been very lonely and miserable in my life as a slave. I had no friends and no one loved me. I was always cold and hungry. You don't trust Cristo. Yet since I met Cristo, I have had plenty of food and warm clothes. I have become free and found many people who want to be my friends. Choosing the Ancient One can only end in joy and freedom."

Tears came to the old man's eyes.

"I do want to be happy and loved, but how can I get to the Ancient One if I am trapped here in the Chasm?"

Simon took the old man's hands into his own. Cornelius looked straight into the child's eyes and was amazed at the love that shone back at him.

"Talk to him, Cornelius, for He will hear you. Don't worry about being so far away because the Ancient One could rescue you with no effort. He is all-powerful."

Cornelius nodded tears streaming down his bearded face. He squeezed the boy's hands and closed his eyes. His heart ached as he mentally pleaded. *I don't know what to say to you, Ancient One. I want to be happy. I don't want to be lonely anymore. Please let me come to You for I am ready to be Your servant. I am stuck here in the dragon's lair, but I want to be on Mount Glory with You. I know You can help me, but I ask You to also help my new friend, Simon.*

Such a feeling of love and joy swelled into Cornelius' heart. He opened his eyes and remembered that he was in a dark hole in the most horrible place in the world. For a moment he had felt so good that he had forgotten that he was a prisoner.

Simon looked back at him in expectation. Cornelius laughed at the serious look.

"I don't know how, Simon my friend, but we are going to get out of here and see the Ancient One face to face."

The boy smiled brightly and jumped into the old man's open arms.

"Aw, isn't that precious?"

Cornelius and Simon glanced up sharply to find a very familiar Demoni. Monstre who had been a part of the group of Demoni that attacked them on the beach smirked at the humans below in the pit.

"Climb the ladder, slave boy. Diablo is ready to deal with you."

Cornelius grabbed Simon's arm protectively. The boy on the other hand glared at Monstre defiantly.

"Make me!"

Monstre huffed before leaping down into the pit easily landing on his feet. Simon backed away frightened by the towering Demoni. Cornelius watched as Monstre grabbed the boy's arm and jerked him toward the ladder. The boy dug his feet against the rock trying to slow the movement, but the creature was stronger.

Cornelius could not bear the sight and he did not want to lose his friend.

Stepping forward, the old man called out, "Stop! You can't take him!"

The Demoni glanced over at the hungry, dehydrated old man and scoffed before turning back to the ladder.

Desperate, Cornelius picked up a loose rock and threw it as hard as he could at Monstre's head. The rock hit the back of the creature's skull hard enough to cause Monstre to cry out in surprise and pain.

With a growl, the monster spun around to face him. His eyes were deadly and Cornelius would have been scared except he wanted to help his friend Simon.

181

"I told you that you're not taking him."

Monstre released his hold on Simon and placed his hand on a sword strapped around his waist. Cornelius stared at the Demoni boldly wishing there was a way for Simon to escape while Monstre was distracted.

"Monstre! What's taking you so long? Lord Diablo is getting impatient."

Monstre glared at the Demoni who called from above.

"This cur is causing trouble. You get the brat."

"Bring the old one too."

Monstre considered the reply and smirked, "Yes. We will see how bold he is in the face of Diablo. Move! Both of you!"

Cornelius hurried over to Simon who took hold of the ladder and began to climb. The old man grasped a rung of the ladder feeling a little shaky for he did not want to be taken before the terrifying dragon. *Oh, Ancient One, please save us.*

The humans were led down a long, black tunnel that seemed to go on forever. Cornelius stumbled along the coarse rock path. The air seemed to increase in heat and humidity. It was so thick that Cornelius felt like he could take a bite out of it.

Suddenly, the tunnel opened up into an enormous cavern with fiery torches scattered around the walls. Demoni were chattering and pointing at the human prisoners. Cornelius frowned at their enthusiasm. *Why are they so excited?*

A hush fell on the cavern leaving it far too quiet. Cornelius looked down at Simon in confusion, but found the boy staring straight ahead with eyes narrowed and a frown on his face. The old man followed the child's gaze. His heart froze when his eyes came to the end of cavern. Standing in complete hatred and gigantic intimidation was the fierce, red dragon.

Cornelius' heart began to pound hard at the sight of the monster, but true fear filled him to his very core when Diablo spoke.

"Why did you bring the old one? He is of no use to me."

The voice held contempt to it. The Demoni behind the prisoners gulped loudly and whispered to each other to tell their master their reason.

"Well?" snapped the dragon impatiently.

Monstre stepped up into Cornelius' view and pointed his gray finger at the elderly human.

"He would not let me fetch the slave boy."

The dragon raised his head and his face shone with amusement.

"Oh? You mean that a strong Demoni like you couldn't handle this feeble, old skeleton?"

Guffaws and snickers rose up among all the Demoni. Monstre glared angrily at his comrades.

"My lord, I would have dealt with him, but they came and told me to just bring him too."

The other Demoni pointed at each other and stammered weakly yet frantically.

"Enough!"

Silence followed the dragon's snarl. Cornelius grimaced as the monster beckoned him forward. The elderly man stepped forward and approached the dragon yet purposely placing himself squarely in front of Simon protectively.

"You are no match for me, old man."

Cornelius nodded and spoke boldly, "You're right. You are more powerful than me, but my Lord the Ancient One could destroy you and rescue me without any real effort."

A gasp followed by chattering rose up among the Demoni. Diablo glanced around the arena and silence returned quickly. The beast smirked at the old man as if an idea had just come to him. He regarded the Demoni behind the prisoners.

"Monstre, summon Avidez."

Avidez sat on a large, comfy bed in his vast new chambers. The luxury and richness of the room amazed the warrior and he truly felt at home here. The man had been given a table full of various foods and his stomach felt so satisfied. Avidez had also been given many fine clothes and he had quickly changed out of his torn rags. Now he wore black trousers and a red silk shirt. His feet were adorned with shiny black boots. A Demoni had brought a black sheath with belt. A silver and red hilt of a sword stuck out of the sheath. Avidez truly believed that this was all what a warrior like him really deserved. He did not regret his decision to leave the company heading to Mount Glory nor did he wish that he was with them. *This is where I belong.*

A knock sounded at the door. Avidez opened it warily and found a Demoni standing there.

"Lord Diablo summons you."

The warrior felt a knot in his stomach as he nodded. He turned and strapped on his sword sheath before following the creature down the dark tunnel. His mind raced as he tried to figure out why the dragon would summon him. None of the reasons were appealing.

Light flooded Avidez's eyes as he exited the dark tunnel. The man blinked several times to help his eyes adjust to the change in light. Looking around, the warrior saw Demoni everywhere forming a perimeter around the area. Near the center, he saw the great dragon in all his ferocity. Then the man blinked again for standing before the creature was an old man that he clearly recognized. *Cornelius? How did he get here?*

"Ah, Avidez, come closer."

The dragon's full attention was on the man which made him very uneasy. However, he obeyed the beast and walked briskly to his new master's side.

"Yes, my lord?"

"I have decided on your task of initiation into our ranks. I want you to kill this pathetic creature."

Avidez looked at Cornelius then back to Diablo uncertainly.

"Don't you want to kill him, Avidez, after all he did to you? He almost made you fall back into the valley. He made you appear weak to the others. Remember how Cristo and the others rebuked you when you came up without the old one. Remember their cruel accusations and how they shunned you. It is all because of him. He ruined everything."

Fury filled Avidez at each word Diablo spoke. By the last word he was boiling over. The warrior charged forward with his new sword raised.

Cornelius closed his eyes and a look of peace crossed his face. That angered Avidez more. With one ferocious swing, the warrior decapitated the old man removing his chance of ever living in peace again. A scream echoed through the cavern and Avidez saw Simon for the first time.

Looking down at the mangled corpse crumpled by his feet, the man focused on what had just happened. Horror filled him at the cheers of the Demoni and the exclaimed "Well done!" from Diablo. *What have I done?*

"No!"

Simon rushed forward as Cornelius' body fell to the hot, rocky ground. Demoni hands grabbed him and struggled to hold onto the fighting, flailing boy as he tried to advance forward. Avidez backed away into the shadows as Diablo moved forward to inspect the old man's body.

Simon exclaimed, "You lying snake!"

Diablo froze and turned his fiery eyes on the boy.

"What?"

The Demoni let go of the child and scurried into the shadows as the others grew silent. Simon did not feel scared for he knew the truth.

"You are a liar and a manipulator! You twist the truth to deceive people. You think you are powerful, but in truth you are nothing! The Ancient One has more power in one finger than you have in your whole body. My Lord is mighty to save and you don't stand a chance against Him!"

"Enough!"

The dragon pounced and slammed a long, sharp talon deep into the boy's chest. Pain screamed throughout Simon's body, but something else had his attention. A light shining behind the dragon filled the child with joy.

"Where is the Ancient One? Where is your precious Cristo?"

Simon moved his gaze to meet the monster's eyes and before death took him, he smiled.

Diablo frowned in confusion at the slave boy's smile. However, the cheers from the Demoni told the dragon that he had restored his reputation. The frown turned into a triumphant smirk as he dropped the boy's dead body to the ground. The cheers of his minions died down suddenly causing the monster to look at his followers. The Demoni were cowering as far into the shadows as they could, but the size of the shadows was diminishing due to a growing light.

Diablo flung his massive body around to face the light and an eerie feeling filled him at the terrible sight.

Cristo stood beside the body of Cornelius completely radiating with light. His sword was drawn and raised. But what brought fear to the great dragon's heart was the look on the knight's face. Cristo's eyes were hard and fierce causing the monster to wince. His face was stern as stone. His usual raggedness seemed replaced by a gaze of nobility and strength. When the knight spoke, his voice held a fury to it.

"Well, Diablo. You wanted to know where I was. Here. I AM!"

The Demoni squealed and fought each other to get to the safety of the tunnels. Diablo knew that he was alone to face his Enemy.

"You have gone too far, Dragon."

The creature's insides were cringing and twisting, but on the outside he showed indifference.

"Has the time come then? Has He sent you for our final battle?"

Cristo returned his sword to its sheath.

"No, it is not time. But your day is coming, Diablo. We will take His Beloved with us."

Diablo wondered who "we" was, but he received his answer immediately. Two Light Warriors of Mount Glory stepped forward. The dragon recognized them as his once friends Andeo and Ingel who had refused to join him in the rebellion against the Ancient One. The two men brought out a shimmery white cloth and wrapped up the remains of Cornelius with a gentleness and care that sickened Diablo. Andeo and Ingel lifted the shrouded corpse and headed for the tunnel exit wordlessly.

Diablo returned his gaze to Cristo.

"And the slave?"

The knight stepped forward with the light increasing with such radiance. Diablo moved off to the side heading for his cave in hopes of finding darkness again.

"Will you come with me, Avidez?"

Diablo spun around to find Cristo, with the dead slave boy in his arms, staring into a far shadow where Avidez crouched. The dragon was about to speak, but the harsh glare Cristo gave him caused the monster to swallow his words.

"Well, Avidez, will you come with me?"

Avidez was amazed at how suddenly Cristo had come out of nowhere. The brilliance of the light blinded the man and he quickly tried to hide in what little darkness was left in the arena. He felt so ashamed at what he had done to Cornelius and knew that the knight would find out about it. He always seemed to know the truth.

The words spoken between Cristo and Diablo were like blurred mumbles to him not that Avidez cared. He just wanted to be back in his new chambers, left alone.

"Will you come with me, Avidez?"

The clarity of the words surprised the man as he realized that Cristo was talking to him. The man's mind raced. He desperately wanted to get out of here now.

"Well, Avidez, will you come with me?"

Avidez frowned. *The knight is only asking because he doesn't know.*

"I know what you have done, Avidez."

The man's heart pounded rapidly as he waited for Cristo to say more. No other words came. *He doesn't really want me to come. He pities me because I am cowering in this hole. What will happen if I try to leave Diablo? Surely the dragon will not allow me to leave...Even if I went with him, there is no way the others will forgive me.*

Avidez's heart darkened at the thoughts. He felt the desire to leave fade to be replaced by arrogance. Standing up, the man faced the knight with a mocking smirk.

"Why would I leave a place with plenty of food to travel again hungry? Why would I give up all my new treasures for a journey of nothingness? I am staying here."

"As always, it is your choice."

Cristo walked towards the Chasm exit with Simon in his arms. Avidez frowned just now realizing that the boy had been murdered by Diablo for he had been too busy cowering in the shadows to know.

"Good choice, my warrior. Well done."

The pride of Diablo caused the man to cringe. *Why didn't I go with Cristo?*

187

CHAPTER 19

ISLAND OF SACRIFICE

Lailani's eyes widened in shock at the sight before her. Out of the forest stepped Victor obviously wounded, supported by a familiar man. The man dressed fully in white had a sword strapped to his waist and he held onto Victor strongly. Lailani remembered the man as Campion who had saved her from drowning in the swamp. That day seemed like a lifetime ago. It was when Cornelius loved her and was willing to die for his friend. The woman blinked away the tears that threatened to escape from her eyes.

What really caused her shock and fear was the fact that neither Simon nor Cristo came out of the forest with them. *Where are they? Why didn't they come back too?*

Lailani watched as Victor climbed the ladder slowly favoring his side. Out of the corner of her eye, she saw Devin rush over to help the battered knight climb onto the deck. The princesses gathered around the man eager for news. A loud whistle rang from the helm of the ship where Iliana stood.

"Let's give the man some room. He needs to rest a bit before we bombard him with questions."

The princesses returned to their seats as Devin led Victor to a bench to rest.

Lailani glanced back at the shore hoping that Campion would have news to share. However, the man in white was gone. There was no sign of where he had gone. The woman looked to the forest edge once more desiring to see Cristo and Simon approaching. No one.

Impatience struck Lailani for she did not want to wait for answers. She wanted to know what had happened now. Marching over to the resting man, the woman confronted Victor.

"What happened? Where are they?"

"What happened? Where are they?"

Victor did not have to guess who "they" were. He knew as he and Campion approached the ship that the other travelers would wonder what had happened to Cristo and Simon. His mind had sorted through all that had happened and he had planned how much to tell them.

At Lailani's questions, Victor hung his head. His shortened story faded from existence. Instead, the complete truth spilled forth to the shock of the others. He told them about how the side-trip had been a way to head away from the Mountain. He explained how he had deceived Simon to leave Cristo and how the boy was taken away by the Demoni. When he finished telling them Cristo's commands, the knight fell silent and waited for the response of the others. It seemed like an eternity before anyone spoke.

Finally, a male voice said, "Welcome back."

Victor's head snapped upward in surprise. *Welcome back?*

"Welcome back."

Devin smiled sincerely at Victor who was now looking at him surprised. He had listened to the man's explanation and had almost condemned him for doing such a horrible thing, but then all he had done in the past flashed through his own mind. *How can I condemn Victor when I have done far worse?*

"Welcome back?"

Devin turned to Lailani who was glaring at him with her hands on her hips.

"What do you mean 'welcome back'?"

The man looked around at the others standing or sitting on the deck. Everyone seemed to be surprised except Iliana who was smiling at the man with a twinkle in her eye.

Devin returned his gaze to Lailani and replied, "I say it because I have done horrible things too and yet I hope to be completely forgiven for my deeds. How can I not accept Victor back into our group? If anyone is completely innocent, then go ahead and stand against this man."

"Well said, Devin."

The man spun around at the voice. Joy filled him at the sight of Cristo until he noticed the small lifeless body in the elder knight's arms.

"Welcome back."

Lailani blinked at Devin's kind words. She didn't think that they should welcome Victor back after all he had done. After all, he had lied and left Simon. What kind of monster would treat a child that way? Her anger at Victor became focused on Devin.

With a glare, Lailani exclaimed, "Welcome back? What do you mean 'welcome back'?"

Devin turned and looked at the woman. He looked evenly into her eyes.

"I say it because I have done horrible things too and yet I hope to be completely forgiven for my deeds. How can I not accept Victor back into our group? If anyone is completely innocent, then go ahead and stand against this man."

Lailani softened at the words for she knew he spoke the truth. Yes, she had messed up before and wanted true forgiveness for her mistakes.

"Well said, Devin."

Lailani's heart fluttered at the voice she had come to know so well yet it turned cold at the sight of Simon's still form.

Victor felt such encouragement at Devin's words. Perhaps he would be accepted back into the group and be allowed to make amends.

"Well said, Devin."

A smile crossed Victor's face at the voice. He quickly looked over hoping to see Simon standing beside the elder knight. His hope was shattered at the sight of Cristo holding a small, still body.

Disbelief filled the young knight as Cristo stepped toward him with a sorrowful, compassionate countenance. Victor slid off the bench falling to his knees desperate to see some movement from Simon. None came.

Tears stung his eyes as Cristo laid the child's body into the man's arms. A large bloody spot stained the chest area of the boy's shirt. The sobs could not be contained any longer nor did the knight feel like trying. He had lost his child because of his own deceit.

Lailani wiped the tears away that were beginning to gather in her eyes. She watched Victor cling to the dead body of Simon before having to turn away. Cristo stood behind her with a look of compassion on his face.

"Cornelius was captured and taken to the Chasm. He was killed by Avidez who believed Diablo's lies. I am sorry, my dear."

The words struck Lailani so hard that she gasped as if she had been punched in the stomach. The tears she had refused to let fall spilled down her cheeks as the truth of what had happened to her friend hit her. She shook her head miserably and turned away knowing that this was all her fault.

Devin stepped closer to her. The man put his arms around her and held her quietly giving her time to cry for her friend. She clung to him heartbroken. Lailani closed her eyes tightly as she laid her face against Devin's chest unaware of what was happening around her. *Why didn't I go with him? I should have been more loyal than that. How could I betray our friendship like that? Oh, what a despicable creature I am! I am so sorry, Cornelius.*

Victor's sobs lessened as exhaustion began to set in. He blinked the tears away as he looked down at the child in his arms. The peaceful expression on Simon's face forced Victor to lower his head and close his eyes. *O Ancient One, I was willing to face whatever punishment You gave me for my crime, but this is too much. Why did You let that creature murder Your child? He did nothing wrong. All he wanted was to go to You on Mount Glory and be in Your service forever. Now it's too late.*

The last two words rang in Victor's ears though they had not been spoken aloud. The man shook his head briskly trying to knock the words out of his head. *No, it is not too late. My Lord, You have the power to bring this boy back to life even now. I believe.*

Simon stood in awe looking around at a place of such radiance and beauty that he couldn't even put it into words. Brilliant light surrounded him. Healthy, happy people were walking or sitting peacefully throughout the area. Some were talking excitedly while others were singing glorious songs.

Simon felt such joy at the laughter and music that he heard. He scanned the groups of people wondering who they could be. Among them sat Cornelius who looked so happy and refreshed. The old man now clothed in rich colors and hair trimmed so neatly did not look at all lonely. Simon was about to go to him when he heard steps behind him.

"Hello, Simon."

The child turned around in surprise. Standing behind him was One that no earthly words could ever describe. At first glance, Simon knew that He must be the Ancient One. The boy's mouth fell open. He felt so speechless and unworthy to reply though he knew that a response was expected.

"H…H…Hello, my Lord."

The child fell to his knees overwhelmed.

The Ancient One smiled, "I am glad to meet you face to face, my son. However, it is not time for you to join me here in the Glory of Glories yet. I have much for you to do back in the mortal world."

Simon frowned, "But I want to stay here with You, my Lord. I feel so safe and happy here."

The Ancient One's eyes twinkled and His smile widened.

"Ah, but you have Me with you there as well. Persevere, my Simon, and I shall see you again soon."

The boy nodded ready to obey and ask how to get back to the mortal world when he heard a song different from what the people were singing. The lyrics were new, but the voice was so familiar.

"That's Cristo!"

The Ancient One took the boy's hand and lifted him to his feet.

"Yes, that is Cristo. Follow his voice and you will find your way back."

Simon nodded reluctantly letting go of the Ancient One's hand and walking toward Cristo's voice.

"Oh, Simon?"

The child stopped and faced the Ancient One eagerly.

"Tell Victor a message for me."

The Ancient One spoke the message to the boy who did not quite understand the meaning. However, he promised his Lord that he would tell Victor the message as soon as he saw him. Then the child followed Cristo's voice into a dazzling light.

No, it's not too late. My, Lord, You have the power to bring this boy back to life even now. I believe.

Victor glanced over at Cristo who had walked over to Iliana. The captain of the Blessed Hope welcomed him excitedly.

"Cristo! Won't you do something?"

The elder knight turned and regarded the desperate man on the deck.

"Won't I? Don't you mean 'can't I'?"

Victor shook his head sharply, "No. I know without a doubt that you can, but will you?"

Cristo's eyes twinkled and he smiled warmly at his fellow knight. Returning to Victor's side, the elder knight knelt down beside him. He placed a hand on Simon's chest gently without hesitation. Then softly Cristo began singing a song that Victor had never heard before. The princesses started humming on their bench matching the tune of the song. Victor listened to the words carefully and found that the lyrics matched the situation perfectly. He thanked the Ancient One before looking down at the small boy whom he loved in his arms. There was no movement yet Victor didn't give up hope. He kept listening and watching.

Then it happened. Simon's eyelids moved slightly. Victor's heart leapt with joy and excitement, but he almost wondered if it was his imagination. *Come on, Simon. Open your eyes, son.*

As if to grant the request, the boy's eyes opened. He looked at the men beside him with a smile. Joy filled Victor at the beautiful sight of the warm living child in his arms. The man looked over at Cristo excitedly to find the elder knight beaming back at him.

Simon sat up quickly and exclaimed, "I saw Him! I saw the Ancient One!"

The other travelers came closer excited to hear what the boy had seen.

"I was in this place that was so bright and beautiful. He called it the Glory of Glories. There were happy people everywhere. Cornelius was there and he was safe and so happy..."

Simon looked over at Lailani who was wiping tears away as new tears flowed down her cheeks. Devin put his arm around her.

"Then He spoke to me. He knew my name! I turned around and saw the Ancient One. Don't ask me what He looks like because no words would be enough. I still have much to do here so He sent me back."

Victor listened in amazement for he had never heard of anyone dying, going to the Glory of Glories, and then returning to the mortal world. Chattering and giggling came from the other travelers and princesses as they returned to their earlier seats.

"A rare blessing you have been given, my dear boy, for not many have visited the Glory of Glories and come back to tell about it. Now, Victor, why don't you take Simon below deck and find some clothes without bloodstains. I'm sure you both have much to talk about."

Victor took a deep breath and nodded. Simon hopped to his feet ready to get cleaned up. He seemed to be renewed and full of energy. The man stood not so energetically and glanced down at his own clothes which were stained with blood too. Simon's blood. The thought made him cringe.

As the knight and the child headed for the trapdoor that led below deck, Cristo called out, "Iliana, let's cast off! We have an island to get to."

Iliana replied equally loud, "Aye, with pleasure, sir."

The first cabin below deck was clean and cozy. To one side was a bunk and to the other side was a large trunk that had a wash basin sitting on it. On the bed two outfits were laid expectantly. One was child-sized and much to Victor's surprise, the other was his size. The clothes consisted of pants, boots, and a shirt. Simon's shirt was emerald green with a golden mountain on it. His pants and boots were black. The boy giggled as he excitedly used the wash basin to clean up his hands and face. Then he picked up the clothes and rushed behind a divider at the far end of the cabin.

Victor smiled shaking his head as he scrubbed the blood off of his hands and arms. Then he turned his focus on his clothes. The shirt was bright blue and it also had a golden mountain on the front. Like Simon's, the pants and boots were black. Victor changed out of his stained clothes and put on his new fresh clothes. Each piece fit perfectly as if made exactly for the man. *How is this possible?*

"Wow! These fit just right!"

Victor looked up at Simon who had come out with his new apparel in place. His little eyes shone brightly with excitement. Victor smiled at the child who had been dead in his arms moments ago.

"You look better."

"You, too…How did you escape Davo?"

Victor told Simon about all that had happened to him in the field. In turn, Simon told about his visit to the Chasm of Misery. Victor cringed at the horrible things Simon had endured.

"I'm sorry you went through all that, Simon."

The man sat down on the bunk so that he was eye level with the boy he loved as his own.

Simon frowned at the knight who suddenly felt afraid that the boy was angry with him still for his lies and deception or worse for allowing him to be taken to Diablo.

"I'm not sorry. If I hadn't gone to the Chasm, then Cornelius would not have called on the Ancient One as his Lord and he wouldn't now be in the Glory of Glories. I may not have liked the Chasm, but I wouldn't change what happened there."

Victor nodded, "I understand. I just hate that I couldn't save you."

The man grew quiet and lowered his head humiliated at his weakness.

"It wasn't your job to save me. I'm not mad at you, Victor. I'm just glad that you survived too."

Victor glanced up relieved to find the child staring at him with his arms open. The man smiled and opened his arms willingly. Simon jumped into his arms. They embraced happily knowing that there were no hard feelings between them.

The knight closed his eyes and sighed.

"Oh, I almost forgot."

Simon's voice lowered to a whisper.

"The Ancient One gave me a message for you." *The Ancient One? What could the message be? Do I really want to know? What if it is bad?*

"What did He say?"

Victor's own voice came out in a whisper. He held his breath almost afraid of the answer.

"He said to tell you that in all things He works for the good of those who love Him."

Tears came to Victor's eyes because he knew that the Ancient One had answered all of his earlier questions of why.

"Do you understand His message?"

Victor laughed through his tears.

"Yes, Simon, I understand what He wants me to know."

The knight wiped his tears away before he let go of the boy. Both smiled at each other.

"Land ho!"

Victor stood up as Simon rushed to the ladder and climbed back up to the deck. *Now where?*

"Land ho!"

Lailani rushed to the side of the ship and looked out to sea wanting to see the land that Iliana was shouting about. On the horizon was a long stretch of land that the travelers had seen from afar before, though now it seemed like a lifetime ago. Lailani's heart leapt at the sight because she knew that they had to go to this island before they could go to Mount Glory. *We're closer than ever before.*

"Listen, Friends, for there is something you must know about this island."

Cristo's words drew the woman's attention from the island. She turned to face the knight and saw that everyone else was doing the same. She noticed that Victor and Simon had returned from the cabin below. Both were cleaned up and wore fresh, colorful clothes.

Cristo smiled at the travelers, "You have come so far, my dears, but a difficult task is yet to come. This is the Island of Sacrifice. Here you must surrender your most prized possession in order to go through the gate that leads to Mount Glory. Be warned that this will not be easy, but nothing worth having is ever obtained easily."

Lailani frowned at the man's words as she wondered what she could give because she had nothing to offer. *What if I can't give anything? Will I have to go back to Terra after I have come so far?*

Devin stared at the land that stood before the travelers. His heart pounded in his anxious chest because the island was not at all what he had expected. He had pictured a bright, welcoming tropical forest with a village of huts. Yet what the man saw now was far from that image.

The island was in fact covered with a dense forest, but it was not at all inviting. The tall, dark trees towered over the people as if they had authority over them. The leaves of the trees were withered and drooped with an air of death. A deep endless fog filled the gaps left between the trees. The entire area held an eeriness that made Devin's skin crawl. Strange sounds filled the creepy jungle. Devin did not recognize the sounds though he had knowledge of many sounds made by a variety of beasts.

"Shall we go?"

Cristo's voice startled the man as he assumed it had the same effect on the others.

"Where?"

Lailani's quiet voice was full of fear and curiosity. Devin glanced over at the woman who stood closer to him than a moment before. He smiled reassuringly though he felt no peace himself. Lailani smiled back and gently took the man's hand into hers. Devin squeezed it tenderly reminding her that he would be there for her.

"At the center of the island, there waits a temple which contains the only gate leading to Mount Glory. We must go to that temple if you are to reach the Ancient One."

Cristo stepped forward toward the foggy forest and began walking down an almost hidden path. The princesses hurried after him not as bubbly and loud as usual. Victor and Simon followed next not separating from each other more than a couple of feet.

"I guess we better go. We don't want to lose them."

Devin hoped his words didn't contain all the fears and doubts he was feeling. The squeeze that came to his hand held such love and courage as Lailani answered.

"Yes. Let's go."

Victor kept his eyes on Simon as the group traveled through the dark, foggy jungle. His heart jumped every time the child faded from sight. The knight's pace quickened when this happened as he was afraid that he would lose Simon again. Perhaps this time for good.

The boy must have sensed Victor's desperation for he slowed down so he stayed in the man's sight. For this, Victor was grateful because he was feeling the exhaustion that came from the long journey and heavy mental distress he had experienced. His feet seemed to drag heavily and he wondered if he was actually moving. His head ached from the previous blow from Davo's sword. All he wanted to do was sit down. Maybe he could rest for just a minute.

Victor fell to his knees and took a deep breath with his eyes closed. He tried to get control of his aching body. The man opened his eyes and his heart jumped. The group of travelers were nowhere in sight. The knight listened hard, but there were no sounds in the jungle.

Panic filled the man as he tried to stand, but his legs were numb. *How is this possible? I have only been here for a minute.*

Grunting and struggling, Victor tried repeatedly to stand, but no matter how hard he tried, the result was the same. He was stuck!

Whispers in the dark startled the knight and fear struck his heart for he knew that the other travelers would not be all around him whispering. Silence followed and the man wondered if he had imagined the whispers. Victor struggled to stand, but to no avail. The whispers erupted around him again though to the man's dismay, they seemed closer and had increased in number.

Frantically, Victor repeated the action to stand, but fell to the ground. Over and over, he tried to get up so he could get away from the whispers that were closing in. Whatever held him tightened each time he moved until Victor felt as if he was choking.

Suddenly out of the forest's shadows came a multitude of creatures that struck fear deeper into Victor's heart. Though the creatures looked like Demoni, they were only a third of the height of Diablo's minions. To a human, these creatures would only come up to an average man's knee. Their skin was a sickly green that would camouflage them in the forest. Their faces and ears were similar to the Demoni, but they didn't seem as dangerous.

Victor felt despair as he realized that these monsters were Diablo's servants known by the name of Grungens. The Grungens were known by the knights of Glory as scavengers who attacked anyone who strayed or fell behind from a group. They lured their prey to sleep before devouring them.

One of the Grungens stepped ahead of the others and smiled in an attempt to reassure him. The green troll-like creature spoke in a wispy, hoarse voice.

"Welcome, ye who are weary. You should rest from this endless journey. Fear not for we will guard you while you sleep. Sleep, Friend, sleep."

Victor frowned at the creature's words knowing this was a trick. However, the words made sense and he felt his eyes closing.

"No!"

Victor jerked his head with a shake. He had to stay awake. If he fell asleep, then he would be done for.

"Oh, my dear friend, do not fight your weariness for you deserve rest. I see you are wounded. Surely the battle was difficult and you have earned a night of sleep without trouble. Close your eyes, dear friend. Let go."

Victor felt so peaceful and the quiet of the jungle added to his calmness. His head began to lower and his eyelids drooped. *Maybe I can rest for just a minute.*

"Victor!"

The sound of his name jolted Victor out of his almost slumber. The Grungens looked around nervously. The knight saw no one, but he heard his name called out again from a distance. It was Simon this time though earlier it was definitely a man. *Cristo? Or Devin?*

"Time is short, Grungens. Lullaby now. No other choice."

Victor tried to understand what the head Grungen was saying. A hum came from the Grungens as they tightened their circle. Then to Victor's surprise, the little green creatures began to sing a song in hushed voices.

"Sleep now, our weary friend; Let your deep weariness end."

The buzz of the voices and swaying tune of the song seemed to cause Victor to feel even more exhausted.

"Close your eyes and go to sleep."

The man tried to force his eyes to stay open, but they felt so heavy. *Cristo!*

"Give in and let yourself go."

Victor's eyes closed as he lay on the ground. His mind drifted off into a world of dreams. He was gone so quick that he did not hear the end of the song.

"And we shall please our lord Diablo."

The green little Grungens hissed with laughter as their leader motioned for them to end the song.

"Grungens, dinnertime!"

With a whoop and a holler, the group of Grungens rushed forward toward the defenseless man.

"Conquered another one, have you, Nob?"

The voice, though soft, froze the actions of the Grungens. Their leader cringed. With a collective turn, the Grungens' eyes widened at the speaker.

Cristo stood leaning against a nearby tree as if out for a casual walk. The Grungen leader, Nob, gulped as he stepped forward to face the knight.

"You wouldn't take what is ours, would you?"

Cristo raised his bushy eyebrows.

"Yours? Is he really yours?"

Nob frowned, "We Grungens found him. We claim him."

Cristo stood up straight and touched the hilt of his sword.

"This man is a knight of Glory. He belongs to the Ancient One."

The Grungens backed up and chattered at each other as the news of this startled them.

On the other hand, Nob was determined to keep the prey that he had worked so hard to obtain.

"He left your group on purpose. Obviously, he didn't want to go to the Ancient One. So he is fair game."

Cristo looked at Nob amused.

"Fair? Do we really want to talk about what is fair?"

Nob glanced at his fellow Grungens for support, but found no help. Instead, the Grungens were shaking their heads trying to persuade their leader to stop.

Nob lowered his head and mumbled, "Fine. Take him and wake him. We care not."

Cristo approached Victor who was still slumped on the ground sleeping. Nob stepped aside with a huff.

"Grungens, home…empty hands, empty tummies."

The green creature led his followers back into the jungle. The other Grungens hurried away eager to be away from the knight Cristo.

A gentle yet firm hand shook Victor's shoulder.

"Awake, Victor, and be weary no more."

The voice caused Victor's heart to leap. He knew who it was before opening his eyes. Cristo was kneeling beside him with a smile. Victor thought about what had happened and his joy disappeared as he realized that he had failed with the Grungens. Irritation and frustration filled him. *Well, I messed up again.*

'Do not be so hard on yourself, Victor, for you did call for me before sleep took you."

The younger knight felt some comfort from Cristo's words. He was grateful that the older man was not scolding him for straying from the other travelers.

"Thank you, my lord, for delivering me from those wretched Grungens. I would be dead without you."

"My pleasure, Victor. You have much to do yet."

Victor frowned wondering what the man could mean, but there was no time to question the knight. The two men stood and headed through the jungle eager to catch up to the rest of the travelers. It seemed like an eternity before they caught up and Victor couldn't believe how long he had been detained.

A clearing came at last and Victor stared up at a stone temple that towered like a giant in their path. He suddenly remembered the last time he had entered this sacred building. Anticipation took control as Simon hurried to his side with a list of questions.

CHAPTER 20

THE GATEWAY TEMPLE

The towering temple looked ancient as if it had been stuck on this island for centuries. Vines and mold were attached to the large stone bricks that made up the structure. Two massive closed stone doors faced the travelers. Simon couldn't help, but wonder how the group would be able to open them without more help.

"Friends, I must leave you now for a time."

Gasps and protests filled the area as the travelers were shocked at Cristo's news. Simon felt less safe at the thought of the knight leaving them alone. His heart started pounding. As he looked around, the boy saw the same kind of panic in the faces of the others.

"Now, now, dear ones. Do not fret for I will meet you past the Gateway. What you must do now is for you alone and no one can help you not even me. You must enter one at a time and make your sacrifice within. If it is accepted, then you will be allowed access through the Gateway and your journey will be nearing its destination. If your sacrifice is not accepted, then…No, you do not need that added worry. Just search your hearts and you will prevail. Until I see you again. Farewell."

Without another word, Cristo walked to the side of the temple. Soon the trees and bushes veiled him from the group.

Simon frowned as he went over to sit next to Victor who had plopped down on the ground to rest. The knight smiled weakly at the boy, but Simon knew that he was just trying to reassure him. Obviously, Victor didn't like the idea of Cristo leaving them either.

Lailani's heart was racing as Cristo disappeared into the forest at the side of the temple. She had an urge to run after him and cling to the man no matter where he went, but she knew that it was not what she was supposed to do. Instead, she would have to wait for her turn to go into the temple and sacrifice something when she didn't even know what it could be.

"Who would like to go first?"

Ziona's question hung in the air as silence followed. Lailani realized that if she went first, then she could get to the other side and be with Cristo again quickly.

Taking a deep breath and speaking before she could talk herself out of it, the young red-headed woman said, "I'll go first if that is alright with everyone."

No one objected so Lailani slowly climbed the stone steps that led up to the doors. With a crack, the temple doors opened. The woman saw only complete darkness inside. She gulped at the frightening unknown before her. Yet Lailani knew that the others were watching so of course she had to go in no matter how terrified she felt. Stepping past the temple doors, the woman was about to turn and ask advice from Ziona. The temple doors slammed shut leaving her in absolute darkness.

Shock filled Lailani at the darkness. In the next moment, torches lit up all around her without anyone lighting them. The room was enormous with nothing in it except a large stone table at the far end of it. Behind the stone table were two massive stone doors closed like the temple doors she had just entered through. Above the doors was strange writing that the woman had never seen before.

Suddenly, a cloaked figure entered from a shadowy corner. Lailani couldn't tell if it was a man, woman, or even human at all. The figure was tall with a red robe that covered the whole body and a hood hid its face. Fear choked Lailani as the figure took its position behind the stone table.

"Welcome, Lailani of Terra."

The voice did not sound at all welcoming and Lailani's fear grew. She nodded her head in greeting, but her mouth felt so dry and choked that no words came. Her stomach was in knots and her mind was racing.

"To open the gateway that leads to Mount Glory, you must sacrifice your most prized possession by placing it on the altar...What do you offer?"

Lailani's heart pounded even more with panic for she could think of nothing to offer and she was afraid that she would not be able to go on after coming so far. She took a deep breath and swallowed hard.

"Sir, I have nothing for I am a poor peasant from the city of Terra. But if I can, I offer my heart to the Ancient One."

Silence followed and the young woman was afraid that she had been rejected. She couldn't blame the Ancient One if He didn't want a common peasant girl in His presence.

"Do you offer it fully? Will you love the Ancient One more than any other? Will you love Him and let your parents' memory lessen in your thoughts and actions? Will you choose the Ancient One and surrender your guilt over Cornelius? Do you give your whole heart to the Ancient One even if it means forsaking your love for Devin?"

With each question, Lailani became more burdened and worried by the situation. She struggled to breathe and tried to gain control or at least collect her thoughts. The woman closed her eyes. *O Ancient One, I do love You and I give You now my whole heart. Only You can change my heart so I love You alone. Please accept my sacrifice.*

Stepping forward, Lailani placed her hands flat on the altar feeling the cold stone on her palms.

"I offer my whole heart."

Looking up at the cloaked figure, the young woman was astonished to see that the gateway stood open.

"Enter, Lailani of Terra, for your sacrifice has been accepted."

The red-haired woman hurried around the altar and rushed up the stone steps. She was eager to move ahead and reunite with Cristo.

Past the gateway, Lailani entered a courtyard of stone that had benches and a fountain though no water sprang from it. Instead of the towering temple in front of her, Lailani found herself facing a mountain more majestic than she had ever seen. The sun shone down on the mountain giving it a brilliance and radiance beyond words. *Mount Glory!*

Simon sat beside Victor wondering what was happening to Lailani. Suddenly the temple doors opened with a thunderous crack.

"Who shall be next, my friends?"

Ziona stood near the steps looking at each traveler in turn. No one seemed eager to go.

"I will."

Simon frowned as the words came out of his own mouth.

"Good, Simon dear. Go on. It is quite safe."

The boy glanced from the encouraging woman to Victor. The man nodded. Simon knew it must be safe if the knight was willing to let him go without debate or concern.

The boy walked cautiously up the steps and entered the dark tunnel. The monstrous doors slammed behind the child. Unwillingly, he cried out in surprise. Complete darkness encircled him and Simon half expected a monster or Diablo himself to spring from the void before him.

Torches burst into flame causing Simon to jump. The boy blinked quickly trying to get his eyes used to the sudden light. At the far end of the room, he saw a stone table. His eyes widened as he saw a figure standing behind the table. Cloaked, there was no face to be seen. The figure stood in front of two enormous doors that Simon thought must be the gateway to Mount Glory.

"Welcome, Simon slave of Aurelius."

Simon bristled at the deep, raspy voice partly at the sound, but more so because of the words spoken. The boy was hurt by the reminder that he was just a slave.

"What do you place on this altar? What do you value the most?"

Simon frowned for he had no idea what he could give up because he had nothing of value.

"I have nothing."

Simon lowered his head in defeat.

"What about your freedom?"

The boy's head snapped up at the suggestion.

"Will you give the Ancient One your newly acquired freedom? Will you become a slave again facing hunger, abuse, and hardships if the Ancient One commands you to?"

Simon felt like he had been punched in the stomach. *Become a slave again? How could I stand that kind of life again?*

His mind recalled being in the presence of the Ancient One in the Glory of Glories and a smile spread across the boy's face. He raised his head and stepped forward.

"I give my freedom fully and completely to the Ancient One."

Simon placed his hands on the stone table. The figure moved aside and turned toward the great stone doors which opened with a crack. Natural light streamed into the dim room.

"Enter, Simon, Guardian of Glory, for your sacrifice has been accepted."

Simon whooped for joy then slapped his hands over his mouth in fear of making noise in such a sacred place. The cloaked figure said nothing as he pointed at the open doors gesturing for the boy to leave. Simon nodded and hurried out the doors. The great slabs closed behind him, but his attention was on what was ahead.

Mount Glory stood before him in all its beauty and majesty. The child's smile widened as he beheld the destination of his journey. However, the smile faded quickly as his eyes fell on Lailani. She was sitting on the ground with tears streaming down her face. Simon hurried over to the distraught woman.

"Lailani, what's wrong?"

The red haired woman looked up and tried to speak without sobbing.

"Cristo's not here."

Victor sat in the grass waiting as patiently as he could. He knew that Simon was safe, but he couldn't help but wonder if the boy would be able to go through the Gateway.

As the man was reflecting on this, the humongous rock doors creaked open again. Victor smiled knowing that his boy had made it through. Standing, the knight approached the steps.

"I'll go next."

The others nodded as the man passed them and climbed the stairs eager to get back with Simon.

Once through the doors, Victor barely noticed the slam of the doors behind him or the instant torchlight. He looked forward recognizing the altar and cloaked figure standing in front of the Gateway.

"Welcome, Victor knight of Glory."

The knight nodded. "What does He want me to offer?"

A number of things had entered his mind as possible sacrifices, but the word that came from the cloaked figure had not been one of them.

"Simon."

"What?!"

A deep panic filled the man as he hoped that he had heard wrong.

"You must give up Simon in your heart in order to pass on to Mount Glory."

Victor frowned suddenly angry.

"Why Simon?"

The cloaked figure cocked his head to the side.

"Because you want to be with him more than the Ancient One. Because you love him more than your Lord. Because you are in a hurry to get back to Simon instead of in a hurry to see the Ancient One. Simon has become your focus and thus you cannot enter Mount Glory unless you give him up."

As the man had spoken these words, Victor started to realize how true they were. He really was trying to get through the Gateway to reunite with Simon. He hadn't even thought about the Ancient One as he entered the temple. There had been a time when all the man wanted was the Ancient One. *What has happened to me? Yes, I am supposed to love others, but not in place of the Ancient One. I can love Simon, but I have gone too far. Ancient One, I beg You to forgive me. I love You more than anyone even Simon. I have become obsessed with him and I know that is not good for him or me. I give Simon to You though it is hard and I know that You will take care of him even without me. Please use me as only You can.*

Tears streamed down Victor's face as he felt the love he had for the Ancient One grow. Deep in his heart, the knight felt ready to let go of Simon if that was the will of his Lord.

With eyes closed, Victor slapped his hands on the altar not in anger, but in surrender and determination.

"I give Simon to the Ancient One with my whole heart."

The knight's eyes opened gently in relief as the heavy burden he had felt since the desert was lifted off of him. Suddenly, he could breathe more deeply than before. Victor did not feel as obsessed about Simon and his heart held a peace that he had never felt before.

"Enter, Victor knight of Glory, for your sacrifice has been accepted."

Victor headed for the open doors of the Gateway eager now to see the Ancient One. He saw Simon standing by Lailani. The man felt love for the boy, but this time it was different for there was no obsessive edge to it.

Simon frowned at the knight who was confused by the expression.

"What's wrong?"

The boy replied softly almost miserably, "Cristo isn't here."

Victor smiled, "He will be."

Shaking his head and ignoring the questions from the other two travelers, the man turned and faced the very familiar mountain before him. His smile grew as he beheld Mount Glory with a new heart and new eyes. *Almost home.*

Devin cringed as the stone doors creaked open for the fourth time.

"Would you like to go next, Devin?"

The man looked into Ziona's eyes with his heart pounding in his chest.

"Oh, no. Ladies first."

The dark-skinned lady in yellow smiled peacefully, "How gracious. Thank you. Come, princesses. We can enter together."

Devin frowned because he had hoped that each princess would go alone which would take longer prolonging his turn. *Well, at least it will take a while for all those women to offer their sacrifices.*

As if to prove him wrong, the doors reopened a few seconds later. Devin frowned. *How could they be done already?*

Shaking his head, the man climbed the smooth stone steps wondering what he was about to get himself into. With uncertainty filling him, Devin stepped into the pitch black darkness that lay waiting ahead. He walked into the temple.

An uneasy feeling hit him at the sudden slam of the temple doors. Devin was not a man known for being cowardly. In fact he had faced many perils while serving Diablo, but he had always known who his foe or his target was. However, here he was faced with the unknown and the brave warrior couldn't quite get rid of the eerie fear that gripped his heart. The silence in the lightless area was deafening.

Torches suddenly came ablaze and the eerie darkness escaped leaving a large stone table and a hooded figure behind. Devin's fear faded away now that he could see his surroundings, but it was instantly replaced by a new fear as the stranger before him spoke.

"Devin slave of Diablo, you dare come? You who have helped Diablo to trap and enslave, torture and murder. Many are the victims you have destroyed. Why should the Ancient One accept any sacrifice you have to offer?"

Devin tried to hold back tears at the harsh, yet true words of the cloaked figure. The question screamed into his mind. He tried to think of an answer that would get him through the Gateway.

In the end all he could do was mutter, "He shouldn't."

"What?"

Devin took a deep breath feeling exhausted and burdened by his past.

"He shouldn't! I am what you say and I have done all the evils you speak of. The Ancient One should want to strike me dead so I can never hurt anyone again. He should have you drive me from this place and allow Diablo to capture me to do with me what he wants. Yet I come with my heart broken and heavy with shame. The Ancient One may not accept my sacrifice, but I will never know unless I offer it. So I offer the Ancient One my life to do with as He wants. If He wants to end my life, then so be it. But if He wants to use me the rest of my life for His purposes, then I am willing to do whatever He will have me do."

Silence filled the temple as Devin grew quiet and waited for the verdict that would determine whether or not he would enter the last part of the journey. The doors stayed still before him. Devin finally concluded that his sacrifice had been rejected.

Heartbroken, the man turned and began to walk back to the other doors. A crack sounded yet it wasn't the doors he had come through before, but instead the doors he had not yet entered. Devin spun around in surprise. A brilliant light shone through the open doors.

"Enter, Devin slave of Diablo, for your sacrifice has been accepted."

Deep relief engulfed the warrior as he stepped forward eagerly almost afraid that the doors would slam shut before he got through. Soon he was outside the temple.

The sight before him filled Devin with great joy. The princesses along with Ziona sat on benches giggling and talking with excitement. Simon and Victor sat near the women on the grass resting peacefully. Devin's' eyes met Lailani's green ones and a warm smile crossed his face. Though the lady looked like she had been crying, her eyes twinkled as she beheld him. But what truly caught Devin's attention was the gigantic mountain where the travelers sat at its base. *Mount Glory! But where is Cristo?*

The cloaked figure lowered his hood with satisfaction. Cristo was pleased with the sacrifices of the travelers. He knew that Lailani was upset that he was not waiting outside for them, but his task had been so important.

As High Priest, Cristo was responsible for the altar and the Gateway. He nodded his pleasure of Lailani's willingness to love the Ancient One over her deceased parents and friend. He chuckled as he remembered Simon's whoop of triumph that the child had tried to recover. Cristo felt such pride in Victor for surrendering Simon, so he could be open to reestablishing his relationship with the Ancient One. However, the knight was most pleased with Devin's response. The man had chosen the Ancient One with a mere hope that He would accept him even though he was unworthy. *That took a lot of guts.*

The knight knew that the group was now excited to be sitting at the foot of Mount Glory. However, Cristo also knew that a great struggle was yet to come.

CHAPTER 21

MOUNT GLORY

Simon glanced around at all of the travelers happy that no one else had been lost. Yet he couldn't help, but listen to the nagging question in his mind. *Where is Cristo?*

"Oh! Look!"

Harmony's cry brought the boy out of his wondering. The dark skinned girl held up the necklace that had been around her neck. It was nothing more than an empty chain. Simon's eyes widened because he remembered that there was still one jewel left before the temple trial. Everyone turned around to locate the last princess.

"Glory, Glory to our Lord for He has rescued me. I was tricked and trapped, but now by Him I've been set free."

The little song rang out with a musical echo. All eyes spun to the doors of the temple where a young tan woman was bowing low and dancing. She had black hair tied neatly in a bun and held in place with a golden headband. Her dress consisted of blue, reddish orange, gold, and dark pink intertwined together.

"Gloria!"

Harmony and the other princesses hurried over to the glorifying princess. Simon smiled as the women embraced and chattered excitedly causing the volume in the courtyard to increase greatly almost to a point that hurt the ears of the other travelers. Ziona hushed them gently. The princesses stopped and listened to the dark skinned woman in yellow.

"Now that we are all here, we can enter Mount Glory and see the Ancient One."

"What about Cristo?"

Lailani's question seemed to mirror everyone else's especially Simon's.

"Cristo will catch up if that is where he is meant to be. Come, friends! The Ancient One is waiting for us!"

Simon looked at the mountain before him and frowned. He could not see any path leading up to Mount Glory nor any cave or door at the base of it.

211

"How do we get in?"

Ziona smiled pleasantly, "Just go up to the base and keep walking. You will walk through the wall of the mountain."

The boy's eyes widened in awe. He quickly looked at Victor for confirmation since as a knight of Glory, the man had been to the Mount Glory before. Victor nodded with a knowing smile.

Taking a deep breath, Simon stepped forward. The natural mountain faded out of view as the boy walked through the wall. What came into view brought a smile to Simon's face.

A massive throne room stood waiting for them with walls and floors of gold. White banners with golden mountains on them draped the walls. At the opposite end of the room was a giant golden throne.

Confusion hit the boy as he looked at the being on the throne. He heard the others entering the throne room behind him. He turned to find Victor who was frowning.

Lailani's eyes widened at the beauty of the throne room. She had never seen any place so magnificent. Her eyes focused on the throne eager to see the Ancient One. On the throne sat a very handsome man with blond hair and blue eyes. He was tall and looked so strong. He wore all white and light seemed to radiate off of him. A deep, luring voice spoke as the man smiled.

"Welcome, dear ones. I have been waiting for you all for so long. I am pleased that you have come to me."

Lailani felt so safe and happy at the man's words. Surely he was the Ancient One. He looked straight at the woman whose heart fluttered at his gentle smile.

"I am the Ancient One."

Joy filled the woman at the news.

"No, you're not!"

A gasp echoed through the throne room as Lailani turned to Simon who stood frowning with his fist on his hips. The woman wondered why the boy would say such a thing. She focused back on the man who still smiled yet there was less of a twinkle in his eyes.

"Of course I am, my dear Simon."

Lailani felt like she could really trust the man because he was so kind even to Simon.

"No. I have met the Ancient One in the Glory of Glories and you are not my Lord."

The woman frowned at Simon wishing he would quit arguing with the Ancient One.

"Ah, but I take on a different form when I am here on Mount Glory. Trust me, my friends, for I am ready to accept you into my service and enrich your lives."

"If you are the Ancient One, then tell us the message you wanted me to give Victor."

Lailani looked at the man in white as he paused and stared at the boy in silence. *Could he be the Ancient One? If so, then why did he hesitate with such an easy task?*

Victor listened to the argument between the man on the throne and Simon. He too knew that this imposter was not the being he met when the knight had come to Mount Glory years before. Yet Victor could not quite picture the One he had seen so long ago. Maybe this was the form of the Ancient One he had encountered on his first visit to the mountain.

"If you are the Ancient One, then tell us the message you wanted me to give Victor."

Simon's demand seemed like a good way to determine who the radiant man really was.

"Ah, that message was meant for Victor. I will not share his secret, private message with all of you."

Victor frowned at the man's way of avoiding Simon's demand. "Then tell me."

The knight was aware of all eyes on him, but he kept his focus on the being on the throne who had slowly turned his attention to Victor. His sparkling eyes were cold and hateful though a smile was still pasted on his face.

"Let's stop this nonsense and do what we came here to do."

Victor wondered about the man's vague words and what he had come here to do.

"Before we continue, please allow us to praise our Lord in song."

Ziona's musical voice and her suggestion brought a smile to Victor's face. The man on the throne tightened his fingers on the armrests as the princesses stepped forward and opened their mouths in continuous praise.

"O Lord of truth and grace; We honor You in this holy place; We praise Your righteous name; Our hearts will never be the same; Your love…"

"Enough!"

Victor jumped at the roaring voice and instantly pulled his sword from its sheath. The imposter was standing before the throne with a look on his face that resembled a madman. The smile had faded and a scowl of pure hatred had replaced it.

Lailani watched the sudden transformation of the man who claimed to be the Ancient One. She was horrified at how unsafe and insecure she suddenly felt. The woman glanced around hoping to see the real Ancient One. Her eyes locked onto the one person among the travelers who made her feel safe. Yet she was surprised by the change that had taken place on him.

"Don't you love to hear my Beloved sing?"

Cristo stood near the wall behind the group of travelers. Lailani looked from his feet to the top of his head taking in his new appearance. He wore shiny, black boots that came up to his knees. Royal blue pants and a clean, white shirt made up Cristo's clothes. A scarlet red cape was tied around his neck. White gloves covered his hands.

The man's beard was no longer scraggly, but perfectly shaped with the rest of his face neatly shaven. The bushy moustache was gone and a thin, neat one had taken its place. Cristo's voice was strong and held no sound of age. On the man's head sat a regal golden crown covered in a variety of jewels. No sword or any other weapons were visible. One would doubt that it was Cristo except that his eyes were the same loving ones that Lailani found peace and comfort when looking into them.

"You know I despise your Beloved."

The man in white spoke with contempt and his face mirrored the disgust that was evident in his voice.

"I know. That is why you didn't deceive them today. You couldn't hide your hatred for these people and they have unveiled your deception. Shall we do this, Diablo?"

A gasp rose among the travelers. The man before them walked away from the throne and suddenly transformed into the despicable dragon. He hissed toward Simon who crossed his arms with a smirk.

"Yes, Cristo. Let us get this over with."

Cristo smiled and approached the throne. Lailani held her breath ready for a battle. What happened next was not what she expected.

Simon watched the royal Cristo approach the throne. The man faced the dragon leaving the throne between them.

"Father, we await Your judgment."

A light shone on the throne as Cristo spoke. *Father?*

The light lessened so as not to blind the humans present. On the throne now sat the very One whom Simon had met in the Glory of Glories. Excitement filled the boy at the sight of the true Ancient One. The beautiful moment was spoiled by the gravelly, despicable voice of the cruel monstrous Diablo.

"You know that those who are flawed and sinful cannot enter Your service. These who have come before You have done many things that disqualify them from Your presence."

Diablo smirked at the travelers. Simon wondered if what the dragon was speaking was true. *Will we be disqualified after coming so far?*

"It is true that no one can enter My service unless they are pure and holy. What accusations do you have against them?"

The voice was the same as when Simon spoke to the Ancient One in the Glory of Glories yet it sounded more formal. The permission given to Diablo to accuse them confused the child for he couldn't believe that the lying snake would be their witness. Simon glanced over at Cristo who was standing with his hands folded and his head lowered waiting.

"Simon ran away from his master. He had unkind, hateful thoughts about his master and his master's family. He was lazy and slothful when the family was gone on a trip. He stole food late at night many times. He spoke lies to his master and was at times disrespectful."

Simon was amazed at the accuracy of Diablo's words. The boy had done many of those things in secret. Guilt washed over him and Simon knew that he was sinful. He knew that he wasn't worthy to be in the Ancient One's service.

"Is this true, Simon?"

The gentle yet firm voice scared Simon for all he wanted was to be a knight in the service of the Ancient One, but nothing he could say would cause his crimes to disappear. The boy stepped forward and knelt before the One on the throne.

He lowered his head and stated, "Yes, my Lord."

The boy closed his eyes dreading the judgment yet knowing he deserved it.

"Victor was a liar and a thief. He did not honor his parents. As a knight, he lost heart in battle and abandoned Your service. He lied about why he was following the Star when he joined Cristo and the slave boy. He tried many times to lead Simon astray. He lied to Cristo about his motive to find Cornelius. He has hated You and blamed You for events that have happened to him. He has loved another more than You."

Victor glared at Diablo as the dragon accused him of numerous sins. At the conclusion, the knight approached and stood before his Lord the Ancient One. The One on the throne looked at Victor solemnly and nodded for his reply.

"My Lord, it is true that I have failed You deeply."

Victor lowered his head anguished yet relieved that he had admitted his failures.

"Lailani has had hatred in her heart. She has thought about how cruel You are to have taken her parents. She started this journey to find her parents not You. She followed the Star because Cornelius did. She was full of pride and vanity as she stared into the mirror. She wished that she were a princess instead of being grateful for who she really is. She reached into the swampy waters in hopes of bringing back her parents. She complained much. She hated Aurelius and his family. She lets sorrow and guilt over Cornelius consume her."

The young woman listened to Diablo and was surprised at the long list though she knew each crime was true.

The redheaded woman came to a place nearer to the throne. She knelt as tears streamed down her face.

"I am what he says, my Lord, and I am not worthy to be in Your presence."

Lailani choked back sobs as she felt such remorse at not being able to finish the journey. *All this way for nothing.*

"Worst of all is Devin."

Devin gulped not wanting to hear what the creature would say about him. He knew it would all be true, but much more horrible than all of the other travelers combined.

"Devin has hated You for many years. He has served in the Chasm most of his life. Devin has lied without guilt, cheated people, and deceived many into leaving their path to You bringing them to the Chasm. He has murdered many of Your Beloved with hatred and loathing in his heart. He tried to kill Lailani and Cornelius in the swamp when he lied about the forms in the water. When that didn't work, Devin lured a wolf monster to attack Lailani because he wanted her dead."

Diablo glared deeply at Devin as he concluded, "Devin broke an oath of allegiance when he abandoned the Chasm."

"Though somewhat twisted, Diablo speaks truth. I am nothing. I deserve to be executed for my crimes. I give myself to Your judgment. Do as You will."

Devin closed his eyes and waited for the blow of death.

"So now I shall take these criminals to the Chasm with me as all others who fail to follow Your ways."

Diablo slunk forward pleased with himself as he saw the fear in the eyes of the condemned. The dragon smirked knowing that he had won a victory over the Ancient One. The holiness of the Mountain Lord would not allow sin to enter His realm. The four criminals would be exiled from the Mountain. Diablo knew this would hurt the Ancient One because He loved all of the people in the world. *Yes, I have won.*

"Any other words before I pass judgment?"

Diablo smirked sure that no one could help them now.

"Father, I have something to say."

Diablo's puffed up attitude fell at Cristo's words. *He wouldn't dare.* "Speak, My Son."

Cristo exclaimed loudly so all could hear.

"It is true what has been spoken about each of these sinners. Yet I have evidence of their atonement which leads to purity and holiness."

A growl escaped Diablo's throat at the promise of proof. *Not again.*

"What evidence do you have, Son?"

Diablo glared at the Ancient One who looked at the dragon evenly, but with a slight twinkle in His eyes at the creature's displeasure.

Cristo took his white gloves off of his hands. Holding his palms up, the man made sure that Diablo could see the single scar in the middle of each hand. Dread spread through Diablo's body for he knew what was coming next.

"Simon, Victor, Lailani, and Devin do deserve death and torment in the Chasm for their crimes. However, I died for each of them and my blood has washed away their sins. I made the atoning sacrifice and purchased them. They belong to me and their hearts are fully devoted to me. No punishment should be given for I have already been punished fully for them."

Diablo gulped as Cristo stared at him.

"They are my Beloved and I will fight for them."

"By the blood of My Son, these four are purified from their sins and forgiven. I remember their sins no more. Their guilt has been washed away."

Diablo roared ferociously at the Ancient One's words though he knew that he couldn't do anything about it. Without waiting for any other words, the monstrous dragon left the mountain in a fury. *I will get my vengeance. I may not get these four now, but I will never rest while these Beloved live especially Devin.*

"Rise, My Beloved children, for you are Mine forever. No one can pluck you out of My hand."

The Ancient One's beautiful words brought tears of joy to the eyes of the four redeemed sinners. Simon stood feeling so excited. He glanced over at Cristo who was smiling at him with a wink.

"Step forward, Simon."

The boy hurried forward eager to obey.

"Simon, my child, you are now one of My Beloved. You shall train to become a knight. Study hard and love much."

Simon whooped with joy causing all in the throne room to laugh in celebration with him. *I get to be a knight!*

"Lailani, approach."

The young woman, feeling unworthy but blessed, faced her new Lord in anticipation.

"Lailani, my daughter, you are now one of My Beloved. You are a princess of Glory and shall be instructed in the etiquette and purposes of one."

Lailani frowned. *I am a peasant. How can I be royalty?*

Cristo came before her and took the woman's hands into his own.

"You are royalty because you belong to me and my Father. Do not doubt your worth for I sacrificed all for you to be with us. Embrace the truth of your nobility."

The prince turned Lailani to a wall with a golden mirror on it. The woman gasped for her reflection in the mirror was similar to the one she saw in the labyrinth. Her red hair streamed down her back in ringlets and she wore a velvet green gown. On her head was a crown of gold with emerald facets. Again Lailani wished that she really looked like that princess in the mirror.

"Look down."

Lailani obeyed and her eyes popped open wide at the velvet green dress that she was now wearing. Her hand flew up to her hair and she pulled a handful into sight surprised at the red ringlets in her hand. She let go of her hair and moved her hand up to the top of her head where she felt a cold, smooth object that could only be her crown. Joy filled her heart as the truth hit her. *I am a princess of Glory!*

"Victor, come forward."

The knight stepped forward eager to have the Ancient One speak to him.

"Victor, my son, you are still one of My Beloved and I welcome you back. You are reinstated as Sir Victor knight of Glory. Our Simon, Guardian of Glory and knight in training, is in need of a guardian himself. You shall be his father and he your son. Guide him in love and be near him as he trains to become one of my knights."

Victor felt as if he had been punched in the stomach and the breath knocked out of him. He couldn't believe that he was now Simon's father.

"Thank You, my Lord. I shall do my best."

With a bow, Victor turned and saw Cristo smiling at him. He nodded gratefully to the prince then looked over to find Simon beaming at him. The knight approached his new son and opened his arms wide as the child jumped into his embrace.

In a whisper, Victor said, "This is what His message means."

Devin watched as the other three in his company were welcomed by the Ancient One. He desperately wanted to be accepted as well, but he knew it was a long shot.

"Devin."

The man took a deep breath and stepped forward hoping to at least be allowed to stay as a slave.

"Devin, my son, you are also one of My Beloved. Your crimes are forgiven and I remember them no more. You are a new creation. Your old life is gone and your new life has begun. You shall train to be a knight so that you will be able to protect others from the evils of the Chasm."

Devin could not contain the smile that came to his face. Relief washed over him.

"Thank You, my Lord and Master. I will do as You say."

Cristo faced the group who had come so far.

"Ziona, please take Lailani to the princess chambers."

The dark skinned woman in yellow nodded eagerly and took the new princess by the hand. Lailani pulled on the hand remembering something that Ziona had said in Terra so long ago.

"Ziona, didn't you say you were bringing something precious to the Ancient One?"

Ziona smiled so warmly, "Yes, and I have delivered you to Him. As Beloved, we have the honor and responsibility to tell others about the Ancient One. Come. You shall learn all about your duties as princess."

Lailani followed Ziona eager to start her training as a princess of Glory.

Cristo smiled as the two women left the throne room. He looked at the two men and the boy in front of him.

"I shall lead you three to the halls of the knights so you may rest before starting your training. Father, I am sure You want to spend time with Your princesses who have been returned to You."

The Ancient One nodded as Cristo led Victor, Devin, and Simon toward a long corridor. The princesses hurried forward to see their King and Father.

Harmony watched the knight trainees head to the halls. She smiled knowing that their journey had just begun.

MEANING OF
CHARACTERS AND SETTINGS

Cristo- Christ

Lailani- heavenly flower

Ziona- goodness

Campion- champion

Cornelius-horn

Victor- to conquer, victory

Simon- listener

Iliana- the Lord has responded

Diablo- devil

Davo- fiend

Monstre- monster

Devin- servant/slave

Aquana- water

Tatianna-fairy princess

Avidez- greedy

Gula- glutton (for punishment)

Aurelius- golden

Keikari- fashion minded

Vano- vain

Korskea- haughty

Mount Glory- when a person's heart is close to God

Glory of Glories- Heaven

Chasm of Misery- when a person's heart has strayed from God

Misery of Miseries- Hell

ABOUT THE AUTHOR

Carrie Rachelle Johnson comes from a family that values reading and education so it is no surprise that she has focused her time on both. She has a Master's Degree in Elementary Education and currently teaches second grade in a small town in Missouri.

Carrie spends much of her time worshiping and serving the Lord at her home church. She is very involved in several children's ministries, sings in the choir, and directs the Drama Team. Carrie has also been blessed enough to teach her series The Glory Chronicles as book studies at her church.

When she is not writing, she enjoys reading, watching movies, and spending time with her loving family especially her nephew Cameron and her niece Allie.

Carrie would love to hear from her readers. Be sure to check out The Glory Chronicles on Facebook or email her at carrierachellejohnson@outlook.com!

SNEAK PREVIEW OF

RETURN TO GLORY
THE GLORY CHRONICLES VOLUME 2

Darkness engulfed her and the cold plagued her. She sat on the hard chilly ground miserable. Once she had been a young beautiful woman with perfect hair and sparkling eyes. She had everything her heart could ever desire yet it was never enough. She always wanted more. Nothing could satisfy her fully. Then came the day when she lost everything. Her family, her home, and in her eyes the most important: her perfection.

A cold, bitter heart now thumped in her chest and her mind dwelled on what she could have done differently. It did not matter because there was no escape from her new home. No hope. No second chances. She was a slave to the darkness. Nothing could free her from her torment. No one cared enough to even wonder what had happened to her. Lonely and hopeless, she waited for another day to pass without happiness. *If only I had chosen Him when I had the chance.*

31839233R00131

Made in the USA
San Bernardino, CA
21 March 2016